HAZELWOOD

by

Rebecca Xibalba and Tim Greaves

(from an original idea by Rebecca Xibalba)

TIMBEX Productions

Hazelwood

CHAPTER 1

Detective Inspector Landis withdrew the broken end of the biro from his mouth and, as he frequently did, silently chastised himself.

Chewing and sucking on pens and pencils had started when he was a child. He'd lost count of the number of times it had earned him a slapped wrist from his mother– 'You'll poison yourself, so help you, you silly boy!' – and even having broken one of his milk teeth on the end of a particularly unforgiving HB pencil at primary school hadn't deterred him. It was a bad habit he had never been able to shake, but the fact of the matter was, it helped him to concentrate.

Landis had been trying to focus on the words in front of him whilst gnawing away at the biro relentlessly for almost 15 minutes, but this afternoon his concentration was playing hard to get. He raised his eyes from the problem he'd been wrestling with and gazed out of his office window on the third floor of the building overlooking Bishopsgate.

Not for the first time recently, he found himself questioning the point of it all. It had become clear some time ago he really wasn't cut out for this sort of thing, and yet here he was still doing it anyway.

He was pulled rudely out of his thoughts by the sudden appearance of a pizza delivery motorcycle weaving dangerously in and out of the traffic on the street below. 'Idiot,' he muttered and absent-mindedly picked up his mug of tea. He took a sip and scowled – it had gone cold – and returned his attention to the matter at hand, sighing as he looked down at the information he'd been provided with. He frowned. The solution was staring him in the face, he knew it. But it just wouldn't come.

There was a light rapping sound and Constable Sharpe's head appeared around the office door. 'Sergeant Hayes says they're here, sir. Interview when you're ready?'

'Thanks, Matt. Tell her two minutes, would you?'

Sharpe nodded and was about to close the door when Landis called him back.

'Here, Matt…'

'Sir?'

Landis tapped the paper on his desk with the chewed end of the biro. 'Remote design meets writers' centre for a high flyer. Nine letters, ends with an E.'

Sharpe shook his head. 'Sorry, sir. Cryptic crosswords aren't really my thing.'

Landis sat back in his chair. 'Nor mine, it seems,' he said thoughtfully, dropping the pen on the desk. He smiled. 'But one feels compelled to persevere.'

Sharpe nodded again and closed the door.

Folding the newspaper, Landis was about to put it away in his desk drawer when one of the front page headlines caught his eye: **COMET RETURNS AFTER 10,000 YEARS**. 'Ha!' he exclaimed, rifling through the paper to find the crossword page again. 'Anagram of remote… plus three letters from the middle of writers.' He smiled as he filled in his answer on the grid. 'Me-te-or-ite,' he said triumphantly. 'A high flyer!' Feeling inordinately pleased with himself, he added, 'It's small victories that steal the battle.' His moment of jubilation evaporated as he looked at the puzzle, which wasn't even half finished. 'Winning the war is another matter,' he sighed. Putting away the paper, he stood up. 'If it took me as long to solve crimes as it does simple crossword clues they'd have given me the heave-ho years ago.' He chuckled.

Picking up his iPad, Landis went down the corridor and knocked on the office door at the end.

Sergeant Hayes looked up from the case file she had been studying and shook her head in disbelief. 'Have you had a look through, sir?'

Landis nodded and closed the door behind him. 'In my 18 years as a cop I don't think I've ever had to deal with anything quite so barbaric. And I've seen a *lot* of bad stuff.'

Hayes didn't reply, lowering her head as Landis took a seat opposite her. He opened the iPad and again flicked through the images which had arrived that morning from the Greek police. The expression on his face was a mixture of sadness and incredulity. 'Where are they, Donna?'

'The two little boys are in the family room downstairs with a social worker and the girl is in the waiting room with her grandmother and PC Keats. The grandmother is a real piece of work.'

Landis snapped the iPad shut and stood up. 'Okay, let's get this over with. We'll speak to the boys first.'

They took the stairs down to the second floor in silence and made their way along to the family room.

'Good afternoon,' Landis said, smiling at the pinch-lipped woman who was seated on the sofa. The two boys seated beside her were engrossed in their comics and didn't look up. 'I'm Detective Inspector Landis, this is Sergeant Hayes.'

The woman reached up and shook Landis's hand. 'Moira Previs,' she said curtly. 'Ms. Are we going to be here much longer? The boys are tired and they'll be wanting something to eat.'

'I'm so sorry,' Hayes said. 'Were you not offered anything?'

'Tea and a biscuit. But that's hardly substantial food, is it?'

Landis exchanged glances with Hayes. 'We'll not keep you long, I promise,' he said, taking a seat facing them. Hayes remained standing. 'I just want to ask the boys a few questions and you can go home.'

'Very well,' Ms Previs replied.

Landis turned his attention to the boys. Evidently of mixed race, their pale brown faces were topped by mops of thick black curls. He could see they indeed looked tired. 'Hello, boys,' he said chirpily. The younger of the two looked up at him, but his older brother remained glued to his comic. 'What you reading there?'

'Batman,' the little one replied. The second boy stayed silent.

Landis smiled. 'Oh, wow. One of my favourites. So which one of you is Jordan and which is Jack?'

The smaller of the two spoke again. 'I'm Jack.' He put down his comic.

'Pleased to meet you, Jack.' Landis turned his attention to the older boy. 'Which must make you Jordan.'

Jordan huffed once and closed his comic. 'Yes.'

'I know you've been through an awful lot the past couple of days,' Landis said quietly. 'But it would be really helpful if you could tell us what happened to you on your holiday.' He noticed Ms Previs was watching him fixedly, her eyes narrowed almost as if she was waiting to pounce should he say the wrong thing.

'Are you able to tell us what happened to your Mum and Dad?' Landis continued.

'We don't know,' Jordan said. 'They had an argument and Dad hit her and she ran off.'

'I see. I'm sorry to hear that. What were they arguing about?'

Jack opened his mouth to speak but Jordan elbowed him in the ribs and cut him off. 'We don't know,' he said firmly.

'Okay, that's fine. What did you do after that?'

'We ran off too,' Jack said in a small voice. 'And Daddy chased us.'

Jordan shot him an angry look.

Landis nodded. 'And what happened when he caught up with you?'

'He didn't,' Jordan said.

'He did too!' Jack exclaimed. 'But then he fell in the Tarzan sand.'

Landis frowned. 'What's Tarzan sand?'

Jordan elbowed his little brother again. 'He means quicksand. Like in a Tarzan film we watched. Dad was trying to rescue Mooch.' He glared at his brother. 'Isn't that right?' The tone was defying the younger boy to disagree.

'What's Mooch?'

'Not what. *Who*. He was Jack's teddy bear. He was on the sand and when Dad tried to rescue him, he fell in and started to sink. We tried to help but we couldn't and he died and that's everything that happened.'

Jack's eyes were wet with tears. 'I miss Mooch.'

'Me too,' Jordan said, placing a conciliatory hand on the smaller boy's arm.

But not their parents? Landis thought. He raised an eyebrow at Ms Previs. If she had any thoughts on the matter, her expression gave nothing away. 'Okay,' he said. 'You've been very helpful, boys. Both of you. If you'd like to wait here for a moment with Sergeant Hayes, I just need to have a quick word with Ms Previs and then you can go and get something to eat.'

The brothers' faces brightened and Landis gestured for the the social worker to accompany him into the corridor.

'We're still waiting for a full report from the Greek authorities, but from what we understand no survivors have been located and it seems more likely than not, to me at least, that Jenny Kinley is as dead as her husband. What's the situation with regard to family over here?'

'We've not yet been able to find any relatives on Grant Kinley's side. There's a grandmother on the mother's side, but she's not interested. From what little I gather there was a rift between her and Jenny some years ago. For now the boys will be taken into care pending a more permanent arrangement.'

'I understand. Well, listen, thank you for coming in, it's been very helpful. Obviously this is an ongoing investigation. As soon as we know more someone will be in touch with you.'

The woman smiled. 'Thank you.'

'I hope the boys will be okay.'

There was sadness in Landis's eyes as he watched Ms Previs and the brothers walking off down the corridor.

'Nice kids,' he said. He turned to Hayes. 'Right then. Let's go see the girl. I hope we can get a bit more out of her.'

'Billie-Jo?' Landis asked as he and Hayes entered the waiting room. He nodded at Constable Keats, who left and closed the door behind him.

The teenage girl sitting forlornly on a corner chair looked up at them, but before she had a chance to answer Landis, the woman standing over near the window butted in.

'How much longer do we have to fuckin' be here?'

Hayes, standing by the door, said nothing. Landis looked at the woman apologetically. 'I'm sorry we've kept you waiting, madam, we just…'

'Madam?!' the woman exploded. 'It's Tracy or Mrs Hazelwood. I ain't no fuckin' madam!'

Landis sized her up. She was wearing a pale pink velour tracksuit and mock sheepskin ankle boots trodden down at the back. She was quite short with a weathered face. Her bleach-blonde hair, plaited into a long ponytail was showing its roots, while the defiant expression on her face looked like that of somebody who'd fought a thousand arguments – and won them all.

'Apologies, Mrs Hazelwood,' he said. 'We'd just like a few minutes to speak with Billie-Jo if that's okay.'

As Tracy was about to reply, there was a pinging sound and she held up a finger. 'Hang on a sec.' She pulled out her mobile phone and looked at the screen and the trace of a smile appeared at the corner of her mouth. Landis exchanged a disbelieving glance with Hayes. Billie-Jo stared at the floor in silence as her Nan's thumbs rattled off a reply to the text. She hit send, slipped the phone back into her pocket and turned her attention back to Landis. The smile was gone. 'And another thing. That coffee they brought us was shit.'

Landis cleared his throat. 'As I was about to say, we won't hold you up any longer than necessary, but it really is very important we ascertain what happened to Billie-Jo and your family on that island.' The phone pinged again. As Tracy started to pull it out of her pocket, Landis said, 'Of course, we can wait until you've finished checking your messages if you like, but that means you'll be here even longer.'

Tracy let the phone drop back into her pocket. 'Don't give me fuckin' attitude. We're doin' *you* a favour bein' here, not the other way round. We've been through all this already in bastard Greece. We had the fuckin' wop coppers on our case for hours and she already told them everythin' she knows.'

'If you can just give me a few minutes, I'll be as fast as I can, then you can go home.'

'Yeah, well, you'd better make it fuckin' snappy. I've got a shit load of arrangements to make to bring my daughter and granddaughter home so we can lay them to rest.'

Billie-Jo looked up at her Nan. Her hair was lank and greasy and the dark red circles around her eyes spoke of several sleepless nights. 'And Dad. Don't forget Dad.'

Tracy turned to face her. 'That man was *not* your father. And if he was any kind of dad... well, we wouldn't be sitting here discussing your mother's and sister's murders, would we?'

Billie-Jo let out a small sob. 'But...'

'But *nothin'*.' Tracy glared at her, then turned to Landis. 'Come on then, let's get this over with.' She slumped down in a chair and pulled a vape out of her pocket. Before anyone could say anything, she'd taken a long draw on it.

'You can't smoke in here, I'm afraid, ' Hayes said.

Tracy stared at her and exhaled a thick plume of white smoke, filling the air with the overpowering scent of chemical fruitiness. 'It's not smokin', you moron. It's a fuckin' vape.' She rolled her eyes.

'Vaping *is* smo…' Hayes began.

'Well, you can't vape either,' Landis interjected. 'Now, if we can please speak with Billie-Jo you can be on your way.' He had taken a dislike to Tracy Hazelwood the moment he set eyes on her. He'd like nothing more than to be rid of her as quickly as possible, but he had a job to do. 'Do you mind if I sit there?' he said, resting his hand on the back of the seat nearest to Billie-Jo.

She shrugged. 'Sit where you like. It ain't my chair.'

Landis sat down. The seat was hard and he felt a fleeting moment of empathy for having kept the two women waiting. He shifted to get comfortable. 'I've read the report provided to us by the Greek authorities and I know you've had a really dreadful ordeal. But I wonder if there's anything more you could tell me about what happened on Mástiga?'

Billie-Jo was staring at the floor and for a moment Landis thought she wasn't going to respond. Then she

11

sighed. 'My Mum and Dad didn't deserve to die, you know. Or my…' – she made a little strangled noise – '…Or Bob.' She shuffled her feet and for the first time Landis noticed the small, black drawstring bag tucked underneath her chair.

'I can assure you, we're going to do everything in our power to ensure the people responsible are brought to justice.'

'For fuck's sake, keep up, would you.' Tracy guffawed theatrically. 'They're all fuckin' dead already.'

Landis shot her a sideways glance, but continued to address Billie-Jo. 'On the contrary, from the little we've managed to ascertain so far, we believe this goes far wider than Terence Hallam.'

Billie-Jo looked at him tearfully. 'Can I ask you something, Mr…?'

'Landis.' He nodded. 'Of course you can.'

Tracy's phone pinged. She sat up and was about to pull it out when she caught sight of Landis looking at her again. 'Alright, alright, keep your bleedin' hair on. Fuck me.' She rolled her eyes.

Landis looked back at Billie-Jo. 'You wanted to ask me something?'

'Yeah. Do you think people deserve to die? Bad people, I mean?'

Landis thought for a moment. 'I believe that if someone has done something wrong they deserve to be held accountable. But die? For being bad? No. I don't.'

'But what if they're *really* bad? Like rotten to the core?'

Landis looked at the girl. *What she must have been through*, he thought. 'Why are you asking?'

The reply was almost a whisper. 'There were a lot of bad people on that island.'

'So it would seem.'

She looked up at him. 'I mean really, *really* bad. Not just that Hallam creep and his slag assistant. It was obvious that we were all invited to the island for a reason and I'd be the first to admit we weren't exactly family of the year, but at least we weren't a bunch of paedos.'

Landis frowned. 'What makes you say that?'

Billie-Jo closed her eyes and she saw her mother, enraged, slaughtering the disgusting creature who'd been spying on her and her sister as they were undressing. She opened her eyes again. 'Doesn't matter. He's dead now ain't he?' she said quietly, looking down at the linoleum. 'I don't want to talk any more.'

Landis leant forward. 'If you could…'

'You heard her,' Tracy said, standing up as if to make it clear the meeting was over. 'She ain't got

13

nothin' more to say.' She reached out and yanked Billie-Jo to her feet. 'Come on, we're goin'.'

It's going to be worth talking with Billie-Jo Hazelwood again, Landis thought. *Preferably without her obnoxious grandmother in attendance.*

But for now he saw no mileage in holding either of them any longer. She'd said all she was going to for today. He got up. 'Thank you both for coming in. We may want to speak with you again, Billie-Jo, but for now you can go home.'

'Speak with us *again?*' Tracy spat.

'With your granddaughter, yes.'

'May I remind you, *we're* the fuckin' victims here?! If you think we're comin' back here you can knob right off!'

'We'll only be in touch again if it's absolutely necessary,' Landis said, knowing full well he'd be crossing swords with this harridan again.

He bent down to retrieve Billie-Jo's bag for her, but quick as lightning she intercepted him and snatched it up. 'I can get it myself. I'm not a fuckin' invalid!'

It was the most animated Landis had seen her. He nodded politely and took a step back. 'As I say, thank you for coming in.'

A little under an hour later, Tracy slammed shut the front door of her three-up-two-down terraced house in

14

Islington and glared at Billie-Jo. 'Right, my girl, just you listen to me. I didn't ask for any of this shit, but you can have the back bedroom until we can get somethin' permanent sorted, which probably won't be till after the funeral.' Billie-Jo watched sullenly as her Nan pulled out the vape and sucked on it. She puffed out a cloud of smoke. 'But I don't want to see you and I don't want to hear you. Not a fuckin' peep, right?'

Billie-Jo shook her head. 'You won't.'

'I don't even want to know you're fuckin' here. I ain't cookin' for you neither.'

'What will I eat?'

Tracy shrugged. 'Not my fuckin' problem. I'll give you some cash and you can sort youself out. How you spend it is up to you, but just remember once it's gone there won't be no more.' She wrinkled her nose and sniffed. 'We'd better go round your Mum's flat tomorrow so you can get some clean knickers. You smell like a tramp's arsehole.' She ignored the tears welling up in Billie-Jo's eyes at mention of her mother. 'And one more thing. If I've got company in the evenin' you make yourself scarce. Is that clear?' She sucked on the vape again.

'I'll stay in my room.'

'You'll fuck off out for a few hours is what you'll do,' Tracy said through another cloud of smoke. 'I don't get much these days, but when I do, the last thing

I want is knowin' someone's in the next room when I'm getting my freak on.'

Billie-Jo had to bite her bottom lip to stop herself sniggering. It was the first time she'd had the urge to laugh for days. She smirked. 'At your age?'

'You cheeky cunt!'

Billie-Jo's smile faded. 'I won't be any trouble, Nan. I promise.'

Tracy squinted at her granddaughter and wagged a finger. 'I'll hold you to that.' She thrust the vape back into her pocket. 'Go on then, fuck off up to your room and leave me in peace. *Tipping Point* is on in a minute.'

Billie-Jo went quietly up the stairs and closed the door of the tiny bedroom behind her. Dropping her bag on the floor, she squeezed between several large cardboard boxes full of clothing and old electrical goods to get to the bed. Pushing a pile of magazines and a motley collection of stuffed toys out of the way, she fell face first onto the mattress and broke down, stifling the sound of her sobbing by burying her head in the musty pillow.

She cried until no more tears would come, then got up and looked out of the window at the small courtyard garden below. It was littered with pots full of dead and dying plants, and the council rubbish bin beside the fence was laying on its side, the contents strewn all over the paving slabs. There was a small back gate leading out into a fenced communal alleyway, but Billie-Jo could see the bolt was padlocked.

She sighed and sat down on the edge of the bed. It had been a rollercoaster two days since she had been rescued from Mástiga and suddenly she was engulfed by overwhelming tiredness. There was something she wanted to do first though.

Retrieving her drawstring bag from the floor, she emptied the sparse contents out on to the quilt beside her. Among the small number of personal belongings she'd brought back with her from Mástiga, there was a sheaf of folded paperwork held together with a paperclip. The small window didn't gift the room with much light, so she flicked the switch on the tiny bedside lamp, discarded the paperclip and laid back on the pillow to read.

CHAPTER 2

It was Jack who broke the silence. 'I'm cold.' He shivered and huddled in close to his brother.

'Me too.' Jordan put his arm around Jack and looked at Billie-Jo. 'What are we going to do?'

Not that she would have admitted it, but Billie-Jo was starting to feel cold too.

They were sitting on the end of the dock on Mástiga where just half an hour earlier they had watched the rescue boat depart, taking with it their one chance of getting off the island. At least ten minutes had passed since the sun had set and the chill breeze rolling in off the sea was beginning to bite.

Billie-Jo stifled a shiver and stared angrily at Jordan. 'How the *fuck* should I know what we're goin' to do, eh? You think I've got some magic solution? *Do* ya?! It's a fuckin' joke they left us behind but there's jack shit we can do about it. Okay?'

Jack started to cry. 'I want to go home. I'm scared.'

Billie-Jo saw the look of hurt in the older boy's eyes as he hugged his brother close. Her tone softened a little. 'I'm sorry.' She reached out and ruffled Jack's hair. 'I didn't mean to shout. I'm scared too.'

'Do you think there's anyone else still here?'

'Maybe. I can't believe my Dad was on that boat. He wouldn't have gone without us.' Billie-Jo frowned.

'I bet it was that Mason lot. They wouldn't give two fucks about abandonin' us here. Selfish cunts.'

'Or maybe everyone went because they thought we were dead,' Jordan said. 'Perhaps they'll come back to check.'

The trace of doubt in his voice echoed what Billie-Jo was thinking. 'Don't hold your breath,' she said. 'But whoever was on that boat will tell the filth what happened here, so at least they should come to investigate.' Her face darkened. 'And someone will have to collect the bodies. That Page creep and my Mum and Bob and…' She trailed off. 'And anyone else who's dead.'

'Do you think Mummy was safe on the boat?' Jack asked, looking at his brother hopefully.

Jordan shrugged. 'Probably.'

Jack stopped crying. He sat up. 'I wish there was something to eat.'

'Okay, listen.' Rubbing her arms to get warm, Billie-Jo stood up, then squatted down on her haunches in front of the two boys. 'Somebody *will* come. But it probably won't be until tomorrow at the earliest or maybe even the day after. It definitely won't be tonight. There's no point us sitting here feeling sorry for ourselves. We're all hungry and it's only goin' to get colder now it's dark.'

'We need to find somewhere warm to sleep,' Jordan said.

'And something to eat,' Jack chimed in.

'Exactly.' Billie-Jo looked up at the night sky and held out a hand. She could feel a light trace of drizzle in the air. '*Bollocks*. It's startin' to rain too. Come on, we have to go back to the chalet before we get soaked. We'll come back down here tomorrow.'

The two boys stood up.

'My legs are tired,' Jack said.

Billie-Jo gave him a weary look. One of her knees, badly grazed from when she'd taken a tumble a while ago, was throbbing badly. 'Fine. You can stay here if you want to, but don't come grizzlin' to me if you've frozen or starved to death by mornin'.'

There was a moment of silence, then Jack giggled.

'What's so fuckin' funny?'

'You said I mustn't moan if I die.'

'So?'

Jack giggled again. 'How *could* I if I was dead?'

Jordan laughed too. 'He's right.'

Billie-Jo shook her head resignedly. 'Whatever. I'm goin' back. Come with me, or not. I don't give a shit either way.' She started to walk away.

The brothers followed and together the three children set off back along the road to the resort. As they walked, the rain started to fall and by the time they reached the line of trees where Bobbi-Leigh's body had been left, it was teeming down. Billie-Jo faltered for a moment as she caught sight of one of her sister's Hi Top trainers at the side of the road; it must have fallen off when she and Jordan lifted the body.

The two boys had set the pace, walking ahead, with Billie-Jo bringing up the rear. When they realised she had dropped back, they stopped.

'What's the matter?' Jordan called out.

Billie-Jo pushed the strands of wet hair out of her face. 'Fuckin' *seriously*?' she shouted.

'Oh.' The boy looked at her apologetically. 'Sorry. I didn't…'

Billie-Jo caught up with them. 'Forget it. Just have a bit of consideration before you flap your fuckin' lips, yeah?' She pushed past the brothers and marched off ahead. The boys stumbled along behind her, trying to keep up.

A hundred yards or so further along, there was a trail leading away to the right that they hadn't noticed when they'd passed by earlier.

'Look!' Jordan exclaimed, pointing. Off through the trees to the right there was a faint glow of light. 'Maybe someone *is* still here!'

'How did we miss that on the way down?' Billie-Jo mused aloud, realising as the words left her mouth what a ridiculous thing it was to say; of course they hadn't

21

seen it, it was broad daylight when they came past earlier.

As if he read her thoughts, Jack said, 'It was nice and sunny before, it's dark now.'

'Yeah,' Jordan said.

Annoyed that she had made herself look stupid in front of two little boys, Billie-Jo still couldn't help smiling. 'Clever little fucker, ain't ya?' She winked at him. Jack just looked at her and shrugged. She pulled at the bottom of her T-shirt, which was now sodden and clinging stubbornly to her skin, grimacing as she felt water trickle down the back of her shorts. 'For fuck's sake!'

She was in no doubt that simply being on the island was dangerous enough, with God knows what in the way of death traps awaiting them. Their ordeal at the ice cream parlour, which had ultimately resulted in the death of her sister, wasn't something she would ever forget.

'Alright,' she said after thinking for a moment. They would have to take shelter from the rain somewhere and they were still some distance from the resort. 'We'll go and take a look. But we've got to be fuckin' careful, okay? For all we know, it's a trap, with that fat cunt and his skanky bitch sidekick just sittin' there waiting for us to walk right into it.'

As they made their way through the trees towards the light, the rain started to ease off and by the time they reached the source of the light it had stopped.

The three children hesitated at the open gates of a compound, their eyes scanning for any sign of life. But there was none. A light above the doorway of the building over to the left was illuminating the expanse of open ground between it and a small portico, beneath which was parked a Rolls Royce. On the far right there was a Mazda with its front staved in. It appeared to have collided with a telegraph pole, which had toppled and was laying on the ground amidst a tangle of wires.

'Okay,' Bille-Jo whispered, turning to the two boys. 'Before we go in there we need to find something to defend ourselves. There's bound to be something we can use in that posh car. If not, that smashed up one.' She cocked a thumb towards the sports car. 'One of them's sure to have a toolkit or somethin' like a hammer in the boot.' Smiling and nodding approvingly, she added, 'You can do a lot of damage with a hammer.' She saw the look of alarm on the boys' faces. 'Don't worry, I'm sure we won't need it.' She turned back towards the compound. 'Okay. Posh car first. Stay close behind me and keep your gobs shut.'

They scuttled across to the portico and stopped beside the Rolls Royce. Billie-Jo looked at Jordan.

'You two check this one, I'm gonna see what I can find over there.'

She ran swiftly across the compound and hopped over the fallen telegraph pole. As she did so, she caught sight of something over to her left. What the hell *was* that? It resembled something that had come off a butcher's slab. She paused and glanced back towards the Rolls, where the boys were just opening the driver's-side door.

There was still no sign of any other activity. With curiosity getting the better of her, she warily approached what were now very evidently the remains of a dead body. Heartbeat racing, she was within ten yards of it when the horror of what she was seeing finally struck her. It was her step-father, Jamie. His bisected corpse – its intestines spilling out of the upper torso, the disembodied legs laying on the ground just behind it – was barely recognisable as human in form. Billie-Jo's mouth opened in terror as she saw the bloodied rictus grin on the face and she let out a piercing scream. 'Daaaaaad!'

Disturbed by the noise, something amongst the entrails moved and a rat – its mouth and fur smeared with viscous red slime – nosed its way out. It saw Billie-Jo, weighed up its options for an instant, then darted away, disappearing out of sight beneath the wrecked Mazda.

Turning away, Billie-Jo dropped to her knees and threw up.

Jordan and Jack came rushing towards her. 'What's happened?' the older boy shouted.

Without looking up, Billie-Jo waved a hand at them to stay back and they skidded to a halt. 'Just...' she swallowed hard, fighting the urge to vomit again. 'Just go and check the fuckin' car!'

'Are you okay?'

Billie-Jo nodded. 'Go.'

After a moment's hesitation, they did as they were told and Billie-Jo got to her feet. She looked fearfully back towards the building, but there was still no sign of life. Surely if there was somebody here, they would have appeared when she screamed.

She walked shakily over to the Mazda. A quick check of the boot and the interior provided her with nothing of any use.

Keeping her head turned purposefully away so as to avoid seeing Jamie's remains again, she walked back towards the Rolls Royce, where Jordan was just opening the boot. As Billie-Jo stepped up alongside him, the boy let out a startled cry and stepped quickly back. Shielding Jack's eyes, he looked at her. 'It's that woman!'

Peering into the boot, Billie-Jo eyes widened as she saw Caroline Smart's broken, partially-clothed body wedged between a large suitcase and a long metal toolbox. The dark eyes were wide open, staring intently but seeing nothing, and there was a bruise on her cheek and traces of dried blood around the nose and mouth. One of the arms was jutting out at an unnatural angle, seemingly dislocated.

Billie-Jo glanced at Jordan and Jack and gestured to the side of the car. 'Go wait over there.' She struggled to remove the heavy toolbox from beneath Caroline's legs, noticing as she did so that the woman had no underwear on. She gagged and doubled her efforts, pulling at the box for all she was worth. At last she managed to drag it free, dropped it on the ground and slammed the boot shut.

'Fuck me!' she gasped. Squatting down and opening the toolbox, the first thing her eyes fell upon was a tire iron. 'That'll do!'

With Billie-Jo taking the lead and clutching the tool as if her life depended on it – which, as far as she was concerned, it probably did – the three of them walked quickly across the compound and up the steps to the imposing building.

Fronting a long, dark corridor, the door was wide open.

'I don't want to go in there,' Jack whimpered.

Jordan put his arm round his brother's shoulders. 'It's okay, I won't let anything happen to you.'

'Nor will I,' Billie-Jo added. 'Promise.' Jack looked as if he was going to start crying again.

They made their way down the dimly-lit corridor trying each of the doors dotted along its length as they went; all of them were locked. At the bottom there was an option to go left or right. They chose right and walked cautiously along to the room at the end where the door was slightly ajar. Ushering the boys to stay back, Billie-Jo tightened her grip on the makeshift weapon and pushed the door wide open.

The store room was in darkness, but just inside the door, splayed out face down on the floor, was Terence Hallam. Billie-Jo gasped and instinctively took a step back. Then she moved forward and reaching out with the tire iron she gingerly prodded the bulky man's arm. 'Hey!' There was no movement. She poked him again, harder this time. 'Hey, are you listening to me, you cunt?' The body remained motionless. Raising the tire iron ready to strike, she kicked Hallam hard in the side of his ribs. He didn't stir. She kicked the back of his head and it lolled to one side.

'What's happening in there?' It was Jordan's voice.

'Wait!'

'But…'

'I said *wait*!' Taking a deep breath, Billie-Jo hopped over the body and spun quickly round to face it. Even in the darkness it was clear that the man responsible for everything that had happened was now dead. Resting on the concrete floor in a pool of dark blood, the head was skewed and Billie-Jo could see a gaping wound in his neck.

It was strange. The discovery of even a single corpse was something most people would never have to bear witness to in their entire lifetime. Yet in the past few hours Billie-Jo had encountered six: the paedophile Warren Page, ripped apart with a broken bottle by her mother, Vicky, in reprisal for his perverted inclinations. Vicky herself, who had melted in front of Billie-Jo's eyes. Her stepfather, Jamie, whose torn body was laying outside in the compound, now just a chunk of meat for vermin to feed on, and her sister, Bobbi-Leigh, who had died in her arms. Then Caroline Smart, the woman whose misguided loyalty to a monster cost her her life. And now Terence Hallam himself, the orchestrator of this nightmare, seemingly murdered by... well, Billie-Jo hadn't a clue. But as she stood staring down at his lifeless bulk, there was no longer a sense of shock. No nausea. No fear. She felt only contempt.

'Are you okay?' Jordan called out shakily.

'Yeah, it's all cool,' Billie-Jo shouted back as she knelt down. 'I'll be there in a moment.'

It took some effort, but by grabbing hold of Hallam's arm and heaving for all she was worth, she managed to roll him over on to his back. She rummaged in the inside pockets of his jacket and found a cigar tube and a moleskine wallet embossed in gold with the initials **GH**. There were half a dozen credit cards inside, but not a lot of cash – 70 Euros perhaps. Without counting it, she stuffed the notes into the back pocket of her shorts and tossed the wallet aside. The jetted hip pockets of the jacket were empty. She moved on down to his trousers, patting the outside. There was the bulge of something soft in one of them. Reaching inside, she withdrew a balled-up scrap of lacy black cloth. 'Ewwww!' she exclaimed as the memory of Caroline's half-naked body flashed through her mind. Hastily discarding the panties, she vigourously wiped her hand on her shorts, shuddering involuntarily as she did so.

'What are you doing?' It was Jordan again.

'For fuck's sake, I said I'll be out in a moment!' Turning her attention to Hallam's hands, Billie-Jo tried to prise the various gold rings off his plump fingers, but not one of them would budge. 'Bollocks,' she muttered. Unsnapping the clasp on the metal band of his wristwatch – a Rolex Milgauss Oyster Perpetual, worth upwards of £11,000 (not that Billie-Jo knew it) – she stashed it in her pocket alongside the cash.

Jordan and Jack were standing in the corridor waiting for her. Both of them looked frightened. 'What were you doing in there?' Jordan asked.

'Just makin' sure the fucker who brought us here is dead, *okay*?' Billie-Jo snapped. She pointed to the open door of the room at the other end of the corridor. 'Come on, maybe there's some food in there.'

'But what if there is and we eat it and it kills us?' Jack said. He was trembling.

Billie-Jo squatted down in front of him. 'Listen. There's nothin' to be scared about any more. The people that wanted to kill us are dead.' Both boys looked at her uncertainly. 'And this was their... I dunno, their secret hideaway I s'pose. They had to eat *somethin'*, so if there's any food here we can be pretty sure it's safe to eat. Make sense?'

Jordan nodded. 'Yeah.'

'Alright then.' She stood up. 'Let's go see what we can find.'

The first thing they saw when they went into the room at the end of the corridor was a bank of TV monitors, which spanned one of the walls. They were all running in screensaver mode, with the **HH** Hallam Holidays logo moving swiftly back and forth. In front of the screens was a desk with... 'A phone!' Billie-Jo cried out. Then she remembered seeing the fallen pole and the tangle of wires out in the compound. She ran to the desk and snatched up the receiver. Hearing the dialling tone, she turned excitedly to the brothers. 'It works! It fuckin' *works!*' Her face fell. 'Bollocks. What the hell is the Greek for 999?'

Jack shrugged, but Jordan squinted at her. 'I think it might be 112.'

Billie-Jo looked at him in surprise. 'What?'

'112. I saw it on a poster when we were waiting for the boat at Piraeus,' the boy said matter-of-factly. 'There was a picture of an ambulance and a fire engine and a police car, and at the bottom in huge numbers was 112.'

Billie-Jo squealed. '*Seriously*?!' The boy nodded. 'You, *beautiful* smart-arse little fucker!' Before Jordan knew what was happening, she had leant over and planted a big kiss on his cheek.

'You got kissed – by a *girl*!' Jack sniggered. 'Jordan and Billie-Jo sitting in a tree, K-I-S-S-I-N-G!'

Jordan felt himself blushing. 'Shuddup!'

Billie-Jo tapped the number in on the phone keypad and only a few seconds passed before a woman answered and said something in Greek.

'Does anyone there speak English?' Billie-Jo asked desperately.

'Certainly,' the woman replied. 'What is nature of your emergency please?'

'Er... rescue?'

'I'm sorry, I don't understand,' the woman said patiently. 'Which emergency service do you require?'

Billie-Jo's brow furrowed. 'Police, I s'pose.'

'Please hold.'

Moments later Billie-Jo was speaking to a man who told her his name was Officer Yiannis Karageorge. He kept silent while she breathlessly recounted everything that had happened to them in the past few days. 'And the boat went without us and we're stuck here,' she concluded.

The line stayed silent.

'Hello? Are you still there?' Exasperated, she looked at Jack and Jordan. 'I think he hung u…'

'Is this a joke?' the police officer said with a note of impatience. 'Wasting police time, it is offence.'

'A *joke*? No!'

'That island, Mástiga, it is private place. It not possible that you are there.'

'I *know* it's private!' Billie-Jo said angrily. 'Didn't you listen to a word I said? *Fuck*! We were invited here by the man who owns it!' She fought back the tears. 'All I'm askin' is someone *please* come and get us.'

'Calm down, please.' Karageorge went quiet for a moment. He was thinking.

Billie-Jo looked at Jack and Jordan again. 'I don't think he believes me,' she whispered.

Karageorge sniffed and cleared his throat. 'Excuse. Very well. I am trusting you this is not joke. I will speak immediately with my superior. Then coastguard come to island to get you. And police. They come too. It will not be soon though. Two hours. Maybe three.'

'*Three* hours?!' Billie-Jo exclaimed angrily.

'You will be safe until then? Where are you now?'

'In some sort of building where Hallam – that's the man who owned the island – where he was spyin' on us, watchin' everythin' we did.'

'How far is from dock?'

'Fifteen minutes walk perhaps? Twenty? I don't know.'

Karageorge made the sniffing noise again. 'Then you stay please. For two hours. After that you come to dock and wait.'

Billie-Jo felt a wave of relief. 'Thank you.'

'Is okay. And do not be fear. Someone come soon.'

The line went dead. Billie-Jo turned to the boys, who were looking at her expectantly. 'We have to wait here for a bit and then go back to the dock. They're sendin' a boat to get us.' She smiled. 'Told you everythin' would be okay, didn't I?'

The brothers' faces lit up and they both cheered.

'But I'm still hungry,' Jack said.

All there appeared to be in the office by way of sustenance was a tall tin of Fortnum & Mason Pistachio

& Clotted Cream Biscuits and a selection of alcoholic drinks.

'What the fuck did they *eat*?' Billie-Jo mused aloud. Jordan and Jack watched eagerly as she examined the seal on the tin. Satisfied that it hadn't been broken, she split it with her thumbnail and removed the lid. She collected a half-bottle of Rémy Martin brandy from the side – 'None of yer cheap shit,' she muttered – and a bottle of tonic water, and the three of them sat cross-legged on the floor and hungrily devoured the biscuits.

When they had eaten, Billie-Jo took a swig of brandy and offered the bottle to the boys. They both shook their heads. Jordan opened the tonic water and handed it to Jack. He took a little sip and screwed his face up – 'Yuk!' – and quickly passed it back to his brother.

Billie-Jo laughed. 'Yeah, pretty disgustin', ain't it? It's much better with some voddie mixed in.' She took another mouthful of brandy and swallowed, nodding approvingly. 'Wow, that shit burns.'

Jordan frowned at her. 'How can you like that stuff? Drinking is a bad habit. It makes people do horrible things.'

Billie-Jo rolled her eyes. 'Get a life, kid.'

Jack poked Jordan's arm. 'Do you think Mummy might be waiting for us when we get back?'

'I told you before, I don't know.'

'You said she might have been on the boat.'

'Maybe. I just don't know, okay?'

Jack sighed. 'I hope so. I miss her.'

'Me too.' Jordan drank some the tonic water and winced. 'There must be *something* else here,' he said.

'Yeah, I know. I mean, they couldn't live on biscuits and booze, could they?' Billie-Jo thought for a moment. 'Although *I* probably could.' She stood up. 'Right, let's see what else is in here.' She went back to the desk and checked the drawers. They were empty. Beside the telephone there was a pile of loose-leaf folders. Each one was labelled with a name of one of the families that Hallam had brought to the island: **MASON** – which was empty – **PAGE**, **KINLEY** and **TROT/HAZELWOOD**.

Billie-Jo rifled through the contents of the last one; there was reams of what could only be considered private information about her family and none of it was flattering. Additionally there were a number of photographs of Billie-Jo, her sister, her mother and her stepfather, all of them clearly having been taken without their knowledge.

There was one additional folder at the bottom of the pile. It was labelled **INVESTORS**. Billie-Jo opened it and pulled out the contents. As she scanned the paperwork, her eyes got wider and wider. 'Fuckers,' she said in a hoarse whisper.

35

'What is it?' Jordan said, getting up to look.

'Doesn't matter,' Billie-Jo said, quickly folding the papers and tucking them out of sight. 'Listen. We've got time to kill now. I'm goin' back to the chalet to collect some of my stuff before we get picked up.'

'But you said the man told us to wait here!' Jordan exclaimed.

'There's my iPod, my phone, all sorts of shit I don't wanna leave behind. I suggest we stick together, but there's nothin' to be scared about now, so if you wanna wait here, well… I won't be long.'

Jordan didn't hesitate. 'We'll come,' he said, bending to help his little brother to his feet.

They made their way back along the corridor to the junction, where Billie-Jo paused. 'Wait here a sec.' She walked back along to the store room, leaned inside the door and looked down at Hallam's body. 'Fuck you,' she said and spat on him.

CHAPTER 3

Billie-Jo opened her eyes. For a fleeting moment she didn't know where she was. Blinking against the glare of sunlight that was shimmering through a crack in the curtains, she stared up at a dusty cobweb, dangling lazily from the cracked styrofoam coving above the bed. Then it came back to her. She was laying on top of the quilt, where she had fallen asleep in her clothes.

She shivered. How long had she been out of it? She turned onto her side and saw the paperwork that she had been reading scattered on the floor beside the bed. She rolled back and sat up, patting the quilt around her to find her mobile phone. Then she spotted it on the bedside table where she must have left it. Grabbing it up, she swiped away the small stack of text messages from the front screen and looked at the time: six thirty-nine. She was shocked to see she had been asleep for over 14 hours. Perhaps it wasn't so surprising though, especially given everything she had been through during the past couple of days. Suddenly she felt hungry.

She went out onto the landing and pressed an ear against her Nan's door. She could hear the faint sound of snoring. As quietly as she could, she made her way downstairs and went out to the kitchen. There wasn't much in the fridge; the only things remotely appealing were a chunk of cheese – which, on closer inspection, had traces of mould on it and the label on which indicated it had exceeded its eat-before date by several weeks – and an open packet of chicken roll. Raiding the cupboards she found some chocolate biscuits and a multi-pack of crisps in a variety of flavours.

Tracy Hazelwood might have made it clear her granddaughter was expected to fend for herself, but she wouldn't have any money until she could get to a post office and change the euros she had pilfered from Hallam's wallet. She certainly couldn't rely on the cash her Nan had said she would give her. Besides, the old bag probably wasn't going to miss crisps and a few biscuits. And if she did? Well, too bad. Billie-Jo would cross that bridge if she came to it.

She crept back to the bedroom to enjoy her makeshift feast.

By the time she finished eating, it had turned seven. She went into the bathroom and stripped off. Tracy's body odour observation might not have been worded very delicately, but she had certainly been right: Billie-Jo *did* smell bad. Turning on the shower, she angled the head and stepped in under the cascade of hot water.

Two minutes later, luxuriating in the simple pleasure of feeling clean, she towelled herself dry and reluctantly put her dirty clothes back on. As she stepped out onto the landing, the main bedroom door opened and Tracy appeared, looking dishevelled in her semi-transparent shortie nightgown. She yawned and broke wind violently.

'What?!' she said, catching sight of the look of disgust on her granddaughter's face.

'It smells like a rat crawled up your arse and died.'

'Watch your fuckin' cheek, you! You're livin' under *my* bastard roof now!'

'Not for any longer than I have to,' Billie-Jo muttered.

'I *beg* your pardon?!'

Billie-Jo hung her head. 'Nothin'.'

'You ungrateful little cow!' Tracy scowled at her. 'You listen to me, my girl! I ain't any happier about this than you are. And I ain't gonna put up with you bein' here one second more than's necessary!' She pushed past Billie-Jo – 'You'd better not have taken all the hot water neither!' – and disappeared into the bathroom, slamming the door.

Billie-Jo went back to her room and gathered up the fallen paperwork from the floor. She had started reading it the previous afternoon prior to falling asleep. Primarily it appeared to identify five individuals who had financially backed Terence Hallam's psychotic scheme to cleanse Britain of what he perceived to be a worthless blight on society. There were also passport sized photos of each of the people concerned.

Furthermore, there was information appertaining to the investors' offshore bank accounts and a succession of payments made to Terence Hallam over a period of several months. Some of it was sickening.

It had occurred to Billie-Jo that it was something she probably ought to give to Inspector Landis. Yet while she had been showering, an idea had come to her. Deciding she would keep hold of it all until she had time to think things through properly, she folded up the papers and stashed them away in her bag. She rummaged around to locate the small internal pocket and pulled out the wodge of money she had taken from Hallam. Counting it, she was surprised to find it amounted to 90 euros; a bit more than she had thought. She folded it properly and tucked it away again. Then she examined the Rolex watch. Given that it had belonged to Hallam, there was no doubt in Billie-Jo's mind it had value. She decided she would show it to her boyfriend later; he probably wouldn't have a clue how much it was worth himself, she thought, but he'd definitely know someone who would. Smiling to herself, she slipped the watch back into the bag and picked up her mobile phone.

Tracy inhaled deeply and rested her vape down on the worktop. She leant over to the open kitchen window and blew out a cloud of white smoke. 'Right then,' she said, turning to face Billie-Jo. 'You can get yourself ready for school. And make it snappy. I've gotta go round the flat and get you some clean clothes.'

Tracy hadn't even bothered to ask if Billie-Jo was hungry, let alone offered her anything to eat. She had wolfed down a thick slice of toast herself; it was burnt to within an inch of its life and smothered in margarine and blackcurrant jam, and Tracy had demolished it with indigestion-baiting speed. Now she was making tea.

'*Seriously?* I *can't* go to school,' Billie-Jo said with a hint of reproach. 'I can't face it. Not after everything that's happened. You can't make me.'

'Oh can't I?' Tracy snapped.

'No!'

Tracy laughed, but it was forced and there was no humour in it. 'I think you'll find I can.'

Billie-Jo started to protest. 'Please, Nan, I...'

'Enough! You ain't fuckin' mopin' round here all day.' Tracy looked at Billie-Jo with undisguised loathing. 'Oh, shitballs! You can't go to school dressed like *that*!' She thought for a moment. 'There's probably some trackies in one of the boxes in your room you can borrow. They'll see you through till tonight.' She huffed and dropped a teabag into the mug. 'I fuckin' *hate* that flat, but I ain't havin' you stinkin' up my house,' she grumbled, pouring on the hot water and stirring.

41

'I had a shower just now. You know I did.'

'Be that as it may, you still stink.' She jabbed a teaspoon at Billie-Jo. 'It's them clothes. You've been wearin' 'em for days. I hate to think what state your fuckin' knickers are in!' She stared impatiently at her granddaughter. '*Well?*'

'Well what?'

'It's almost seven-thirty. If you're gonna get to school on time, you'd better go get your lazy arse dressed and get movin', hadn't you?' Tracy rolled her eyes. 'Oh, hang on.' She went to her handbag and pulled out her purse. Withdrawing three £10 notes, she was about to hand them to Billie-Jo when she thought better of it. She returned one to the purse, rummaged for a couple of pound coins and handed them over with the two bills. 'And fuckin' make it last. I don't get no more benefits till the end of the week.'

'Thanks, Nan.' Billie-Jo took the money and stuffed it into the pocket of her shorts. She chewed her bottom lip apprehensively. 'When you go to the flat, are you gonna bring Bronson and Stella back with you?'

'The dogs?'

'Yeah. They're probably getting hungry by now.'

'What the fuck are you wittering about?' Tracy scowled as the realisation of what Billie-Jo was saying dawned on her. 'Don't tell me they was left on their own in the flat?'

'Dad said there was no way he was payin' to have them put in kennels.' Billie-Jo smiled weakly. 'We left them plenty of food and water though.'

'That *fuckin'* Jamie!' Tracy exclaimed. She didn't like dogs, she never had. She had made her opinions clear the day they got them that Jamie couldn't even look after himself, let alone two young puppies. He clearly only wanted them – and opted for those breeds specifically – because in his head they were status symbols. And Vicky had never listened to anything her mother had to say. So Tracy had left them to it and the subject never came up again. Nevertheless, she would never condone cruelty and neglect.

'So will you get them then?' Billie-Jo pressed.

'Absolutely not! There's no fuckin' way they're comin' here and that's that.'

Billie-Jo looked at her Nan sadly. 'Can you at least give them something to eat? And some fresh water? *Please*?'

Tracy sighed. 'Of course I will. I'll not see them starve to death.' A thought crossed her mind. 'I suppose I'll have to call the dog people. Fuck me, that's more shit I don't need!'

Billie-Jo's face fell. 'But then they'll be taken away. I'll never see them again.'

'Just be thankful they'll end up in a good home! Now, no more faffin' about, get yourself upstairs and ready for school.'

Realising there was nothing more to say, Billie-Jo silently returned to her room. She rummaged through several of the storage boxes and found the tracksuit bottoms. Quickly changing into them, she got down on her knees and retrieved the drawstring bag from its hiding place under the bed.

Billie-Jo had no intention whatsoever of going to school. Before she had come downstairs, she'd texted her boyfriend.

Tyler James lived in a two bedroom flat directly above the chicken shop where he worked. The air inside was always heavy with the lingering odour of chip fat and fried food, which Tyler insisted he didn't notice, much to Billie-Jo's incredulity. The curtains seemed to be permanently closed too. On the many occasions she had visited, she had certainly never once seen them open.

The carpet in Tyler's bedroom was threadbare, and there was an ugly patch of black mould on the ceiling above his bed; how many times had she laid there on her back staring up at *that*?

Tyler actually shared the flat with an older man named Gav and his druggie girlfriend, Courtney. Billie-

Jo had only met them once, but she had taken an immediate dislike to them both. That had been one evening when she had only been there a few minutes before Tyler left to get some cider from the off licence down the street.

He had been gone for about ten minutes and Billie-Jo was slumped in front of the TV, when one of the bedroom doors opened and Gav and Courtney emerged; up to that moment, she hadn't even been aware they were home. Courtney, clearly high on something, had been half asleep. She just leant against the door jamb and didn't say a word. However, during the two minutes of awkward conversation that had ensued with Gav, he had spent the entire time staring hungrily at Billie-Jo's chest. Fortunately, when Tyler got back, the odd couple had gone out. After that, she only ever agreed to go round to the flat if they weren't there.

Billie-Jo hadn't really expected Tyler to reply to her text until later; he was rarely out of bed before ten. But less than a minute after she had sent it, her phone pinged. His short reply said that she should drop by the shop to see him at lunchtime. That suited her just fine. It would give her the chance to find a post office and exchange the euros.

She stood at the bus stop on the corner feeling highly conspicuous dressed in a purple velour tracksuit.

Waiting nearby with their mother, two small boys wearing school uniforms kept looking at her, whispering to each other and giggling. She looked across the street towards the house, where she could see Tracy watching from the bedroom window. *Why don't you just piss off?* she thought. She hadn't intended to get on the bus, but since she was being spied on she realised she had little choice but to continue with the deception.

The bus appeared around the corner and with a hiss of brakes it drew up at the kerb. Playing for time, Billie-Jo stood back for a few moments to allow the woman and her boys to get on first. She glanced over at the house again. 'Bollocks,' she said under her breath. Prickling at the sight of Tracy, still standing in the window watching her, she reluctantly got aboard.

When she told the driver she only wanted to go as far as the next stop, he gave her a sarcastic smile. 'Legs not working today then?'

'Says the man whose job it is to sit on his arse all day,' Billie-Jo said under her breath.

The man's smile faded. 'Oi! I'm not obliged to let you on my bus, you know.'

'Sorry.'

'Two pounds forty.'

'Two pounds forty? To go *one* stop?!'

'It's that or Shanks' pony.' The driver shrugged. 'Makes no odds to me.'

Billie-Jo pulled out one of the £10 notes Tracy had given her.

'What's that for?' the driver said.

'To pay my fare.'

'Can't take cash.' The driver pointed to the ticket machine. 'Contactless only.'

'I haven't got a card.' Billie-Jo noticed the man sat in a seat at the front looking at her impatiently over the top of his newspaper. '*What?!*'

'You're holding up the bus,' the man said testily.

'Fuck off, you prick.'

'Right, you,' the driver said sternly. 'Off!'

Billie-Jo looked at him imploringly. 'Please. It's only one stop.'

'I said *off*! Now!'

From where she was standing, Billie-Jo could see up to the bedroom window. There was no sign of Tracy now.

'You can fuck off too then,' she said, sticking up her middle finger at the driver and alighting.

As the bus pulled away, she crossed over the road and headed off in the direction of the Essex Road tube station. On the way, she spotted a post office. She bought a bottle of Coke from a nearby newsagent, then hung around outside for almost an hour waiting for it to open.

As soon as the doors were unlocked, she went straight up to the bureau-de-change counter. A woman whose name badge identified her as Leslie was just taking a seat. 'How can I help you, Miss?'

Billie-Jo handed over the euros. 'I want to change this wop money.'

Leslie looked distinctly affronted, but she took the cash anyway and counted it out.

A few minutes later Billie-Jo walked out with just over £70 in her pocket and made a beeline for the tube station.

*

As far as Tracy was concerned, Churchill Hamlets was a cesspool of scum and she absolutely detested it. On those occasions that she and Billie-Jo's late mother, Vicky had got together, it was never at the flat. She hadn't actually seen a lot of her over the past few years. Wherever they went and whatever they did, they always seemed to end the day arguing. Always, those arguments would start with something trivial, but they never failed to come back to the presence of Jamie Trot in her daughter's life; Tracy despised him even more than she did the Hamlets. Or, if not him, the absence of

Vicky's ex-parter, Curtis Whitlock. Yes, Curtis had been a chronic philanderer who Vicky kicked out just after the second of her two girls was born; given she had learned he was sleeping with another man, it was understandable. Nevertheless, Tracy had always had a soft spot for Curtis. The way he smiled at her always made her feel young and desirable.

Swinging a carrier bag and mumbling irritably to herself, Tracy hurried up the stairwell in Churchill Hamlets, breathing through her mouth so as not to inhale the pervasive smell of urine.

Following an incident some years earlier when Vicky had locked herself out – which resulted in a late-night call-out to a locksmith and a not insubstantial bill – Vicky had given her mother a spare key for safekeeping. Now, as Tracy turned the key in the latch and pushed open the door, she was met by the overwhelming stench of excrement. Putting a hand over her nose and mouth to prevent herself from gagging, she stepped into the living room and slammed the door shut behind her. Immediately she saw the piles of dog faeces scattered all over the carpet.

As she gingerly stepped over an unfeasibly large deposit, there was a low snarling noise from one of the bedrooms and Bronson, the Hazelwood's Rottweiler, appeared in the open doorway. His head was low and his eyes were fixed on Tracy. He snarled again. More aggressively this time.

Tracy stopped still in her tracks.

CHAPTER 4

Tracy stood her ground and pointed a warning finger at the dog. 'Oi! Don't you *dare* bare your teeth at me, you mangy little fucker!'

Undaunted, Bronson growled again and took a pace towards her.

'Oi!' Tracy repeated angrily. 'Stay!'

Bronson paused and peered up at her warily. At the same moment, Stella, the family's Staffordshire Bull Terrier, sauntered into view behind him, her tail wagging excitedly.

The last time Tracy had seen either of the dogs was when they were pups. She had never had much faith in Vicky's ability to do the right thing; she would always put herself first, before everyone and everything. And as for Jamie, he took selfishness to a whole new level. All the same, Tracy still couldn't understand how either of them could have jaunted off on holiday without making sensible provision for the dogs. Yet here in front of her was damning evidence to the contrary.

As Stella came into the room, Bronson snapped at her once and she submissively laid down behind him, her tail still wagging. The Rottweiler looked back up at Tracy and barked once.

'Quiet!' she commanded. 'Sit!'

Much to her surprise, although Bronson made a little growling noise of protest, he did exactly as he was told.

Walking around the outside of the room so as to keep as much distance between herself and them as possible, Tracy went into the kitchen. There was a row of ten empty bowls lined up along the skirting board; at least it seemed they'd been left a decent amount of food, she thought – even though they had probably scoffed down every scrap the moment the front door closed. Beside those, there was a plastic washing-up bowl, half full of water, with small fragments of food floating about in it. Tracy picked it up and emptied the contents into the sink, then she refilled it and put it back down on the floor.

Bronson and Stella were watching her intently from where they remained obediently seated beside the bedroom door.

Tracy reached into her carrier bag and pulled out the four cans of budget-price dog food she had picked up at Baddi's convenience store on the way over. She retrieved a couple of the empty bowls from the floor and forked out the vile-smelling contents of the cans. 'Come on then,' she called. 'Grub's up.' She set the bowls down and both dogs came rushing over and buried their noses in the mush.

Taking advantage of the distraction, Tracy hastily went into the bedroom that Billie-Jo had shared with her sister. She filled two carrier bags with as much fresh clothing as she could carry and went back out to the living room.

Bronson and Stella had finished their meal and were now laid in the cardboard boxes that Tracy assumed must be their beds. Grimacing as she deftly sidestepped another prodigious mound of fecal matter, she saw the two dogs looking up at her. There was a palpable sadness in the Staffie's eyes and Tracy's expression softened as, for a moment – just one tiny moment – she felt empathetic towards them. 'Don't worry. There's a better life away from this shithole waiting for you.'

Bronson whined loudly and hung his head. Stella wagged her tail and made a little whimpering noise.

As Tracy got to the door, her countenance returned to what Vicky had once laughingly called her resting bitch face. 'But if ya think for one second I'm hangin' around to clean up all this shit, ya can jog the fuck on.'

It might have been a mess, but it had still been her daughter's home, and with a last sorrowful look around the room, Tracy let herself out.

Pausing on the doorstep, she set down the carrier bags of clothes to lock the door. Just as she was putting the key away in her purse a voice called out.

'I say!'

Tracy looked up to see an old man with a Chihuahua on a short leash hurrying along the outside walkway towards her.

'Good morning,' he said breathlessly as he stepped up alongside her. 'I heard the door bang a few minutes ago. I assume you're here to sort out those dogs.'

Tracy eyed up the man dismissively. He had a head of whispy, thinning grey hair and at least two days' worth of silver stubble on his gaunt face. If she had been asked to age him, Tracy would have guessed he was in his mid-to-late seventies. Although he had on a suit and tie, he wasn't wearing it well; the shirt collar beneath which the necktie hung limply was frayed and ill-fitting around his scrawny neck, while the jacket bore a number of indefinable stains. When he stepped up close to Tracy she caught the reek of cheap cologne and tobacco.

She took a step back. 'You assume wrong then,' she said curtly, picking up the carrier bags.

'Well someone needs to,' the man persisted. 'In there whining away day and night they have been. This is a nice neighbourhood and...'

Tracy guffawed in disbelief. '*Seriously*? A *nice* neighbourhood? Are you kiddin' me, mate?' She waved a hand at the myriad of colourful obscenities on the graffiti-strewn walls. 'It's a fuckin' shithouse!'

54

The man was slightly taken aback at her ferocity. 'Well,' he spluttered, 'I don't...'

'And who the fuck are you anyway? The bastard Paw Patrol?'

The man stared at her, a perplexed expression on his face. 'I'm sorry,' he said, with a note of genuine apology in his voice. He extended a hand. 'I'm Reg. Reg Avery. I live directly underneath – one floor down, that is.' Quickly realising Tracy wasn't going to shake his hand, he sheepishly withdrew it. 'I didn't mean to appear rude. It's just that I haven't seen the family who live here for several days and it's clear that the dogs have been left to fend for themselves. It's impossible to sleep with all the noise they've been making, and it sets off young Rupert.' He glanced fondly at the Chihuahua.

Tracy gave it a look of disdain.

'I actually spoke to someone at the RSPCA yesterday,' he continued. 'They promised to send someone round, but nobody came. That's why I thought...' He trailed off and smiled broadly, displaying two rows of perfectly aligned white teeth that were patently dentures. 'So, are you a friend of the family? Will they be returning soon?'

'Mind your own business, you nosy old git,' Tracy said dismissively. 'I'll call the RSPCA later.'

'Later *today*?' Reg asked hopefully.

Tracy gave him a disparaging look. '*Later*!' And with that, she turned and strode off.

As the whining inside the Hazelwood's flat started, Reg watched her disappear down the stairwell. 'What a thoroughly unpleasant woman.' He looked down at the Chihuahua and his face brightened a little. 'Come on then, Rupert. Let's get you to the park for wee-wees.'

*

'Why you wearing them dodgy threads?' Smirking at Billie-Jo's purple tracksuit bottoms, Tyler lit up a limp roll-up and inhaled deeply.

'Don't take the fuckin' piss!' Billie-Jo snapped back.

Tyler chortled. 'Really, babe. Have you had a look at yourself?'

'There's a very good reas…'

Tyler cut her off. 'I can only give you two minutes. Pauly called in sick again. Waste of *fuckin'* space. Adbul tried callin' Kez, but she wasn't pickin' up.' He took another puff. 'So it's just him and me, and he's in a right shitty mood about it too.' Catching sight of the drawstring bag on Billie-Jo's shoulder, he breathed out the smoke through his nostrils. 'So then, did ya bring me back somethin' nice?'

56

Billie-Jo stared at him in disbelief. Was that really all he had to say? No *It's good to see you*? No *How was the break*?

They were standing on the pavement outside Cluckin' Crayzee, the chicken shop where Tyler had worked since he was 16 years-old. After leaving school, he had been a mere five weeks into a business studies course when he decided he couldn't stand the tedium any more. Answering an online job ad for part-time work at Cluckin' Crayzee, he'd been offered the job by the proprietor, Abdul Mukherjee, immediately. Tyler's parents didn't approve, of course, but what they thought had never troubled him too greatly, and their protestations that he was wasting his life fell on deaf ears.

One day, Abdul told him that Gav and Courtney, the couple who lived above the shop, were looking for a third person to help split the escalating rent. Tyler had jumped at the chance and, following a night on the beer where he had bonded with Gav, he moved in later the same week. Within days, Gav had identified Tyler as a kindred spirit and introduced him to some of his unsavoury aquaintances. Before long Tyler was dealing drugs. Nothing hard, just cannabis and amphetamines – or twigs and seeds as he quickly learned to call them – but the cash it put in his pocket was enough to cover his weekly rent, with some left over.

After moving in with Gav and Courtney, Tyler never saw his parents again. That had been three years ago now, and he had never felt the inclination to better himself. And why would he? Cluckin' Crayzee put some legitimate money in his pocket, not to mention free food in his belly, and he could roll out of bed late and simply walk downstairs to get to work.

Surprisingly, given its location on the end of a row of distinctly run-down eateries – several of which seemed to be courting closure notices – Cluckin' Crayzee served pretty decent takeaway meals; at an attractively affordable price too. Today, the lunchtime queue extended out of the door.

Tyler took another draw on his cigarette. 'Come on, did ya?'

'*Seriously*, TJ?! It was a fuckin' island in the middle of the sea! There wasn't nowhere to buy *nothin*'. All you ever think about is yourself, you cock. How about askin' me what happened?'

Tyler breathed out another dense plume of smoke. His face darkened. 'Don't go givin' me grief, bitch. Why should I give a fuck about your holiday when you couldn't even be bothered to send me no pics like you promised.'

'I *couldn't*. Our phones were bricked. I'm fuckin' lucky to even be alive! Not that you'd give a shit!'

Tyler glowered at her. 'What the fuck you chattin' about?'

Before Billie-Jo could answer there was a banging sound on the shop window and they turned to see Abdul glaring at them through the glass. He tapped his watch and mouthed something to Tyler.

'Alright, alright, one minute!' Tyler exclaimed, turning back to Billie-Jo. 'I can't even have a fuckin' fag break in peace. What d'ya mean, you're lucky to be alive?'

Billie-Jo stared at him.

'*Well*?'

'Never mind. Doesn't matter now. I'll tell you later.'

Stubbing out his cigarette on the wall, Tyler tucked the snipe behind his ear. 'Whatever. Come round the flat about six.' Giving her a lascivious look, he dropped his hand down and squeezed his crotch. 'You and me, we's got some catchin' up to do.'

He was about to go back inside when Billie-Jo pulled his arm. 'Hang on.' She opened her bag and pulled out the Rolex watch.

Tyler's eyes lit up. 'Sweet! You *did* get me somethin', you fuckin' tease!'

'It's not for *you*. I need you to see what you can get me for it.' She held it out towards him. 'Here.'

Tyler's eyes narrowed. He took the watch from her and turned it in his hands. 'Looks like a knock-off to me.'

Billie-Jo's mind flashed back to Hallam's dead body. She shook her head. 'Trust me, it ain't no knock-off.'

'Where'd you get it?'

'Does it matter?' She looked at Tyler imploringly. 'I need the cash. You gonna help me or not?'

There was another bang on the window. Abdul angrily beckoned to Tyler.

'Alright, I'll get Gav to give it a look. He'll know if it's worth somethin'. And where to fence it if it is.'

Billie-Jo shook her head. 'Not Gav. I don't like him, you know that.'

'He's sound, babe. Just don't hold your breath that it ain't a cheap piece of crap.' Before Billie-Jo had a chance to protest further, Tyler kissed his index finger and touched it to her lips. 'Trust.'

She watched sullenly as he slipped the watch onto his wrist and fastened the clasp.

Admiring the look of it, he nodded approvingly and turned away. 'Laters.'

Tyler went back into the shop and Billie-Jo stood for a moment and watched through the window as he appeared to exchange a few heated words with Abdul. 'Prick,' she muttered.

CHAPTER 5

Billie-Jo had drifted around aimlessly for a couple of hours before returning to the house. She walked in to find her nan drinking tea and watching *Tipping Point*.

Without even looking up, Tracy waved a hand at the kitchen. 'Your stuff is in there.'

'Thanks, Nan.'

Delighted to find the two carrier bags bulging with fresh clothing, Billie-Jo was about to retreat upstairs when Tracy casually asked about her day at school. Engrossed in the TV show, she barely acknowledged Billie-Jo's non-commital reply.

She turned her head lazily to Billie-Jo. 'Anyway, I've got company comin' tonight, so you'd better make yourself scarce.'

Without bothering to mention that she had planned to go out anyway, Billie-Jo went up to her room. Extracting a £20 note, she returned the drawstring bag to its hiding place under the bed and emptied out the contents of the carrier bags.

Then she went and took a shower, which cost her another tongue-lashing from Tracy, who yelled at her from the bottom of the staircase: 'You had a shower this mornin' for fuck's sake! My water bill is gonna be humungous!'

Twenty minutes later, dressed in a pair of jeans, a T-shirt and her favourite hoodie – and feeling fresher than she had done for days – Billie-Jo came back downstairs. Although it aggrieved her to do it, she apologised about the shower.

'Yeah, well, just wait till it's *you* payin' the fuckin' bills. It won't be so funny then!'

Tracy's programme had finished and she was preparing herself something to eat. As had been the case at breakfast, she failed to offer her granddaughter anything.

'And speakin' of bills,' she added, as if thinking aloud, 'I'm gonna have to look into seein' if I'm entitled to benefits now I'm stuck lookin' after you.'

Billie-Jo should have set off for Tyler's there and then, but she made the mistake of asking about Bronson and Stella. A dispute about the impending fate of the two dogs had ensued, and quickly escalated to a screaming match. Armed with the painful knowledge that she would probably never see the dogs again, Billie-Jo had left the house in tears. Stopping at McDonald's to grab a burger and a drink, it had turned half past six by the time she got to Tyler's.

He wasn't happy.

He was wearing a scruffy hoodie and jogging pants and clutching a tumbler of vodka over ice when he opened the door to let her in. 'I said six. Where the fuck have you been?' He turned away from her dismissively.

'Sorry. I got into a bust up with my Nan.' Billie-Jo stepped into the flat and closed the door.

'I've got better things to do than hang about waitin' for you to show,' Tyler said angrily. As he sat down heavily, he registered what Billie-Jo had said. 'Hang on. You went to see your Nan on the way over? What the *fuck*, BJ? Why would you do that when you knew I was waitin'?' He glared at her and drained the glass of vodka.

'I wasn't *visitin'* her. I'm livin' there now.'

'Yeah, right.' Tyler scoffed. 'Since when?'

Billie-Jo exploded. 'Since my whole fuckin' family got killed on that fuckin' Greek island! *That's* since when!'

Tyler frowned. 'What the fuck you chattin' about? You trippin' or somethin', bitch?'

With a heart-rending wail, Billie-Jo crumpled in a heap on the floor and sobbed her heart out. Tyler stared at her in dismay, unsure what to say or do. He got up and went over and knelt down beside her. 'You serious, babe?' he said softly.

Trying to compose herself, Billie-Jo rubbed the back of her hand across her face, streaking it with mucus. 'Yeah.' She was trembling. 'I am.' She wiped her hand on her jeans.

'Shit.' Tyler helped her to her feet. He guided her to the stained sofa. 'Come and sit down. I'll get you a drink.'

He poured a generous measure of vodka into a tumbler and refreshed his own, then he came over and sat down beside her. 'What happened?'

Taking the tumbler from him, Billie-Jo emptied it without pausing for breath. She handed it back. 'Another.'

Tyler refilled her glass and sat down beside her again. He placed a hand on her leg. 'Tell me, babe. What the fuck happened?'

He sat in silence, listening in disbelief, as Billie-Jo spent the next ten minutes describing everything that had happened to her and her family on Mástiga.

She emptied her glass. 'So now I'm stuck livin' with my Nan, and she's made it perfectly clear she doesn't fuckin' want me there, and my life is hell.'

Puffing out his cheeks and exhaling loudly, Tyler sat back. 'What a shitshow.' He was having difficulty processing everything he'd just heard. 'I can't believe Bob is dead.'

Billie-Jo scowled at him. 'Not just Bob, you prick! My Mum and Dad too. All of them, for fuck's sake!'

'Yeah, sorry. I know.' He shook his head sadly. 'But Bob though…' A thought suddenly occurred to him and his face brightened. 'Hey, there has to be a shitload of compo to be had outta this!'

'*What*?'

'Compo. You must be entitled to a fuckin' wedge!' He slipped his arm around her shoulders. 'Every cloud, eh? If it's enough we could think about gettin' ourselves a place together.' He saw the look on her face. 'If you wanted to.'

Billie-Jo was about to explain to him why that would never happen when a mobile phone pinged. Tyler pulled it out of his pocket and looked at the screen. He sat bolt upright. 'Shit.'

'What is it?'

'I got a customer comin' round.' He quickly tapped a reply to the text and hit send.

'Now?'

'Yeah.' Tyler got up and went to the sideboard. 'It won't take long.'

Billie-Jo shook her head. 'I can't believe you're okay with junkies coming here.'

'Safer than dealin' on the streets, babe.' Opening a drawer Tyler pulled out two small wraps. 'And it's only regulars come here. People I trust.'

'You're a fuckin' idiot. That's playin' with fire.'

Tyler laughed and withdrew a handgun from the drawer. 'Nah.'

Billie-Jo's eyes widened. 'What the fuck is *that*?'

Tyler turned and grinned at her. 'What does it look like?'

'It *looks* like a fuckin' gun!' Billie-Jo exclaimed.

'It's protection.'

'Protection from *who*? I thought you just said the people who come here are regulars!'

'They are, babe. But it pays to be cautious.' Tyler playfully pointed the gun at her. 'Blatt blatt!'

'Don't fuckin' point it at me!'

Tyler laughed. 'Relax. It ain't loaded.' He lowered the gun and winked at her. 'Yet.'

Getting up, Billie-Jo walked over to him. 'Show me.'

Tyler handed her the gun. 'Pretty cool, huh?'

'Yeah, it is actually.' Billie-Jo examined the weapon. It was about twelve centimetres long, between seven and eight high, and barely more than two centimetres wide. Cast in silver with a black grip – on which there was an emblem identifying it as a Beretta – she felt the weight of it in her hand. It was remarkably light. 'How long have you had this thing?'

'It ain't mine. It's Gav's.' Tyler took it back from her and looked at it admiringly.

'Have you ever fired it?'

'Nah. But Gav has. At least he said he has. Reckons he put a cap in some guy that refused to pay for his fix.'

Tyler shrugged. 'Not sure I believe him, but what the hey.'

Billie-Jo thought for a moment. 'So why d'ya need a gun? Who's comin'?'

'One of my less predictable regulars,' Tyler said, taking a magazine out of the drawer and sliding it into the butt. It loaded with a soft click. He saw the look of concern Billie-Jo was giving him. 'Your face!' He laughed. 'Don't sweat it. It'll be fine.'

Billie-Jo peered past him into the open drawer, where, as well as a small stash of amphetamine wraps, there were several rolls of banknotes with elastic bands around them and at least half a dozen boxes of ammunition. 'Fuck! You've got enough bullets for an army!'

'Hardly.'

There was a knock on the front door.

Tyler quickly slid the drawer shut and put a finger to his lips. Tucking the Beretta into his hoodie pocket, he whispered, 'Go wait in the bathroom.'

'For fuck's sake!' Billie-Jo hissed.

Nevertheless, her stomach churning, she did as he said. Quietly closing the door behind her, she pressed an ear to it. She could hear talking, but it was indistinct and she couldn't make out what was being said. Then she heard the front door bang shut.

'It's okay, you can come out now,' Tyler called.

As Billie-Jo went back into the living room, he was returning the gun to the drawer.

'I was absolutely shittin' myself in there!'

Tyler chuckled. 'I told you not to worry, babe. Tariq is just a big pussy, but I've seen him get a bit heated sometimes. Like I said, unpredictable. But that's dopeheads for you.' He closed the drawer and waved a fistful of notes at her. 'Not bad, eh?' He stuffed them into the pocket of his pants.

Seeing the money reminded Billie-Jo about the Rolex. 'Hey, did you show that watch I gave you to Gav?'

'Oh, yeah, I was gonna tell you about that.' Avoiding making eye contact with her, Tyler went back to the sofa and slumped down. 'It was just like what I said. A knock-off.'

'Really?' Billie-Jo frowned. A 24-carat motherfucker Hallam may have been, but she couldn't believe for one moment he would have entertained a fake watch. 'You're fuckin' lyin'!'

Tyler looked at her innocently. 'Nope. Knock-off.' He patted the cushion beside him.

Billie-Jo went and sat down. 'Well it still must be worth somethin',' she said. 'Even a knock-off is worth *somethin'*!'

Tyler rummaged in his pocket and pulled out the money again. 'Gav gave me a score for it.' He handed her a £20 note. 'He said he knows someone who'll probably take it for thirty.'

'Thirty quid?! So how come I only get twenty?'

'*Really?*' Tyler shook his head and grinned at her. 'Gav's commission, babe,' he said, as if it was obvious.

'Fuck's sake!'

'Don't be like that.' Tyler slipped his arm around her shoulders. 'Come here. I've missed ya.' He pulled her close and took hold of her hand, guiding it unceremoniously to his crotch.

Through the material Billie-Jo could feel he was already hard. She quickly withdrew her hand.

'Come on, babe, y'know you want it,' Tyler persisted. He tried to kiss her.

Billie-Jo turned her head away. 'I don't!' He tried again and she recoiled. 'Get off me! We ain't fuckin' havin' sex, okay?!'

Tyler stood up. 'Why the fuck did you bother comin' round then?' he said petulantly.

Billie-Jo looked up at him. 'I just wanted to ask you somethin'.'

'BJ has to give me a BJ first. Then we talk.' Tyler pulled down the front of his jogging pants and his erection popped into view. 'I've been waitin' for this all day.' He reached out with both hands and tried to pull Billie-Jo's head forward, but she squirmed free. Tyler's expression changed. 'Don't be a bitch,' he said impatiently. 'Get your fuckin' mouth down here and suck my junk.'

Billie-Jo suddenly looked up at him and smiled flirtatiously. It momentarily disarmed him.

'What you smilin' at?'

'You like havin' your little thingy sucked, don't ya?'

Tyler grinned at her. 'You know I do, babe. And you do it soooo well.' He chuckled. 'And it ain't little neither.'

Billie-Jo got down on her knees, took his hardness in her hand and leant forward. Her mouth was inches away from him when she paused.

Tyler could feel her warm breath on him. 'Aww, don't tease me, babe!' He closed his eyes, anticipating the sensation of her soft mouth enveloping him.

'Did Bob do it better than me?'

'*What*?' Tyler opened his eyes.

'I said, did Bob suck your cock better than me?'

Tyler took a step away from her. 'What you chattin' about now?'

'Surely you haven't forgotten already.' Billie-Jo's eyes were burning into him. 'Your birthday last year? When my sister was in the exact same position as I am now?'

Tyler looked at her nervously. He tried to brazen it out. 'Yeah, right. In her dreams.'

'No, no. For real.'

He squinted down at her. 'Who told you that?'

Billie-Jo was trying to contain her anger. 'Who the fuck d'ya think told me? *Bob*!'

'She wouldn't. I mean…' He faltered. 'I mean, she *didn't*. If she said that she's a lyin' sket!'

'Don't you *dare* fuckin' diss my sister.' Billie-Jo's head darted forward and she bit down hard on the end of Tyler's manhood.

He screamed and reeled away from her. 'What the *fuck*?!' Cradling his injured member, he looked down. His eyes widened and his face filled with rage. 'You've drawn blood, you fuckin' psycho cunt!'

Wiping her mouth, Billie-Jo stood up. 'That'll teach you for fuckin' around behind my back, you worthless piece of shit! And with my little sister of all people!'

Tyler took a step towards her and struck her hard across the face. She stumbled back onto the sofa and he towered over her, his clenched fist raised to strike again. But then, as quickly as it had come, the anger drained from his face.

'Get the fuck out,' he said through gritted teeth. Pulling up his pants, now spattered with blood, he strode to the bathroom. He paused at the door and looked back at her. 'I don't never wanna see your skank face round here again.' He went into the bathroom and closed the door.

71

As soon as he was out of sight, Billie-Jo jumped up and hurried over to the sideboard. She pulled out the Beretta and checked the magazine was still loaded. It was. She was about to gather up the boxes of shells when Tyler reappeared in the bathroom doorway.

'What you still doin' here?' Then he spotted the gun in her hand. 'Hey!' he said angrily, starting forward.

Panicking, Billie-Jo pointed the gun him. 'Stay away from me.'

Tyler stopped and raised his hands. 'Woah! Easy, babe.' He eyed her up nervously and took a step forward.

'I mean it. Stay back! Or else!'

A cocky smile appeared on his face and he dropped his hands. 'Or else *what*? Didn't daddy ever tell you little girls shouldn't play with guns?' He took another pace towards her.

Billie-Jo waved the gun at him.

Tyler flinched.

'I won't warn you again, fucker!' She took a step back. 'Don't test me.'

'You wouldn't shoot me.' Tyler's voice dropped to almost a whisper. 'You couldn't.'

Billie-Jo was struggling to keep her hand from shaking. 'Yes I could. And I *will*!' Her palm was beginning to sweat and she no longer felt as if she had a proper grip on the gun. She tightened her finger on the trigger. 'I will,' she repeated quietly.

Tyler seemed to relax. 'Well, okay, sure. Maybe you *could*.' He grinned and nodded at the gun. 'But you'd have to take the safety catch off first.'

As Billie-Jo's eyes dropped to look at the gun, Tyler launched himself at her. Before she knew what was happening, she had squeezed the trigger and there was a loud bang.

With a look of genuine surprise on his face, Tyler staggered backwards. He glanced at his shoulder, where a dark stain was spreading outwards from the black hole in his hoodie. 'You fuckin' *cunt*!'

Billie-Jo was probably even more shocked than Tyler was. Still gripping the gun tightly, she took a step towards him, her eyes tearing up and her face full of regret.

But then he raised his fist. 'You're fuckin' dead, bitch.'

Instinctively, Billie-Jo pulled the trigger again.

Nothing happened.

As Tyler grabbed hold of her, she urgently squeezed it again. Twice. On the second attempt the Beretta fired, taking half of Tyler's bottom jaw clean off.

He stumbled back and dropped like a stone to the floor. He jerked once, then lay still.

Billie-Jo stood, staring in disbelief at his prone body. Then she ran to the bathroom and was fiercely sick.

CHAPTER 6

Unsurprisingly, Billie-Jo didn't sleep a wink that night. Every time she closed her eyes she saw Tyler's jaw separating itself from his face in an explosion of viscera that had showered her face and clothes.

She could barely remember what she had done with herself between leaving the flat and arriving back at Tracy's house several hours later. Everything that had happened immediately after she had killed Tyler remained vivid though.

She could recall staring at herself vacantly in the bathroom mirror as she washed Tyler's blood off her face. Although the two gunshots hadn't been loud, she'd still half-expected somebody to come banging on the door. But nobody did. She wasn't sure how long she was in the bathroom, but before she left she had been sure to clean up all traces of her vomit.

She had emptied the drawer of the rolls of banknotes, all the wraps of amphetamines and the ammunition. Then, having the wherewithal to remove the magazine from the gun, she had stuffed it along with everything else into her pockets.

Keeping her eyes averted from the mangled remains of Tyler's face, she had gone to relieve him of the cash he had on him only to discover the Rolex watch. Cursing at his dead body – 'You dirty robbing bastard,

I bet you never even showed it to Gav!' – she slipped it on her wrist and snapped the clasp shut. It was a loose fit, but not so much that there was a risk of it coming off.

As she was about to leave, a thought had suddenly came to her; there was something far more obvious she could do here. Putting some of the pills and a few notes back into the drawer, then hastily returning the remainder of Tyler's cash to his pocket, she had left.

She clearly remembered leaving the flat, making a conscious decision to leave the door ajar a couple of inches. Then she had removed her blood-stained hoodie and bundled it up before hurrying down the stairs, stepping onto the street and slipping away unnoticed amidst the meandering flow of evening pedestrians.

But, aside from disposing of the ruined hoodie in a wastebin about a mile away, everything else after that – including the tube journey back to Essex Road – was little more than a blur.

It was well past four in the morning now and she lay restlessly tossing and turning in bed, with Tyler's last few moments of life replaying in her head, round and round on a relentless loop.

She tried desperately to focus on something else. Tracy was oblivious to where Billie-Jo had been, so there was nothing to worry about there. Had anybody actually seen her arrive at Tyler's flat? Passers-by, possibly, but why would any of them have really noticed her? No, she was confident that wasn't a problem. And she was fairly certain nobody on the street had given her a second glance when she left either. Of course, Abdul had seen her with Tyler outside the shop at lunchtime. It wasn't impossible he'd have mentioned to his boss he was seeing her that night.

Of more immediate concern though, when Tyler had spoken to Gav about the watch – if he actually had, of course – it was likely he'd have mentioned she was coming over. She wouldn't have put it past him to brag about how eager she always was to put out either. *Would* he have actually done that? Of course he would, she thought, feeling a prickle of shame; not so long ago, it would have been the truth.

Well, she decided as she checked her phone to see what time it was, both Gav and Tyler dealt drugs. Who would the police trust? If she denied going there, it would be Gav's word against hers.

It was almost four-thirty. Deciding there was no point worrying about what Gav might or might not know or say until it came to it, she rolled over again and sleep finally took her.

As it turned out, Billie-Jo's thinking wasn't too wide of the mark. When she came downstairs a couple of hours later, Tracy was sitting eating her breakfast and listening to the radio. The lead story on the local seven o'clock news was a report on the murder of a London teenager:

'The body of 19-year-old Tyler James, known to his friends as TJ, was discovered late last night in a flat above the Cluckin' Crayzee takeaway in Hackney by his roommates, Gavin Hughes and Courtney Moore. He had been shot dead in what police are treating as a drugs deal gone wrong. A 35-year-old man is helping them with their enquiries.'

That guy Tariq, Billie-Jo thought. *I bet it's him.*

She wasn't stupid enough to think she was out of the woods yet, but for now at least she could breathe easy.

As she left the house on the pretence of heading to school, a curious sense of calmness descended upon her. Shooting Tyler had unquestionably been more accident than premeditated murder, but she had no regrets whatsoever that he was dead. On the contrary. She was glad.

*

Billie-Jo spent some considerable time deliberating over where she should take the watch. Any of the more upmarket establishments would immediately smell a rat. And they would have CCTV surveillance too.

It had been a while since she had visited Soho, and it was the first time she had actually ventured there on her own. Having mooched around for a couple of hours sizing up several possibilities, she bought a chicken salad sandwich and a bottle of Coke in lieu of late breakfast and found a bench in Golden Square to sit and eat.

When she left the park, she took what she figured might be a shortcut back towards Piccadilly. It was then that she passed Julian Hart & Son. The premises were so inconspicuously situated along the narrow side street, that if someone were not to walk right past, they would never know it was even there.

What little Billie-Jo could see of the interior, beyond the displays of new and second-hand jewellery that filled the window, was shrouded in darkness. Disappointed that the place appeared to be closed, she was about to turn away when she caught sight of a sign on the door that indicated otherwise. She tried and it opened.

As she stepped inside, heartbeat racing, the old-fashioned bell overhead tinkled, announcing her arrival. She was immediately greeted by the overpowering scent of yesterday's fry-up and cheap air freshener.

The shop was small. Sitting behind a glass display case filled with all manner of bijouterie, was a man eating a Cornish pasty and reading a tatty paperback book.

He looked up at her over the top of his rimless spectacles. 'Morning.' He made a throaty noise that could have been a chuckle. 'You'll forgive me if I don't get up.'

Billie-Jo could see that he was occupying a wheelchair.

Putting aside his book, the old man tried to turn the wheelchair so that he was facing her. There wasn't a lot of room for manoeuvre and it bashed into the glass cabinet, which shuddered. A couple of the pieces inside fell off their display stands. 'Buggeration!' he exclaimed loudly. 'Oops.' He grinned at Billie-Jo apologetically, revealing a row of yellowing teeth flecked with traces of pastry. 'Pardon my Français!'

Perfect, Billie-Jo thought. *A doddery old fart.* She didn't know whether she was looking at Julian Hart or Son; the establishment gave the impression of having been here a long time, so it could feasibly be either of them. But it didn't matter. All she knew was that this was going to be far easier than she had initially anticipated.

There wasn't a hair on the man's head, making it difficult to age him with any accuracy, but if she had

80

been pressed, Billie-Jo would have said he was 75 if he was a day. There was a horizontal scar about an inch and a half long on his chin, running almost parallel with his thin lips. It was so prominent that it gave him the bizarre appearance of having a second mouth.

'So how can I help you?' He licked his lips and wiped away a long thread of spittle from his chin. 'Looking for anything in particular today? A pretty necklace for a pretty neck perhaps?'

'No.' Billie-Joe rummaged in her drawstring bag and pulled out the Rolex. She laid it on the counter top and slid it towards him. 'How much will you give me for this?'

The man leant forward. Even though she was standing several feet away, Billie-Jo could smell onions on his breath.

'Let's see what we've got here then,' he said, picking up the watch. 'Rolex. Very nice.' Almost imperceptibly, as he inspected it, the corner of his mouth twitched. Pushing his spectacles up on top of his head, he withdrew a loupe from the breast pocket of his waistcoat and screwed it into his eye. He turned the watch in his hands, examining it carefully and making little noises of approval. Billie-Jo noticed the telltale orange stains of a heavy smoker on his fingers.

Half a minute passed, then he slipped the eyeglass back into his pocket and laid the watch back down on the counter top. 'Where, may I ask, did you get yourself an eleven thousand pound watch?'

Billie-Jo nearly choked. 'Eleven *thousand*?!'

'Yup. Give or take a few pounds. So come on, where'd you get it?'

Billie-Jo had decided on the story she was going to tell before coming in, but the shock at what the man had just said completely threw her for a moment. 'It was… it's… I mean it *is* my Grandfather's,' she stammered.

'Uh-huh.' The man lowered his spectacles back onto his nose and peered up at her. 'You stole it, didn't you, little lady?'

Billie-Jo was beginning to realise coming in here had been a mistake. The man's faculties clearly weren't as shaky as she had presumed.

'I didn't,' she said. 'It's my Grandfather's. He hasn't been able to work recently because he's been sick. It's the only thing of any value he owns, so he asked me to sell it for him.' She could tell from the way the man was looking at her that he clearly didn't believe a word of it. 'He needs the money,' she concluded quietly.

The gimlet eyes studied her. 'Your Grandfather, eh?'

Billie-Jo looked down at her feet. 'Yeah.'

The man scratched his chin. 'Alright. It's a legal requirement I check with the police when I'm offered expensive items.'

Billie-Jo tried to sound matter-of-fact. 'Yeah?'

'Yup. Protocol. To ensure they aren't on any stolen goods lists.' The man could see Billie-Jo was starting to look uncomfortable. 'That's not a problem, is it?'

'No.'

'Because it's completely legit, right?'

'Yeah.'

The man stared at her in silence for a moment, as if he was waiting for her to break. He'd been in the trade long enough to know when something was stolen. 'Okay then. If you want to come back in an hour, I'll see what I can do for you.'

Billie-Jo's mind was racing. All she wanted was to get out – and there wasn't a chance in hell she was coming back.

'Tell you what, mate.' She snatched up the watch and thrust it into the pocket of her hoodie. 'Don't worry about it, yeah? I'll take it somewhere else.' She turned to leave.

'Five hundred.'

'Huh?' Billie-Jo turned back to face him.

Rather disconcertingly, there now seemed to be a hint of menace in the smile. 'I said five hundred. I'll give you five hundred pounds for it. Cash. No questions asked.'

'You said it was worth eleven thousand!'

The man shrugged and sat back in his wheelchair. 'Non-negotiable. Take it or leave it.'

Billie-Jo shook her head. 'I'll leave it.' She turned her back on him and started towards the door.

'You'll have your work cut out for you trying to shift that thing, you know.'

Her hand on the door handle, Billie-Jo paused. She looked back over her shoulder at him.

'But I kind of think you *do* know, don't you?' he continued. 'No reputable dealer will touch it. If I were you, I would seriously reconsider my offer before walking out of here.'

There was wiliness in the old man's greedy eyes now. He knew he had Billie-Jo on the hook; all he had to do was gently reel her in.

'Come on. You don't look stupid.' He smiled. 'Then again, coming in here trying to hawk a stolen watch wasn't all that smart. You should know you can't kid a kidder, little lady.'

'Eight hundred,' Billie-Jo said.

'You don't hear too good, do you? I said it's non-negotiable. Take the five. It's a generous offer.'

'Forget it.'

The man chortled. 'You've got spunk, little lady. I'll give you that.' He appeared to think for a moment. It was just possible she was actually going to walk away after all. A little sweetener was needed. 'Okay. Six fifty. Final offer.'

Billie-Jo pulled the watch out of her pocket and set it back down on the counter. She kept her hand on it. 'Cash?'

'Right here, right now.'

'Okay.'

The man snatched up the Rolex and hastily tucked it away in a drawer behind him. Billie-Jo watched as he counted out the £650 in a combination of £20 and £10 notes – then counted it again just to be sure.

As he handed her the money, he noticed her looking up at the ceiling behind him. He glanced round at the CCTV camera mounted in the corner. 'Don't you go worrying about that old thing. It hasn't worked for years and it's way too expensive to get it fixed.' He grinned. 'You'd be surprised how effective it is having a camera on the wall though, regardless of whether it's a dummy or not.'

Dropping the cash into her bag, Billie-Jo pulled the drawstring tight. 'You're a fucking thief, do you know that?'

The man chuckled. 'I've been called worse in my time. And by far sassier fillies than you.'

As Billie-Jo left the shop, his voice rang in her ears: 'Pleasure doing business with you, little lady. You be sure to have yourself a nice day now.'

*

Detective Inspector Landis pressed the doorbell of Kevin Smart's small, semi-detached house in West Hampstead. While he was waiting for someone to answer, he caught sight of his reflection in the glass and straightened his tie.

The investigation into what had happened on Mástiga was progressing well. The Greek authorities were proving difficult to liaise with, but Landis was managing to work around that. He had spoken extensively with Nick Mason, his wife Kirsty and their boy Charlie, and he now believed he had a pretty clear picture of events.

He had also been tasked with speaking to the relatives of the dead, but that had sounded much simpler that it was turning out to be.

The only surviving member of the Page family, the teenage daughter Hollie, had returned to the UK with the Masons. But after spending one night with them at their home, she had taken off and disappeared. She hadn't yet gone back to the family house, but Landis was fairly sure she would do eventually; after all, she was only 14. He hadn't yet indentified any contactable next of kin for the family.

The only traceable relative for the Kinleys had been Helen Watling. She stated she hadn't seen Lisa for some time. And, though ostensibly distressed over the news that her daughter and son-in-law were dead, she reiterated what she had told Moira Previs from Social Services: under no circumstances was she prepared to take in her little grandchildren, Jack and Jordan.

Landis intended to see Billie-Jo Hazelwood again – even if it meant having to go through her insufferable grandmother. But this afternoon he wanted to speak with Kevin Smart, the husband of Caroline, whose abused body had been found by the Greek police, stuffed into a car boot on Mástiga.

According to what Landis had been told by Nick Mason, Caroline had appeared to have been Terence Hallam's right-hand woman, and he wanted to learn more.

A woman in her mid-to-late 30s wearing a plastic apron answered the front door. She looked at Landis inquiringly.

He introduced himself and she said she was Kevin's carer, Gillian Edmondson. Telling him that he had been expected, she invited him in – a little reluctantly, Landis felt.

'Kevin's just had his afternoon nap. I'm making tea. Would you like one?'

Landis nodded. 'That's very kind.'

Gillian showed him through to the lounge where Kevin was watching a television programme. He pressed a button on the remote to mute the TV and Gillian introduced him to Landis: 'This is the policeman who called yesterday.' Then she went out to the kitchen to make the tea.

Kevin listened as Landis explained what had become of Caroline with as much tact and compassion as he could.

As he finished, Gillian returned with the tea. Kevin's was in a stainless steel container with a straw. She set it down on the table beside him – 'Be careful, it's hot.' Then, after plumping up the cushions behind his back, she politely retreated to the kitchen, leaving them to it.

'I don't think Caroline loved me,' Kevin said tearfully. 'She did once. At least I think she probably did. But not any more.'

Landis raised his eyebrows. 'Why would you say that?'

Kevin spread his hands wide as if to say "look at me". 'I mean, I can't say I blamed her. It can't have been easy. By day, chief breadwinner doing a job she couldn't abide. And by night, slave to someone who can barely wipe his own arse. She always came home so stressed and I know I was a burden she could have done without.'

Landis looked a little awkward He didn't quite know how to respond to that. He picked up his tea and took a sip. It was lukewarm. He set the cup down again.

'We haven't been able to find any of Hallam's employee records yet. But from what we've been led to believe, your wife was his full-time personal assistant. Is that correct?'

Kevin made a little noise that was a cross between a laugh and a sob. 'Yes, that's right. Caroline always said she hated that job – maybe she did, maybe she didn't. If anything, it was probably more likely frustration at being trapped out of necessity. She was certainly well paid though. And she clearly admired Terence Hallam. I never met him, by the way. And Caroline never said much about him. But whenever she did, there was always... well, I suppose you'd call it a sort of deference in her voice. She seemed to idolise him. She worked long hours too and of course sometimes there were overnight stays.'

'Overnight stays?'

'Yes, you know, business trips and that sort of thing.'

Landis raised an eyebrow. 'Well, Mr Smart... May I call you Kevin?'

Kevin nodded.

'Please accept my apologies if I'm speaking out of turn. I certainly don't mean to be insensitive. But it very much sounds to me as if theirs might have been more than a working relationship?'

Kevin sighed. 'I may need someone to clean up my shit and piss for me, Mr Landis, but I'm not blind. I don't know if anything was going on, but of course I suspected.'

'You never confronted her?'

'I suspected,' Kevin repeated. 'That was enough. I suppose deep down I really didn't want those suspicions confirmed. Does that make sense?'

'I'm not sure it does. If it were me, I'd want to know.'

Kevin turned his head away and stared out of the window. 'Yes, well. I loved Caroline. She was my world. But I had nothing to offer her. Physically, I mean. I guess ultimately she found more comfort in the bed of a wealthy, influential man than she did in that of a worthless invalid. Who could blame a woman for that?' Quickly wiping away another tear, he turned back to face Landis. 'Gillian has been a Godsend though. I am able to look after myself to a point. She usually only comes in twice a day for an hour, but she's always been willing to stay overnight if Caroline was away.' He saw the look on Landis's face. 'No funny business. Just to look after me.'

Landis nodded. 'Of course.'

'We get on well. She couldn't have been happier to move in for a few days when Caroline swanned off to Greece. And now…' He trailed off. Picking up his tea, he sucked some through the straw. 'Well. That will need to be discussed.'

Landis stood up. 'Well, thank you for your time, Kevin. I'm really sorry for your loss. If you need anything else, or you think of anything at all that could help with our investigation into Hallam's activities, please give me a call.' He handed over a business card. 'Day or night.'

Before leaving, Landis returned his cup to the kitchen where Gillian was washing up.

She broke off to show him to the door. 'He's a lovely man, Detective Inspector. He just got dealt a bad hand.'

Landis returned to his office in Bishopsgate feeling a lot sadder than when he had arrived. This was fast becoming one of the most arduous and upsetting cases he'd ever been assigned to.

CHAPTER 7

Repatriating a dead body is not a complicated process. Essentially, one must obtain a translation of the death certificate issued in the country where the person died. Permission must then be sought to remove the body, which will be issued by the coroner, once again in the country where that person died. Under normal circumstances this shouldn't take longer than between five and seven days. However, when a death has occurred under violent or unnatural circumstances, the coroner in England needs to be notified, and naturally enough it becomes a little more complicated. Multiply that by three and you're dealing with a stressful and not inexpensive situation.

The bodies of Jamie Trot and Vicky and Bobbi-Leigh Hazelwood were not released and returned to England from Greece until the end of September.

Their joint funeral took place on October 3rd.

Tracy had allowed Billie-Jo to choose the three songs to be played at the service.

Picking something for Vicky was simple. It had to be Luis Fonsi's *Despacito*, which she had adored. Bobbi-Leigh was just as easy. Billie-Jo would never forget the laughter as she and her sister used to prance around their bedroom to the beat of Rhianna's *Only*

Girl in the World when they were small. Jamie was a little more difficult though; his taste in music had been pretty awful in Billie-Jo's opinion. In the end she settled for *Old Town Road* by Lil Nas, which he had listened to often and once drunkenly performed at a karaoke night. Badly at that.

The humanist service was emotional and both Billie-Jo and Tracy wept.

Curiously though, it brought them closer together. Not to a level that could be called harmonious as such; there were still little eruptions and there was always an air of acrimony whenever they spent any length of time in the same room. But after the funeral they mostly managed to remain civil to one another.

Two days later, much to Tracy's annoyance, Detective Landis telephoned and arranged to visit Billie-Jo again.

The meeting was brief. It quickly became apparent there wasn't much more she could tell him, and she ended up going over the same ground as the first time they had spoken.

Then, one morning less than a week later, Tracy was on a bus and spotted Billie-Jo in the window of a café when she should have been at school.

As soon as she got home, Tracy phoned the school and gave them a mouthful for not having chased up their absentee. The woman she spoke with claimed they

93

had tried to contact Billie-Jo's parents, but to no avail. Truant officers had visited the flat too, she said. In their defence, she added, the school had no idea she was living with her grandmother now and she strongly recommended Tracy speak with her granddaughter – because otherwise, as guardian, she could be on the receiving end of a fine.

That afternoon when Billie-Jo got home, Tracy was waiting for her in the kitchen.

'Good day at school?' she asked with a hint of sarcasm.

'It was okay.'

'Just okay?'

Billie-Jo sensed something was up. Tracy barely even usually spoke to her when she got in. 'A bit shit I s'pose,' she said.

'What was shit about it?'

There was definitely something going on here. Billie-Jo shrugged. 'Dunno.'

'You don't know cos you wasn't even there, you lying little cow!'

An almighty row ensued, resulting in Billie-Jo being given an ultimatum that she couldn't see any way past: 'You get your fuckin' arse into school. Every day, mind you. Or you can find somewhere else to live! Is that clear?'

Billie-Jo returned to school the very next day.

With the money she had made selling the watch and the various sums she had purloined from Hallam and Tyler, there was well in excess of £3000 hidden away in Billie-Jo's room. Naturally enough, the temptation to spend some of it proved too difficult to resist; almost £300 went in one hit on a trip into town with a friend, Carly, after which she had returned home with a new pair of trainers, several pairs of jeans, some T-shirts and a Vans shoulder bag.

Tracy had been watching TV when she got back to the house, so Billie-Jo had easily managed to smuggle her purchases upstairs without her noticing. It wasn't a one-off occasion though, and her extravagance had eventually led to yet another confrontation.

She had been on her way out one Saturday morning when Tracy called her back.

'That bag. It's new, ain't it?'

Billie-Jo paused at the door. 'Eh?'

'That shirt you've got on too. I definitely haven't seen you wearin' it before.'

Billie-Jo huffed. 'God, seriously? You eyeballin' everything I fuckin' *wear* now? Haven't you heard of charity shops?'

Tracy's eyes blazed. 'How many times have I gotta tell you to watch your fuckin' mouth in my house?' She looked at Billie-Jo suspiciously. 'That twenty quid a week I gives you seems to be goin' a long way. You'd better not have been out chawin'!'

'I haven't!'

'Woe betide you if I find out you have. Last thing I want is the filth round here bangin' the door down!'

'Honest, Nan. It's charity shops.'

Tracy evidently didn't believe her and Billie-Jo left the house making a mental note to be more circumspect in future.

There was something else she invested in too. Tyler had once mentioned to her that he always used burners. She hadn't even known what he was talking about. He'd explained that a burner was a cheap mobile phone which people used for anonymous online activity and then disposed of. At the time, she had ribbed him about visiting porn sites. But now she wanted to keep a close eye open for any news on the investigation into his murder, having a burner made perfect sense.

A few days after their spat, further information was released to the media about the death of Tyler James.

It transpired that it was indeed Tariq – Tariq Ahmad – who had been helping the police with their enquiries. He had been almost comatose when the officers broke down the door of the house he shared with seven other men. All of them were illegal immigrants. A search revealed that he had the same type of drugs in his possession that had been found in the drawer in Tyler's flat.

Taken into custody, when Tariq's lucidity returned he'd admitted that he had been to the flat that night, but claimed it had been a legitimate transaction. He said he hadn't seen anyone else there and that Tyler had been very much alive when he left. He had returned home, where he took several of the pills, after which he couldn't remember anything until becoming vaguely aware of being manhandled into the back of a police van the next morning.

During the ensuing interview, Tariq made the mistake of remarking that he sometimes heard voices in his head. Coupled with the fact he had no clear recollection of the evening in question, this was enough for the police to formally arrest him under suspicion of Tyler's murder. There were questions raised about the fact Tariq had left some of the drugs behind, also that he hadn't taken the money from Tyler's pocket. Moreover, an extensive search had failed to turn up the murder weapon. But as far as investigating officers were concerned, Tariq Ahmed was their man and he was now in custody awaiting trial.

Billie-Jo heard all this on the radio one morning while she and Tracy were eating breakfast. One thing that had changed over the weeks was that they had actually started eating meals together. There was little doubting this mostly came down to the fact Tracy had started to receive a generous allowance towards Billie-Jo's keep.

As she listened to the report about the investigation into Tyler's murder, Billie-Jo could hardly believe it. Although she suspected Tyler played the field, she had been sleeping with him for months and somehow she'd slipped under the radar; the police hadn't even worried themselves to contact her. The investigation had started and ended with Tariq Ahmad.

Once again she was consumed with relief. Yes, there was the tiniest twinge of guilt that Tariq was going to be tried for something he didn't actually do, but not so much that it would impact on her day. She went off to school that morning feeling better than she had done for weeks.

And so, life went on. The next few months passed quickly and relatively quietly. Until early one Friday evening between Christmas and New Year when everything suddenly changed.

Although it had been snowing heavily for most of the day, by the time Billie-Jo got in from school mid-afternoon it had more or less stopped. Nevertheless, it was bitterly cold, and Tracy had rustled up a couple of warming bowls of chilli and some thick slabs of crusty bread for their dinner.

She and Billie-Jo had been sitting, eating from trays on their laps, and watching *The Chase*. The programme finished and Tracy muted the sound.

'One step away from twenty-fuckin'-seven thousand! They'd have taken it too if that twat hadn't said Henry the Sixth.'

Billie-Jo rolled her eyes. 'And I s'pose you knew the answer.'

Tracy laughed. 'Course I fuckin' didn't! But I wouldn't go on telly in front of millions of people and make a twat of m'self in the first place.' She stood up. 'Fancy sharin' the last of that apple pie?'

'Yeah, please.'

'I'll heat it up.' Tracy took both trays and went out to the kitchen.

Curling her feet up beneath her, Billie-Jo picked up her phone and started browsing through the posts on her Facebook page. She paused to look at a photo of one of her friends, arms wrapped round the neck of a poncey-looking guy at some concert or other she'd been to. 'Fuckin' bitch,' she muttered, idly scrolling on.

Tracy reappeared carrying two dishes of dessert. She handed one to Billie-Jo and settled back in her chair. The six o'clock news had started on the TV and she unmuted the sound.

'...and following the hearing today, a spokesperson for Partridge and Swann said that they conceded there had been negligence in not identifying what was happening sooner, but were pleased that the case had finally come to court.' There was a quick shot of a man leaving a court building with a briefcase raised in an attempt to shield his face from the assembly of journalists and photographers. 'Mr Partridge has strongly denied all the allegations of embezzlement and stands by his statement that he is confident he will be found innocent. Our reporter, David Marshall, spoke to him earlier this week.'

As the man who had been filmed leaving the court came on screen and started to speak, Tracy hit the mute button.

'He can knob right off,' she said through a mouthful of apple pie. 'I tell you, it makes me fuckin' sick. There ain't no justice in this world. All these pricks are interested in is lining their own pockets. They probably rake in more money in a year than I'll see in my whole fuckin' life, but, oh no, it's never enough is it? Gotta have more.'

Still looking at her phone, Billie-Jo wasn't really listening to Tracy's rant, but she made a little noise of agreement.

'Doesn't matter how many laws they break doing it neither,' Tracy continued. 'They've got the money to hire the best lawyers and surprise surprise, they get away with it. And even them that does get banged up bounce back with a bastard TV show or a fuckin' book. Like that politician who went down for two years for somethin' or other. He probably had a whale of a time getting' bummed in the showers, he gets out, and what does he do? Writes a load of books called *My Prison Diaries* or some shit like that. Bestsellers. Even more fuckin' money in the bank! And it's *always* the so-called respectable ones. You never know what's goin' on behind those cocksure smiles. I tell you, they're cunts, the lot of 'em.' She waved her spoon at the TV set. 'Look at that smarmy little fucker. Whatever he done wrong, I'll bet you a pound to a pinch of shit he'll get away with it.'

Billie-Jo finally looked up at the TV. What she saw made her blood run cold. She stared at the man on the screen in disbelief. She had seen him before and she knew exactly where too.

'Put the sound up, Nan.'

'Why?'

'Please!'

Tutting, Tracy unmuted the sound.

'…next week.' The interview had just finished and the picture changed to another shot of reporters milling around outside the courts.

'The trial continues,' the voiceover said.

Almost knocking her dessert dish off the arm of her chair, Billie-Jo jumped up and ran to the stairs.

'Oi, where are you goin'? You haven't eaten your puddin'.'

'Gotta go toilet.'

Her heart racing, Billie-Jo bounded up the stairs two at a time. When she got to her room, she knelt down and felt about under the bed, pulling out the paperwork about Hallam's investors that she had brought back with her from Mástiga. Her fingers shaking, she rifled quickly through it and extracted one of the pages. She stared at it and her stomach turned.

There was a photograph clipped to the top of the page, and now there was absolutely no doubt about it – it was the man whose face had flashed up on the TV. Billie-Jo scanned the information on the page and there too was the name she had heard on the news report: Crispin Partridge. The information in the paperwork was scant, but it identified the man as a partner in a private firm of financial advisors, Partridge & Swann. He was married to Cressida and they had one son, Dominick. *So*, Billie-Jo thought. *Not only pouring money into Hallam's twisted scheme, the scumbag had his fuckin' grubby little hands in the till too.*

She suddenly felt a bit sick. Folding the paperwork and stashing it back under the bed, she nipped into the bathroom to flush the toilet, then went back downstairs.

Tracy looked up at her. 'That took you long enough!'

Billie-Jo pulled a face and rubbed her stomach. 'That chilli went straight through me. I've got the shits.'

Tracy cackled. 'You must've had a dodgy kidney bean.' She pointed to the dish of apple pie on the arm of Billie-Jo's chair. 'You gonna eat that?'

'I don't think I can face it now.'

Setting her own empty dish aside, Tracy leant over and picked up Billie-Jo's. 'Waste not, want not.' She started to tuck in.

CHAPTER 8

With Tracy's angry outburst over criminal injustice still playing on her mind, Billie-Jo went up to bed that night with a seething rage inside her unlike anything she had ever felt before. Unable to sleep, she spent some considerable time on her burner phone, researching and reading every piece of information she could find online about Crispin Partridge.

There was plenty.

It transpired he was one of the Norfolk Partridges, a highly respected family that had made its fortune in arable farming. He was privately educated at Beeston Hall, before moving on to Wymondham College and then Cambridge University.

Young Crispin had always had a remarkable talent for numbers. After he graduated with honours, substantial funding from his parents enabled him to establish his own business in London as a private financial advisor. For no other reason than their names – Hector and Melissa – Billie-Jo instantly despised his parents.

By the age of just 23, Partridge was living in a flat in Westminster, owned a private two-seater plane and two cars, and was often photographed at the swankiest nightspots – always, it seemed, in the company of a different young lady. On top of that, there were the extended holidays in far-flung, exotic climes that most normal people could only ever dream of being able to afford to visit. In short, he was basking in the glory of a charmed life.

It was the more recent information about him that Billie-Jo found interesting. As his business had taken off and the workflow became increasingly unmanageable for a one-man outfit, Partridge had gone into partnership with Tobias Swann, a fellow Cambridge graduate who he had remained in touch with. Before long, Partridge & Swann had become *the* go-to concern for those with money who wanted the very best available financial advice. Three previous Prime Ministers had been known to use them. Furthermore, their clients over the years had included a famous actor, a best-selling author who Billie-Jo had never heard of, a disgraced former TV presenter who was now serving jail time for sexual misconduct in the workplace, and a number of prominent figures in the city, among them Aristotle Parker, Genevieve Forsythe and –

Billie-Jo, whose eyes had started to droop, was suddenly wide awake again.

– Terence Hallam.

Partridge & Swann continued to flourish over the years, eventually moving to larger premises off The

Strand and building a valuable base of seven employees.

At the age of 41, Partridge had married Cressida Harlington-Forbes and they had taken up residence in Tunbridge Wells, where, a year later, their son Dominick was born.

As Billie-Jo had been reading, a plan had started to take shape in her head, and it didn't take much digging to discover that the Partridge's home was a beautiful detached property in Calverley Park, just a few minutes' walk from the mainline station.

It had turned midnight by the time she started to read about the embezzlement charges that had been brought against him. A lot of it was going over her head, so when she started to zone out she set her phone alarm for early the next morning and settled down to get some sleep.

Billie-Jo got up to find it had been snowing hard again overnight.

She showered and dressed for the cold weather, then, making sure she had everything in her bag she was going to need, she went downstairs.

At the breakfast table, unable to disguise the hint of ulterior motive, Tracy casually enquired as to what plans she had for the day.

'I'm gonna meet Carly,' Billie-Jo lied.

'Where you going?'

'Dunno. Carly said somethin' about going to see that new Keanu Reeves film. I can't really afford it though, so I expect we'll just go get somethin' to eat in McDonalds.'

'Here.' Tracy went to her purse and handed Billie-Jo a £10 note. 'You've been doin' better at school. You deserves a little treat.'

'Wow, really?'

'Go see your film.' Tracy smiled at her. 'Hang on a sec, give me that back.' She fumbled in her purse and exchanged the £10 note for a twenty. 'You can have lunch on me too. And treat your mate.'

Billie-Jo smiled appreciatively. 'Aww, thanks.'

'Just make sure you keep yourself entertained all day. And I mean *all* day, okay?'

Billie-Jo looked at Tracy knowingly. 'Expecting company, are we Nan?'

Tracy looked slightly indignant. 'Not that it has fuck all to do with you, but as it so happens I am. I've got my friend Lionel comin' over.'

'*Lionel*?' Billie-Jo sniggered. 'What sort of name is that?'

'What's wrong with Lionel? It's a nice name.'

'It's a fuckin' *ancient* name. How old is he, ninety?'

Tracy pointed a warning finger at her. 'Oi, don't you take the piss or I'll have my fuckin' money back! I'll have you know he's a lovely man.'

Bundled up against the biting wind, Billie-Jo trudged through the snow to Essex Road and boarded a train to London Charing Cross. From there, the onward journey to Tunbridge Wells took a little over an hour.

She spent most of the time staring out of the window at the views as they flashed past; built-up towns punctuated by stretches of beautiful countryside, all clothed in a barely disturbed blanket of white that stretched away onto the horizon for as far as her eye could see.

She tried to think about anything and everything except what lay ahead; more than enough consideration had been given to that, and she knew that if she didn't banish it from her thoughts for a little while she would probably chicken out.

Before leaving the house, she had rummaged through the storage boxes in her bedroom and found an old pair of reading glasses. It was remarkable how wearing them changed her appearance. Although they made her vision ever so slightly blurry, she had put them on when she arrived at Charing Cross station. Having boarded the train and found a seat in the rear coach well away from any other passengers, she had taken them off.

Now, as the announcement came over the tannoy that the next stop would be Tunbridge Wells, she put them back on again.

Stepping off the train onto the platform, lightly dusted with snow and sprinkled with salt to prevent travellers from slipping, she glanced up at the station clock: two minutes past ten.

From Google Maps she had ascertained that Calverley Park was only six minutes' walk away. Adjusting her scarf so that it masked the bottom half of her face – which provided the dual benefit of both concealment and protection against the wind and snow – she zipped up her puffa jacket and put on a pair of fingerless mittens. Then she quickly tucked up her long hair under a woolen beanie and lowered it at the front so that it aligned with the top of the spectacles. Finally, after assessing the contents of her bag one last time, she slipped it onto her shoulder and set off.

Due to the weather, it was hard going covering the short distance to Partridge's house and it took Billie-Jo longer to get there than she had anticipated. Given the ferocity of the wind and snow, she hadn't really expected to see anyone as she crossed the park. However, there was someone bundled up and braving

109

the elements – she didn't get close enough to see if it was a man or a woman – walking two big dogs. Other than that she didn't encounter a soul.

The house she was looking for was located at the end of an L-shaped close lined with naked oak trees. There was a double-width open driveway fronting the property, on which was parked a metallic black Bugatti. As Billie-Jo approached, she could see tracks leading away from the empty space beside it. Despite her carefully considered plan, this was a turn of events that hadn't even occurred to her; what if Partridge wasn't at home? *Well*, she thought, *it's too late now. I'm here*.

Taking a deep breath, she strode confidently up to the door and rang the bell. The chimes inside jingled a familiar tune. Billie-Jo vaguely recognised it, but she wouldn't have been able to name it to save her life. A few moments later, she heard the safety chain rattle and the door opened.

Billie-Jo's stomach tightened. The man stood in the doorway was much taller than she had expected. Less immaculately presented than the one she had seen on television the previous afternoon too. Dressed casually in a chunky, green woolen pullover and loose-fitting grey sweatpants, his mop of hair was badly in need of a brush and he evidently hadn't bothered to shave that morning either. But there was no doubt whatsoever who it was.

Crispin Partridge sized up the figure on his doorstep. The face was all but hidden by a scarf across its mouth and a snow-caked hat pulled down low.

He frowned. 'Yes?'

'I'm really sorry to bother you. I was supposed to be meeting my friend, but I left my phone on the train and I don't know Tunbridge Wells at all.'

Partridge's eyes narrowed suspiciously. 'Is this some sort of set-up?' He looked past Billie-Jo, scanning the close as if he was expecting to see someone else. 'Are you press?'

'Press?'

'Don't play stupid. Press. A journo.'

'No, I'm...'

'You must think I was born yesterday. I've said all I have to say to you people.' He looked at her scornfully. 'Meeting a friend? Is that the best you can come up with?'

'It's true!'

'Sure it is.' There was derision in his voice now. 'Just bugger off!'

Billie-Jo pulled the scarf away from her mouth and took off the spectacles. 'And I *did* leave my phone on the train.'

Partridge had been about to close the door on her, but now he could see that the person he was talking to was a young girl, curiosity got the better of him.

'The station is at least five minutes away. Why on earth did you come knocking here?' There was still suspicion in his tone. 'If all you've told me is true, why didn't you speak to someone at the station?'

'My friend lives round here somewhere, but I couldn't remember the exact address. It's on my phone...'

'Which you left on the train?' Partridge clearly wasn't buying it.

'Exactly. I tried a few doors along the road.' Billie-Jo gestured behind her. 'But nobody was answering. All I know is she lives right near Camden Park, so...'

'Ah!' Partridge's expression changed into a half-smile and he shook his head. 'I'm afraid you've come the wrong way, young lady. This is *Calverley* Park. Camden Park is a good twenty minutes' walk from here.'

Billie-Jo assumed an expression of dismay. 'Oh no!'

Partridge chuckled. 'Oh *yes*. Sorry.' He started to close the door.

'Wait! I know it's an imposition, but do you think I could come in quickly and use your phone to call my friend?'

'What for?'

'To see if her Mum can come and pick me up. You said it's twenty minutes to Camden Park and without my phone I haven't got a clue where I'm going.'

Partridge still wasn't entirely convinced by Billie-Jo's story. He shook his head regretfully. 'I'm sorry, I'm afraid not.'

The cold wind was making Billie-Jo's eyes water. It couldn't have been more advantageous. She shivered. '*Please*, mister?'

Partridge appeared to consider the situation for a moment. 'Alright,' he said, suddenly taking pity on the somewhat bedraggled-looking and clearly freezing-cold girl. 'But I'm extremely busy, so you'd best be quick.'

Billie-Jo smiled. 'I will be, I promise.'

Stamping her feet to get the accumulation of snow off her trainers, she stepped into the hallway and Partridge closed the door.

There was a faint scent of roses in the air and the quiet sound of classical music was emanating from what Billie-Jo presumed to be the living room.

'Shall I take my shoes off?'

Partridge shook his head. 'You'll not be here long. Phone's over there.' He pointed to a small wooden table with ornate fretwork on its legs. It looked like it could be an antique.

'Thanks.'

As Billie-Jo picked up the receiver and was about to dial, Partridge appeared at her shoulder. 'You can remember your friend's phone number then?'

'Uh-huh.'

'But not her address?' He was looking at her suspiciously again.

Billie-Jo shrugged. 'Yeah.'

Partridge raised his eyebrows and went over to the stairs. He sat down on the bottom step and watched Billie-Jo while she made the call.

'Where exactly is this?' she asked as she punched in a random selection of numbers.

'Just say Honeywell Close. You can go and wait for your friend at the end.'

'Calverley Park?'

'Well remembered.' There it was again – that trace of suspicion in Partridge's voice.

However, with her back to him, Billie-Jo made such a convincing show of the brief, one-sided conversation that by the time she hung up Partridge was satisfied the story she had fed him was true. So much so that he apologised for having been suspicious of her when she arrived. Then, when she told him her friend's mum wouldn't be able to pick her up for half an hour, he even offered to make her a hot drink while she waited.

'That's *so* kind of you. It's lovely and warm in here.' Billie-Jo took her bag off her shoulder, slipped the spectacles inside and put it down on the doormat. She pulled off her scarf and mittens and dropped them beside the bag, then removed her beanie and shook out her hair – which tumbled down loose around her shoulders – and unzipped her jacket. All she had on underneath was a cotton T-shirt. The outlines of her nipples were pressing against the thin fabric.

She knew precisely what she was doing. Just as she had anticipated they would, Partridge's eyes flicked down to her chest.

'Yes, well…' The tip of his tongue flicked out and moistened his lips. 'Come on out to the kitchen.' He lingered in the doorway, a slightly dopey smile on his face.

In that moment, Billie-Jo knew she had him. *Fuckin' men*, she thought, struggling to maintain an expression on her face that didn't betray the contempt she was feeling for him. *They're* so *easy!*

Partridge stepped aside and waved a gentlemanly hand, ushering her past him. 'After you, young lady.'

Offering him a sweet smile that conveyed both an innocent unawareness of what she'd allowed him to see and maybe – just maybe – the tacit promise of availability, she started to walk towards him.

That was the moment when her plan suddenly went awry.

CHAPTER 9

Twenty minutes later, as she made her way back across the park, Billie-Jo was still cursing her stupidity. It had only been one tiny little oversight. But she had failed to do something that now seemed so blindingly obvious, she could hardly credit that she hadn't.

One little flick of the switch on the side of her phone to put it on silent; that's all it would have taken. But it had never even entered her mind.

Partridge was standing in the kitchen doorway. As Billie-Jo stepped over, preparing herself to brush seductively against him as she went past, the pinging noise announcing the arrival of a text rang out from her shoulder bag.

She froze on the spot, inches away from him.

'What was that?'

'What was what?' As the words left her mouth, Billie-Jo knew it was a facile thing to say.

Partridge was glaring at her. 'I thought you said you left your phone on the train!'

Billie-Jo's mind was racing. 'I did. I mean, I thought I had. I must have…'

Partridge took a step back and pushed her away with such force that she stumbled backwards and fell over. 'I knew it!' He towered over her, his face like thunder. 'Who the fuck are you?'

Billie-Jo started to get up. 'I...'

'Stay down!' Partridge put a foot on her shoulder and pressed down hard.

'Get off me!'

Partridge pressed harder. 'Not till you tell me who you are and what you're doing here.' A thought suddenly struck him. 'Wait! Did some scum-sucking journo pay you to come here? Hoping to get covert photos of the inside of the accused man's house?'

Billie-Jo was squirming about beneath him, trying to get free.

'Or did they think they could set me up in a half-arsed honeytrap and sling even more mud at me?' Partridge's face darkened. 'Send in an underage kid to flash her little titties at me and make me out to be some sort of paedo!'

'Well ain't that exactly what you are?' The pain pulsing through Billie-Jo's shoulder was so intense that she thought she was going to pass out.

Partridge looked a little taken aback. 'What the hell is that supposed to mean?'

Billie-Jo stared up at him angrily. 'You had a fuckin' good gawp, didn't ya? Now get the *fuck* off me!'

'Hah!' The expression on Partridge's face changed to a look of triumph. 'So I was right then. This whole

117

thing was a set-up.' He lifted his foot off her shoulder and took a step back. 'Get out!'

Gasping for breath, Billie-Jo rolled away and scambled up onto her knees. Without taking her eyes off him, she stood up, put on her scarf and beanie, then zipped up her coat. 'You're wrong, you know.' She bent down to collect her bag. 'I didn't come here to set you up.'

'I don't care,' Partridge said calmly. He pointed at the front door. 'Just get out of my house.'

'You *really* don't want to know why I came?' Without waiting for a reply, instead of picking up her bag, Billie-Jo reached inside and withdrew the Beretta.

Partridge's eyes widened and he stepped back, instinctively raising his hands. 'What the hell...?!'

Billie-Jo was pointing the gun directly at him 'You honestly haven't got a clue who I am, have you?'

Partridge shook his head.

'I suppose I should have figured that. Does the name Hallam ring a bell?'

A look of confusion appeared on Partridge's face. 'Wait. You mean you knew Terence?' The confusion changed to a smile and he started to lower his hands. 'Well, why on earth didn't you say so?'

Billie-Jo waggled the gun at him. 'Keep your hands up!'

Smiling nervously, Partridge raised his hands again. 'Listen here, I don't know what all this is about, but if you think I had anything to do with Terence Hallam's unfortunate death you're very much mistaken. He was one of my clients. We did a lot of business together. I'd go so far as to call him a friend. A bloody good man.'

'A bloody good man?!' Billie-Jo made no attempt to hide the bitterness in her voice. 'He killed my whole fuckin' family, you cunt!'

The colour appeared to drain from Partridge's face. He had seriously misjudged what Billie-Jo was saying. For a moment he'd thought she had come here to misguidedly avenge Hallam's death. Now, as the penny finally dropped, he could barely bring himself to ask the question. 'You... You were on Mástiga?' There was a tremor in his voice.

'Too fuckin' right I was on Mástiga. And your *friend* Hallam is responsible for murdering my...' – Billie-Jo stifled a sob – '...my Mum, my Dad and my little sister! And so are you.'

'Woah, now hold on there, young lady. What happened on that island had nothing to do with me.'

'You gave him money to fund his psycho idea didn't you? Far as I'm concerned, that makes you pretty fuckin' responsible too!'

Partridge frowned as a thought occurred to him. 'Just a moment. What makes you think I gave Hallam

119

money?' He started to lower his hands again and Billie-Jo motioned for him to keep them up. '*Really*? This is ridiculous. I'm not going to do anything rash, I assure you.' He continued to lower them and this time Billie-Jo let him. 'So, come on. What makes you think I had anything to do with that business on Mástiga?'

'There was a file in Hallam's office naming you and a bunch of other shitbags as investors.'

Partridge almost laughed. 'Really? Oh, Terence. You bloody fool!'

'It's not fuckin' funny!'

'It actually is. I'll tell you, I had a lot of dealings with Terence Hallam. All manner of investments, shifting his money around for him, that sort of thing. Not all of it was... well, shall we say strictly legal? And Terence was old school. He insisted on keeping hard copy records of everything. I mean, who the hell does that in this day and age? I told him it was folly and it would be his undoing one day.' Partridge shook his head and chuckled. 'And now it's become mine.' Still shaking his head, he looked at Billie-Jo. 'Don't you think that's a little bit funny?'

Billie-Jo was having trouble keeping the gun steady in her hand. 'You and those other fuckin' privileged cunts *paid* to have innocent people get murdered.'

'Oh, come on. They were hardly...' – Partridge made little air quotes – '...innocent. Everyone on that island was a blight on society. Terence Hallam's project was absolutely inspired. And when he said he needed extensive funding, he certainly didn't have to ask *me* twice. It was worth every penny of my five million investment for the opportunity to watch some of the scum of society get wiped off the face of the planet.'

'*Watch*?!'

Partridge now seemed to be remorseless. He chuckled. 'My dear girl, you don't think I'd pour my hard-earned money into a project like that and not get to reap the rewards? Of *course* I watched. It was sensational.'

Billie-Jo was almost lost for words. 'You sick fuck!'

Partridge shrugged his shoulders and squinted at her. 'Alright, let's cut to the chase, shall we? How much?'

'What are you talking about?'

'How much is it going to cost to make this go away?' He gestured at his pocket. 'I have over five hundred pounds in my wallet. It's yours. All of it. Just take it and leave.'

'You think you can just buy me off?'

'You wouldn't be the first.' He smiled at Billie-Jo superciliously. 'And why don't you put that gun away, eh? You're not going to shoot me.'

'You wouldn't be the first.'

Partridge guffawed. 'Touché.' The smile faded. 'So are you going to take the money or not?'

Billie-Jo waggled the gun. 'Show me.'

Partridge went to remove his wallet from his pocket.

'Wait! Slowly. Don't try anything stupid.'

Partridge grinned again. 'You've been watching too many movies, young lady.' He reached into his sweatpants and carefully, so that she could see what it was, pulled out the wallet between his thumb and forefinger. Opening it, he withdrew a bundle of notes and offered them to her.

Still pointing the gun at him, Billie-Jo took the money with her other hand and, without even looking at it, stuffed it into her jacket pocket.

'Now what?'

'I came here to kill you.'

Partridge laughed mockingly. 'Did you *really*? I don't think so.'

'You're mistaken then.'

'Oh, don't get me wrong. I suppose it's possible you came here with the *intention* of shooting me down. Some silly notion of getting revenge. But having a gun in your hand and having the guts to pull the trigger are two very different things.'

'I told you,' Billie-Jo said. 'It wouldn't be the first time.'

But she knew he was right. Yes, she had shot and killed Tyler James, but she had never intended for that to happen. It had been an accident. And now, standing here in the hallway of a strange house, pointing a gun at a man she had never set eyes on before, suddenly seemed terribly wrong.

With tears brimming in her eyes, she lowered the gun.

Partridge smiled. 'There you go. Sensible girl. You have your blood money. So I'd suggest you leave now and we can both pretend today never happened.'

Billie-Jo bent to pick up her bag.

'And let's be honest. That family of yours wasn't really worth avenging anyway, was it?' he continued. 'You're much better off without them.'

'What did you say?' Billie-Jo stood up again.

'I think I do remember you now. Your father was Jamie, or something? And your mother... Nicky, was it?'

'Vicky. Her name was Vicky.'

'That's it. Vicky. Such a shame she got melted.' The tone was mocking now. 'Still, them's the breaks. It was pretty bloody magnificent watching the flesh sliding off her bones.' Partridge licked his lips. 'Bit of a waste really I suppose. I certainly wouldn't have said no. Gorgeous body.' He winked at Billie-Jo. 'Like mother, like daughter, eh?'

Billie-Jo squeezed the trigger. The gun kicked once and a black hole appeared just above Partridge's left eyebrow. He reeled backwards, a look of surprise on his face, and hit the wall. Then his legs buckled beneath him and he dropped to the floor.

Grabbing up her bag, Billie-Jo stashed the gun and retrieved her spectacles and mittens. Putting them on, she quickly wrapped the scarf around her neck and pulled it up to cover the bottom of her face.

As she adjusted the beanie on her head, she heard the rumble of a car pulling up outside.

Her heart pounding out of her chest, she opened the front door a couple of inches and cautiously peered out.

An olive green Range Rover, the size of a small tank, was pulling in alongside the Bugatti. The engine shut off and Cressida Partridge climbed out. Her pale face was topped by a mane of jet black hair that was pulled back tight and hung in a long ponytail at the back. Looking elegant in knee-length leather boots, a fleecy winter coat, slender gloves, and a vivid pink neckscarf, she made her way round to the boot.

Billie-Jo shut the door and hurried across the hall. Hopping over Partridge's body, she ran into the kitchen.

The ends of her fingers protruded from the fingerless mittens, from the just below the first knuckle. Being careful that they didn't make contact with the handle on the back door, she wrapped her palm around it and pushed down.

She let out an exasperated groan: the door was locked. Looking around desperately, she spotted a key holder on the wall beside one of the cupboards; it was studded with six hooks, most of which had more than one key dangling from them.

There were three windows spanning the length of the countertop. Her hands shaking, she leaned across and tried the handles, but they too were locked.

Suddenly she had an idea: the safety chain on the front door! If she could just get back and slide it on! She raced back across the kitchen, but as she got to the doorway she heard the sound of a key rattle in the lock and the front door opened.

Cressida Partridge, carrying a bag of shopping in each hand, stepped into the hall. As she tapped the heel of her boot on the door and it swung shut, she caught sight of Billie-Jo.

She frowned. 'What...? Who...?' Her look of puzzlement at the sight of the togged-up figure standing rooted to the spot in her kitchen doorway changed to one of horrified disbelief as her gaze fell upon her husband's body. Her eyes widened, she dropped the shopping bags and a gloved hand flew up to her mouth. 'Crispin!' Then, with a wail, she ran forward and dropped to her knees. She instantly saw the bullet hole and her head shot up to look at Billie-Jo. 'You killed him,' she screamed. 'You killed my husband!'

'I… I can explain…'

Cressida stared at the figure, not quite able to process what was happening, her eyes brimming with tears and searching for answers.

Billie-Jo suddenly felt a sense of calmness descend on her. She shook her head resignedly. 'Actually, you know what? I *can't* explain.'

In one swift movement, she pulled out the Beretta from her shoulder bag and aimed it at Cressida.

The bullet found its target in the woman's right eye, which exploded in a spurt of aqueous humor and blood. With a guttural cry, she lurched forward and fell face down on top of her husband's body.

All that was going through Billie-Jo's head as she returned the gun to her bag was how surprisingly easy it was to take a life. Not 15-minutes earlier, Crispin and Cressida Partridge had been living, laughing, loving, breathing human beings. Now they were nothing more than nugatory lumps of flesh and bone, which would soon be reduced to ash. They would never cheat again, they would never lie again… they would never do *anything* again.

'Mummy? Daddy?'

The small, frightened voice came from away to Billie-Jo's left. She stepped out into the hall. Standing beside the banister at the top of the stairs was a small boy, perhaps nine or ten years old. He was dressed in pyjamas and had on a pair of padded headphones. He was staring down at his parents' bodies.

The stab of remorse that descended on Billie-Jo for having orphaned the child disappeared as quickly as it had come. After all, wasn't that precisely what Partridge and his cronies had done to her?

She crossed the hall to the front door, where she paused and looked back up the stairs at the boy. Deepening her voice to a growl in a slightly feeble attempt to make herself sound like a man, she said, 'Dominick, right?'

The boy just stared at her in shocked silence.

'Trust me, kid, you're gonna be better off without them. You'll be absolutely fine.' Opening the front door, she added, almost to herself, 'You sure as fuck ain't gonna want for nothin'.' Stepping outside into the snow, she pulled the door shut behind her.

CHAPTER 10

Much to Billie-Jo's relief, the Hasidic Jew who had graciously stood back to allow her to board the train before him at Tunbrige Wells, alighted at Sevenoaks.

He was wearing a traditional gaberdine frock coat, and his hair hung from beneath a wide-brimmed felt Hoiche, the intricate plaits framing an immaculately trimmed beard.

He had taken a seat opposite Billie-Jo and pulled out a hardback novel from the briefcase he had with him. Oddly, it then remained on his lap unread, and he instead proceeded to stare at her for the entire 20-minute journey. At least that's how it had felt to Billie-Jo. She fought to concentrate on the view through the window as the world sped past, but she could feel him watching her and, sure enough, every time she glanced over he nodded at her politely and smiled.

A little girl wearing a bright red duffle coat and matching pom-pom hat now occupied the man's seat alongside her mother, and she had assumed staring duty with a vengeance.

Billie-Jo could feel the eyes burning into her and the more she tried to ignore it, the more discomfited she felt. She poked out her tongue at the child, half expecting to elicit a smile – or, at the very least, a mirrored response – but there was no reaction whatsoever; just that solemn, unwavering gaze.

The woman kept leaning over to her daughter and whispering that it was bad manners to stare at people, but it didn't make any difference. There was accusation in those small eyes, Billie-Jo was certain of it; condemnation even. Looking out at the passengers dotted along the platform as the train pulled in to Orpington station, she told herself not to be so paranoid; it was nothing more than her guilty conscience needling her over what had taken place in Honeywell Close that morning. It was to be expected. She had, after all, shot and killed two people in cold blood. Nobody could do that and not expect to experience some kind of emotional fallout. It was guilt, she told herself, and nothing more.

All the same, rationale failed to prevent the cloying unease spurred by the girl's stare from gnawing away at her. Billie-Jo was again consumed by relief as they approached London Waterloo East and the woman got up to leave the train. Looking slightly flustered as she rebuked the child for her rudeness, she all but dragged her to the doors and they got off.

From there it was only three minutes to Charing Cross.

It was just before midday and Billie-Jo suddenly felt at a loose end. Tracy had made it abundantly clear that she wasn't to return to the house until later. The mental image of her nan locked in a slobbering embrace with a wrinkled old man flashed through her mind and she quickly banished it.

The spectacles were beginning to make her eyes hurt. She took them off and dropped them into her bag, then she found a bench on the platform and sat down to phone her friend. As luck would have it, Carly wasn't doing anything that afternoon and was delighted to be invited to go and see a movie – Billie-Jo's treat.

By the time she met up with Carly outside the Empire cinema in Leicester Square, Billie-Jo was actually feeling weirdly euphoric about the morning's events, which were already starting to feel very surreal.

They bought some snacks – trays of nachos smothered in cheese and salsa, a big bag of wine gums and two go-large Pepsi-Colas – and made their way up to the auditorium. At the top of the stairs, Billie-Jo spotted a CCTV camera. 'Hang on, Carls.' She stopped and took off her coat and beanie. 'Fuck me, it's hot in here.' *Evidence I was here if it comes to it*, she thought.

Popping into the toilet, after which they both dallied in front of the mirror to apply some lipstick, they went on through and found their seats. There they spent the next couple of hours chattering and giggling their way through the film, much to the annoyance of the man sitting nearby. His irritability was like a red rag to a bull and, for the two girls, only made the situation funnier.

By the time Billie-Jo went to catch the train back to Essex Road, any hint of guilt over her morning in Tunbridge Wells had vanished. Stopping at the chicken shop opposite the station to grab some dinner, she got back to the house just after four forty-five.

As Billie-Jo put down the bag of food on the kitchen counter, Tracy eyed it disapprovingly. 'You got worms or somethin', girl?'

'Eh?'

'McDonalds not filling enough?'

'Oh, no,' Billie-Jo said, taking off her coat. 'We didn't go to McDonald's in the end. Carly wasn't hungry. Nor was I. But I'm fuckin' starvin' now.'

As she watched Billie-Jo forking the food out onto a plate, Tracy had to concede it smelt quite appealing. 'What you got there then?'

'Hot'n'spicy chicken strips, chips, onion rings, and a couple of wallies.' Billie-Jo saw the look on Tracy's face. 'There's loads here if you want some.'

'I was just gonna have m'self some beans on toast...'

Billie-Jo shrugged. 'Okay.'

'Hear me out! As I was sayin', I was *gonna* have beans on toast. But that chicken actually looks a bit of alright.'

Billie-Jo smiled at her nan and took down an extra plate from the cupboard. She split the food between them and they sat down in front of the TV to eat.

The adverts were on and Tracy dipped the sound low. 'You have a good day then?'

'It was alright, I s'pose.'

Tracy nibbled on an onion ring. 'What was your film like? I love that Keanu Reeves.'

'A bit shit.'

'Aww, that's a shame.'

Billie-Jo quickly changed the subject. 'How about you? Did you have a nice time with old man Lionel?'

'He's not old,' Tracy said, sucking the grease off her fingers. 'Well, not *that* old anyway. Besides, there's somethin' to be said for older men. They're kinder. More considerate, if y'know what I mean. Lionel is very…' – a wistful smile appeared on her face as she sought for the right word – '…very *attentive*.'

Billie-Jo almost choked on a chip. 'Tryin' to eat here, Nan!'

Tracy rolled her eyes. 'He brought me flowers.' She pointed to a vase full of red and yellow roses on the side.

The advert break came to an end and the news started. Tracy raised the sound as the presenter started to speak.

'The lead story tonight, police are investigating the murders of a London financier and his wife at their home in Tunbridge Wells this morning.'

Billie-Jo's stomach churned and she thought she was going to throw up. She stared wide-eyed at the screen as a photograph of Partridge appeared.

The report continued: 'Crispin Partridge made the news this week over charges that he embezzled hundreds of thousands of pounds from Partridge and Swann, the financial advisory firm he co-owned with Tobias Swann. We go over live now to our reporter, Susan Bright, in Tunbridge Wells. What are you able to tell us, Susan?'

The picture changed to a shot of a woman standing on the street in front of a building. Behind her, there was police tape visible across the front door. It was dark, but Billie-Jo immediately recognised the house in Honeywell Close. The woman looked cold.

'Not much, Graham. Police are currently trying to establish exactly what happened here this morning. The only witness is Mr and Mrs Partridge's nine-year-old son, Dominick, and so far he hasn't been able to provide much information. It seems he was in his bedroom listening to music on his headphones when somebody broke in downstairs and shot both his parents dead. From the top of the stairs, he caught a glimpse of someone in the hallway leaving the house, but he's understandably in shock and regrettably hasn't yet been able to provide police with much of a description. I spoke to one of the officers just now and she told me the incident is believed to be related to those charges of embezzlement Mr Partridge had been facing, and that will be the focus of their investigation.'

The picture changed back to the newsreader in the studio. 'Thank you, Susan.' Shaky footage of the Partridges dressed up to the nines at some event or other appeared on the screen. 'Crispin and Cressida Partridge were familiar faces on the London social circuit…'

'Well, fuck me!' Tracy muted the sound. 'What was it I was sayin' yesterday? Crime pays, was it?' She chuckled. 'How wrong was *I*? It sure didn't pay for him.'

She glanced at Billie-Jo and saw her ashen face. 'You alright?'

'Yeah. Just felt a bit queasy there for a sec. Dodgy onion ring, I think.' She took a breath. 'I'm okay now.'

Tracy turned her attention back to the television just as a photo of Partridge shaking hands with a prolific member of parliament flashed up. 'Well, that just about says it all, don't it?' She waved a chip at the screen. 'These people, they get away with murder. If it was you or me, we'd be banged up before we had time to stop and take a piss! But, oh no, not them. They think they're untouchable. Well, I don't mind tellin' you. Far as I'm concerned, whoever it was what killed 'im deserves a fuckin' knighthood!'

'What about his wife though?' Billie-Jo said quietly.

'Good riddance to bad rubbish if you ask me.'

'But surely she didn't deserve to die? Not really?'

'Course she did! Any bitch thick enough to let a slimy cunt like that between her legs is a fuckin' waste of oxygen!'

If Billie-Jo had felt an ounce of remorse at having shot Crispin and Cressida Partridge, it dissolved away to nothing in that moment.

She dipped a hot'n'spicy chicken strip into the blob of tomato ketchup on the side of her plate. People getting away with murder? It seemed possible that Billie-Jo had literally done just that. Not only once, but twice. She couldn't help smiling to herself. She had done a good thing. Justice had been served.

Crispin Partridge had been made to pay the ultimate price for what he'd done. But he hadn't been the only one involved in Hallam's sordid initiative. There had been four others. And Billie-Jo knew their names. By the time she climbed into bed that night, her head was swirling with ideas. Things hadn't gone exactly as she had intended at Partridge's house. Before setting off, she believed that she had thought about every eventuality. But she had been fooling herself; for one

135

thing, she hadn't factored in the presence of Cressida and Dominick. How could she have overlooked that? It had been a costly oversight, and one that ended badly for Cressida.

As Billie-Jo snuggled down under the blankets, thinking about the myriad of ways the situation could have gone terribly wrong for her – and thanking her lucky stars that she wasn't spending the night in police custody – she made herself a promise that next time she would be more meticulous.

Next time? Oh yes, there was going to be a next time. Of that Billie-Jo was certain. Furthermore, it would be soon.

CHAPTER 11

Michael Bamford, now aged 74, had for many years been a respected Professor of Archaeology at the University of Bath. He had retired to the New Forest eight years ago, where, having been a confirmed bachelor all his life, he had taken up residence in a beautiful thatched cottage in a rather enviable location on the outskirts of Stoney Cross.

Something of an eccentric, and fluent in six languages – including, rather impressively, Mandarin – he was a popular figure around the village, where he could often be seen handing out leaflets for the local church. An enthusiastic member of the choir, a volunteer at the village hall's pop-up library, a dedicated scoutmaster, and an active member of the neighbourhood watch scheme, it would be fair to say that everybody in the community knew "Mike". And he knew them.

The University had bestowed upon him the honorary title of Emeritus Professor and, according to the online article Billie-Jo was reading on her burner phone, he very much delighted in being acknowledged as such.

What the article failed to mention was that sweet little old Michael got his jollies watching innocent men, women and children being butchered.

It was Sunday morning. Having spent some time examining Hallam's paperwork, deliberating over whom should be dealt with next, Billie-Jo had found this information pertaining to the retired Professor with relatively little effort. Further probing uncovered a fairly extensive profile piece. At first, it looked as if it might be quite dull, but as Billie-Jo wanted to be sure she was equipped with as much information on Bamford as possible before planning her visit to Stoney Cross, she started to read it anyway.

Bamford had been an only child. Something of a tearaway, serendipity had intervened when, in 1959, his parents took him on holiday to Coombe Martin in Devon. One day, on a coastal walk, they all stopped to eat their sandwiches and soda pop. He had just been reprimanded for some misdemeanour or other and was idly digging in the earth with a stick when he had discovered a strange glass bottle with a marble in the top. Hoping it might be worth a few pennies, a few weeks later he had cajoled his father into taking him to an antiques fair, where its value had astounded them both.

Called a Codd-neck, the bottle dated from the late 1800s and the marble in the top had been part of the clever design to keep it airtight. The man on the stall explained it was rare to find an example in such good condition, because after children had consumed the contents – often ginger beer – they used to smash them to retrieve the marble. The man had given Michael two pounds for it. Right there and then, standing at an antiques fair in Chipping Sodbury clutching a pair of crisp one-pound notes, his future was mapped out.

As he progressed through his teenage years, solitary archaeological excursions all over the world had proven financially rewarding, and by the age of 21 his bank balance had been bigger than his mother and father's combined. It continued to soar in the years ahead. A bright young man, his remarkable good fortune in uncovering and selling valuable finds notwithstanding, he had also decided to follow a scholarly path; at the age of 27 he had earned his master's degree in the subject. Seven years on from that, he had been offered the post of Deputy Head of Department of Archaeology at Bath University. There followed many field trips abroad with his students, during which time he expanded and perfected upon his talent for multilingualism.

In 1987 there had been a whiff of scandal when Bamford was accused of an inappropriate relationship with the twelve-year-old brother of one of his sophomore students...

Fuck me, another *kiddie-fiddler!* Billie-Jo thought. *What is it with these fuckin' wealthy cunts?!*

…Rumours persisted that a substantial financial settlement ensured the matter was buried and, not coincidentally, the student had transferred to another university.

Billie-Jo had read enough. Aside from the sleazy incident involving the boy, unlike Partridge – who'd had a trail of corruption and abused privilege hanging over him – everything else about Michael Bamford seemed to indicate he was a really nice guy. Which just went to prove what Tracy had said: it was impossible to know what was going on behind the face of respectability.

Billie-Jo couldn't for the life of her think how this esteemed academic and pillar of society had become tangled up with Terence Hallam. All she knew was that he had invested some of the fortune he'd made selling antiquities in satiating his inhumane penchant for voyeurism, not to mention the thrill of playing judge, jury and executioner.

Now it was time to decide what form of action she was going to take.

She knew she wouldn't be able to do anything until the following weekend, which gave her five days to plan things thoroughly. Nevertheless, she ran a quick Google search to find the nearest train station to Stoney Cross; she was alarmed to discover it was 18 miles away in Ashurst – almost two and a half hours on foot.

She couldn't risk getting a taxi; it would probably take 20-minutes, there would be unavoidable interaction with the driver, and he would have a record of the fare.

She was about to shelve Bamford in favour of one of the other investors when a thought occurred to her: it was the New Forest, tourists' cycle hire outfits were all over the place, surely there had to be one somewhere nearby. Within a couple of clicks she had ascertained there was one directly opposite Ashurst station. The cycling time to get from there to Stoney Cross was 45-minutes.

Billie-Jo hadn't ridden a bike since she was ten and she didn't relish the prospect, but it seemed as if it was going to be her only option. However, checking the times of the trains from Waterloo to Ashurst for the following Saturday morning, she hit another obstacle: there was a warning notice of disruption due to a scheduled train strike. 'Fuck me!' she exclaimed aloud. '*Really?*'

*

'I must say, you picked a beautiful day for it!'

The old man on duty at Pedal Power Bike Hire gave Billie-Jo a toothless grin from behind his wispy white beard. 'It warms my heart to see youngsters getting themselves out in the fresh air. Kids these days, I tell

141

you, they spend far too much time glued to their computer games, running around shooting people.' He rolled his eyes.

Due to train strikes, which wiped out Billie-Jo's plans for two weekends on the trot, it was three weeks after having read up about Michael Bamford that Billie-Jo finally made it down to the New Forest.

It was a Saturday morning and once again she had risen with the lark. Gathering up everything she needed, including the spectacles for disguise purposes and, of course, the Beretta, she had left the house quietly to avoid waking Tracy. Being the middle of January, it was freezing cold and still dark when she made her way to Essex Road. Her plans immediately got off to a bad start when she managed to miss the seven thirty-five out of Waterloo Station and had to kick around for an hour waiting for the next one. It was a 90-minute run down to Ashurst and she spent the best part of the journey listening to two men sitting behind her bemoaning the state of the country and the shortcomings of the Conservative Government.

'Here, Dave, did you see that Tory twat on *Question Time* last night?'

'Did I? *Did* I?' The second man sounded angry.

'I dunno, that's what I'm asking. Did you?'

'Too right I did, John. Made me seethe. Bloody nerve, telling us we need to tighten our belts whilst they're cutting funding to the NHS and pushing up inflation to the point where the ordinary man will be living in poverty!'

'Yup. And there he is, living it up in a country mansion with his fingers in more pies than Mrs Miggins!' The first man blew his nose. 'They're so outta touch with what's going on in the real world it defies belief. I tell you, John, something's gotta give.'

'You said it, my friend.'

'I *did* say it. Wages are going down, prices are going up. Have you seen the price of bananas?!'

'Don't eat 'em, Dave.'

'It's scandalous! And don't even get me started on the cost of fuel. Old girl next door to us, Mrs Jenkins – lovely lady she is, lives on her own – she was talking to Sonia last week and she literally has to choose between turning her radiators on or having a hot meal. What kind of country are we living in where that's okay? Tell me it ain't wrong!'

'It's a bloody disgrace, my friend. Something needs to be done about these elitist tyrants.'

As irritating as she was finding the conversation, Billie-Jo had smiled to herself at that last remark.

By the time the train arrived in Ashurst, the sky was blue and the sun, though low on the horizon, was sparkling through the trees. It was only the middle of January, but already winter seemed to be losing its grip.

143

Having done her research well, Billie-Jo had discovered that she needed to book the hire of a bike in advance. She had called on her burner phone and spoken to a man who wanted to take payment there and then. Explaining she didn't have a debit card, Billie-Jo sweetly managed to persuade him to accept her booking and agree that she could pay cash to the attendant upon her arrival.

The grounds where the Pedal Power outbuilding was located had been deserted when she arrived. Tucking her scarf up around the bottom of her face, she had knocked on the door. After a few moments, it had opened and, with a cheerful good morning, the old man had stepped out.

Keen to take advantage of the respite from what must have been a lonely vigil, he had tried to engage Billie-Jo in conversation, but she had kept her responses to a bare minimum. She gave him the name under which she'd made the booking – Maya Robinson – and with a little grunting sound, he bent and removed the security chain from one of the bikes.

'Maya. A pretty name that. I saw you on the booking system when I got in. You're our first customer of the day, don't you know. We don't get so many this time of year. Not that I can see why.' He chuckled and waved a hand at the sky. 'What could be better than being out on two wheels on a day like this?'

Billie-Jo didn't reply. Smiling politely, she handed over the £22 all-day hire charge in two ten-pound notes and a two-pound coin.

'Thank you muchly.' The man gave her a friendly wink. 'Headed anywhere special?'

Shaking her head, Billie-Jo slung her bag over her shoulder and straddled the bike.

'Just a little mosey around then, is it?'

Billie-Jo nodded, and without waiting for any further questions that might require a verbal response, she took off.

'We close at four today!' the man called after her as he watched her speed away.

According to Google, the estimated cycling time to Stoney Cross had been three-quarters of an hour. It took Billie-Jo an hour and 10 minutes; she hadn't got far before realising how exhausting riding a bike can be when you're not used to it. To ensure she could see properly where she was going, she had taken off the spectacles and, as she hurtled along, the cold wind in her face was making her eyes water.

Panting heavily, and with the muscles in her calves and thighs screaming at her for mercy, she pulled over to the side of the road and took a swig of Coke from the bottle she'd bought at Waterloo. Several more stops for refreshment and to consult Google Maps, meant she

145

didn't peddle into Stoney Cross until just after eleven-thirty.

Exhausted, and cursing aloud at the prospect that she would soon be making the return journey, Billie-Jo left the bike leant up against a wooden sign post at the end of the lane where Bamford's cottage was situated. It did cross her mind someone might steal the bike, but she shrugged it off; *fuck it, it ain't mine*. Putting the spectacles back on, she pulled down her hat, wrapped her scarf tightly around her face and completed the last quarter of a mile on foot.

The Hollies – so named, Billie-Jo assumed, because of the two vast green bushes laden with red berries on either side of the garden gate – was easy to find, nestled on the edge of woodland.

Taking a quick look up and down the lane to be sure there was nobody around to see her going in, she pushed open the gate. It creaked loudly. Head down, she walked purposefully up the short path, bordered with flowerbeds full of snowdrops and pansies, and stopped at the front door. From inside the house, she could hear the sound of a vacuum cleaner. There was no apparent sign of a doorbell, only a large, ostentatious brass knocker in the shape of a boar's head. Making sure she didn't touch it with her fingers, Billie-Jo wrapped her gloved hand around it and knocked twice. The sound of hoovering ceased.

In her head, Billie-Jo had pictured Michael Bamford opening the door. She would spin him a story about having been on a walk in the Forest with her parents, but that they had accidentally become separated and now she was lost. He would invite her in, she would reveal why she was really there, and...

The door swung open wide with a blast of warm air and, looking hot and flustered, a young woman stood looking out at Billie-Jo. 'Yes?'

About twenty-years-old, if that, she was a little taller than Billie-Jo and had long, wavy blonde hair fastened up in a topknot. She was wearing a white blouse that was at least one size too small – its buttons were straining to contain her sizeable breasts – sheer black nylons and a pleated black skirt so short that it scarcely covered her modesty.

She brushed away a comma of hair that had fallen over her right eye. 'How may I help you please?' The accent was distinctly Eastern European.

Billie-Jo was slightly thrown. Had she come to the wrong place? The woman was looking at her enquiringly. Billie-Jo deepened her voice. 'Hi,' she said, glancing at the carved wooden plaque mounted on the wall beside the door: 𝕿𝖍𝖊 𝕳𝖔𝖑𝖑𝖎𝖊𝖘. No, she *hadn't* made a mistake. 'Sorry, this *is* Mr Bamford's house isn't it?'

'Yes, this is his home.'

Billie-Jo's plan was falling apart in front of her eyes. Wait, the sound of the vacuum cleaner... Bamford had a housekeeper! Of course, someone like him *would* have; he wouldn't be caught dead doing the ironing or putting a duster round himself.

Billie-Jo's mind was racing. How the hell was she going to get him alone? Could she maybe coax him into leaving the cottage with her under the pretext of helping her to find her parents? That was more than a long shot. And, even if she could, that wouldn't solve a problem that she could have well done without: This woman was now a witness to her visit. Was she going to end up as collateral damage, just like Cressida Partridge had?

The warm air wafting from the inside of the house was causing the lenses on her spectacles to steam up. Billie-Jo wiped the back of a mitten across them. 'I wonder if I might speak to him please?'

'Sorry, he's not here now. It's Saturday. He's at village hall with cub boys.'

'Cub boys?'

'Yes, the little boys.'

It took Billie-Jo a moment to register what the woman was saying. Then the penny dropped. Of course! She had read that Bamford was a scoutmaster. Maybe there was some kind of activity session with the cubs on a Saturday morning. Another chink in her carefully thought-out strategy.

'Oh, sorry, yes. The cub scouts.'

'Cub boys. That's what I said.'

'Is he going to be long?'

The woman shrugged. 'An hour perhaps. Maybe two. Mr Bamford always comes home for lunch, but usually only a sandwich, there's no set time for this. I make for him. Then always he like to spend the afternoon...' – her full lips appeared to form a kittenish smile and her blue eyes widened – '...relaxing. No interruption.' Her expression reverted to the slightly flustered look. 'It's not often visitors come here. Who shall I say called?'

'It doesn't matter.' Billie-Jo felt deflated. She had come all this way, and for what? Only to find out that Bamford wasn't even at home. 'Sorry to have bothered you.'

'It's no bother.'

Before Billie-Jo could say anything more, the woman shut the door in her face.

In the five minutes it took her to wearily walk back up the lane to retrieve the bike and pedal the 18 miles back to Ashurst, Billie-Jo's resolve had returned.

So Bamford was at the village hall, was he? Then that's where she would go. She would find a spot to watch and wait and, when the cub scouts went home, she would confront him there.

CHAPTER 12

The wooden signpost beside which she had left the bike helpfully pointed the way to the village hall. Ignoring the shooting pain in her right knee, Billie-Jo swung her leg over the saddle and set off.

Ten-minutes later, with every muscle in her legs protesting, she pedalled up the gentle incline towards the village hall.

It was an old brick building set back from the road amongst a cluster of beech trees with a slate roof stippled with clumps of moss. There were several cars parked out on the lane and as Billie-Jo got closer she could hear the hubbub of voices.

There were around thirty or more people standing around outside the hall. Assuming they must be parents waiting to pick up their little angels, without turning her head, Billie-Jo cycled on past and pulled over several hundred yards further down the lane. She wheeled the bike up into the undergrowth and stashed it behind a tree, then made her way back through the woods on foot and found a knoll where she could hunker down out of sight of the people and keep watch.

She lay down on her front among the damp leaves. The cold made her shiver, but fortunately she didn't have a long wait; only a few minutes passed before the door swung open and a procession of cubs – each clutching, from what Billie-Jo could see, pieces of wood – filed out of the hall. Appearing behind them were two portly women, both wearing scout uniforms. Chattering excitedly, the children all reunited with their parents.

'Bye Bagheera! Bye Baloo!' one of the little ones shouted. 'See you next week!' He was waving frantically at the two women. Smiling, they paused beside a green Smart Car parked out on the lane, gave the boy a cheerful wave back, then climbed in and drove off.

Gradually, all the people drifted away and the cars departed until, except for the twitter of birds overhead, the air fell silent.

Billie-Jo waited another full minute, just in case there were any stragglers, then she stepped out from her hiding place and cautiously made her way down across the now empty car park towards the building. The door was still open and as she got to the steps, she could hear voices inside. For an instant she hesitated, then darted across to the right and disappeared round the corner of the building.

There were several windows at intervals along the sidewall, their wooden frames exposed beneath flaking paint. One of them was slightly ajar, and by standing on tiptoe Billie-Jo was just able to see inside.

Taking off her glasses, she immediately recognised Michael Bamford, not so much from the pictures she had seen online, but certainly from his photograph in Hallam's file.

He was sitting on a stool at a long workbench covered with tools. There was a boy dressed in a cub scout uniform beside him, watching intently what the old man was doing. Bamford was holding a small wooden mallet and a chisel, and in front of them there was a block of wood clamped in a vice.

Billie-Jo cursed under her breath: another unforeseen hitch.

Bamford appeared to be showing the boy how to use the chisel. Smiling, he stood up and handed the tools over, urging the lad to have a try himself. Moving round behind him, Bamford wrapped his arms around the lad and took the small hands in his own, gently guiding them into the right position.

The boy tapped the mallet against the end of the chisel once and looked over his shoulder at the old man for validation. 'Like that?'

'Bravo!' Bamford exclaimed. He reached down and pulled off the boy's scout cap, ruffling his blonde curls. 'Carry on, you're doing marvellously.' The voice was urbane, with a distinct edge of superiority.

Looking rather pleased with himself, the lad returned his attention to the piece of wood.

As she watched, Billie-Jo felt herself go hot and cold. Instead of removing his hand from the boy's head, Bamford continued to caress his hair, playing with the curls, wrapping them round his fingers. His eyes were closed and there was an unmistakable look of rapture on his face. Then the hand slipped casually onto the boy's shoulder and gave it a little squeeze of encouragement, traced its way down his back and came to rest just above the buttocks, where it rotated, the index finger tracing out little circles.

Lost in concentration, the boy seemed to be oblivious to what was happening.

The fingers carefully pushed up the bottom of the jumper and snaked underneath…

There was a clattering sound over to the left of the hall. Bamford abruptly withdrew his hand and took a step away. He smiled cheerfully. 'Ah, Mrs Garrett.'

The boy stopped what he was doing and looked up. 'Hey, Mum.' He put down the mallet and chisel on the bench.

As Billie-Jo craned her neck to see, a woman came into view and hurried over towards them. 'I'm *so* sorry, Mike. We're doing the place up and I got caught up helping John paint the ceiling in the spare bedroom, and the time just ran away with me, and …'

Bamford smiled and waved a dismissive hand. 'No apology necessary.'

Mrs Garrett looked at him apologetically. 'That's very gracious of you, but I really *am* sorry. I hate being late for anything.'

You got here just in the fuckin' nick of time, lady, Billie-Jo thought.

'I hope Tom's been behaving himself,' the woman continued.

Bamford nodded. 'Good as gold. We've been helping young Thomas improve his woodworking skills, haven't we m'boy?'

'Yep. I want to make Dad something nice for his birthday.'

'Is that so?' Mrs Garrett crossed to a row of hooks on the wall and collected the boy's coat and scarf. 'Well, not today. We're not going to hold Mike up any longer.' She helped Thomas into his coat and apologised to Bamford again.

'Honestly, Mrs Garrett, think nothing of it. Thomas is a delightful boy and his talent for working with wood is well worth cultivating. I'd be more than happy to spend some time with him if that's something he would like.'

'That's really kind of you, Mike. Maybe that's something we can talk about next week.'

Billie-Jo slipped away from the window and crept back up the side of the building. She waited for Mrs

Garrett and Thomas to leave, then swiftly crossed over to the door and stepped in.

Inside the hall there were multiple stacks of chairs lining either side of a large open space. A two-foot-high dais spanned the end wall. There was a rhythmic grinding sound echoing around the room.

Bamford was bent over the bench in the left-hand corner with his back to Billie-Jo.

Withdrawing the Beretta from her bag, she stealthily moved around the perimeter of the hall with her back to the wall. As she drew level with Bamford, she could see what was making the noise. He was wearing a dust mask over his nose and mouth and his attention was focused on a short length of wood, which he was running back and forth across a large vertical sander that was standing beside the bench.

Catching a movement out of the corner of his eye, Bamford turned his head and gave a little start. 'Oh, my word! You made me jump.'

He reached over and flicked a switch and the sander came to an abrupt stop. Pulling down the mask so that it hung on the elastic beneath his chin, he turned to face her. 'Humble apologies.' He smiled. 'I didn't hear you come in.' It was then that he spotted the gun in her hand and the smile disappeared. 'Hey, what *is* this?'

Billie-Jo slipped her bag off her shoulder and set it down. Holding the gun out in front of her, she took a single pace towards him and stopped. 'I'm here to kill you.'

Bamford stared at her for a moment, apparently lost for words. Then he threw back his head and laughed.

Billie-Jo pulled the scarf away from her face and glared at him. 'You won't be laughin' in a minute, fucker.'

As quickly as the laughter had begun, so it ceased. Bamford studied the figure in front of him. 'Surely you can't be serious, you silly little girl.' He frowned. 'Why would you – or anyone else for that matter – want to kill *me?*'

'Think real hard. I'm sure you'll come up with *something.*'

A look of concern appeared in Bamford's eyes. 'How long have you been here?'

'Long enough.' Billie-Jo motioned at the stool beside the bench. 'Sit down.'

Bamford did as he was told. 'Now, just you listen to me.' His voice sounded shaky. 'I don't know what you *thought* you saw, but I can assure you that you're very much mistaken.'

Billie-Jo took another step towards him. 'What is it you *think* I saw?'

'You tell me.'

Billie-Jo could feel her blood rising. 'I saw you touchin' up an innocent kid, you scumbag nonce!'

157

'You saw no such thing!' The tone had changed to one of indignance.

'Is that so?'

'Absolutely. You've made a mistake.'

Billie-Jo's legs were killing her. Keeping the gun levelled at Bamford, she squatted on her haunches. 'Is that the same mistake as when you were caught messin' around with the little brother of one of your students?'

Bamford looked taken aback. How could she possibly know about that? 'I'll have you know that was a misunderstanding,' he stammered. 'I... now, just you look here.' He looked angrily at Billie-Jo. 'I don't have to explain myself to *you*. I don't even know who the hell you are!'

'Mástiga.'

Bamford stared at her in disbelief. '*What* did you just say?'

'Mástiga,' Billie-Jo repeated calmly.

Bamford's shoulders slumped and he leaned back against the bench. 'Oh my God.'

'He aint gonna help you.'

'You were part of Terence's initiative?'

Billie-Jo glared at him. '*Your* initiative too! You fuckin' gave him a shit ton of money to make it happen. I lost my whole family! My little sister. My Dad. My Mum. She was beautiful and you cunts melted her fuckin' face off!'

'So you're one of the kids who survived. I saw that on the news.' Bamford sighed. 'You know, after everything went wrong on the island, I feared that someone would come for me. But nobody did. I thought that surely the police…'

'The police don't even know you exist.' Billie-Jo stood up again.

'I have to say though, I certainly wasn't expecting some little girl to show up. How on earth did you find me?'

'It wasn't difficult. Hallam kept records. Finding your house was a doddle. When I got there your maid was very helpful, she told me you was here.'

'You spoke to Anneka?'

'If that's your maid's name then, yeah, I spoke to Anneka.'

'She's a *housekeeper*, not a maid. She takes care of me.'

Billie-Jo shook her head in disgust. 'Yeah, I bet she does.' Bamford was smiling at her. She held out the gun towards him. 'What you smilin' at? You think this is *funny*?!'

'You spoke to Anneka.'

'Yeah, I just said that. So fuckin' what?'

'Silly child. Don't you see? If anything were to happen to me, Anneka would tell them about you

159

turning up at my home asking for me and you'd be the first person the police came looking for.'

Billie-Jo was unfazed. 'They'd have a hard job findin' me.'

'Do you think so?' The expression of superiority appeared on Bamford's face. 'I have a suggestion to make. And I recommend you give it serious consideration before doing anything silly. How about you just put down that gun and run along home. I shall say nothing to anyone and it will be just like none of this ever happened. You don't really want to go to jail for shooting an old man, do you?' He gazed at her keenly, waiting for a reply.

Billie-Jo thought for a moment. He was right. Even though she had planned her visit to Stoney Cross carefully, she hadn't accounted for Anneka and if she shot him now there would be a hunt for the killer that could potentially lead the police to her doorstep. If she *shot* him that is…

Bamford suddenly stood up. He took a step towards her. 'Give me the gun. If you were going to shoot me, you'd have done it by now.'

Billie-Jo pointed it at him threateningly. 'Don't count on that. Back off!'

Bamford looked at her uncertainly. Nodding, he raised his hands to half-mast and as he backed away he stumbled against the bench. He threw his arm back to steady himself and inadvertently caught the switch on the electric sander.

With a rasping sound, it burst into life, shredding the sleeve of his jacket.

He yanked his arm away and looked at Billie-Jo with surprise. 'Oops!' He chuckled nervously. 'Nearly a nasty accident.'

Billie-Jo didn't hesitate. She dropped the gun, rushed forward and grabbed hold of Bamford's hair. He wriggled sideways, but she was far too quick for him, and before he knew what was happening, she had wrenched his head down and across the bench. His face struck the rolling belt and he let out a high-pitched scream as, amidst a spray of blood, the coarse sandpaper took the flesh off his cheek. 'No… please. Nooooooo!!'

Billie-Jo couldn't look. Turning her face away, she pushed down for all she was worth, putting the full weight of her body behind it.

Bamford continued to struggle and scream as his face jiggled and bounced against the unyielding machine.

The smell of burning pork reached Billie-Jo's nose and she almost gagged. The grinding noise sputtered momentarily under the immense pressure being put on the belt, but then it picked up speed again and tore Bamford's ear clean off the side of his head, depositing it on the bench. The screams had mutated into guttural moans as his hands scrabbled about wildly for something – anything – to fight back with. Howling with agony as his temple was ripped away to expose the white of his skull, his fingers found the chisel Thomas Garrett had been using. Gripping hold of it, he blindly thrust it behind him and it found its target.

Shrieking, Billie-Jo let go of him and stumbled back against the wall, twisting her ankle and clutching at the tool jutting out of her shoulder.

Bamford slumped forward across the bench. Weakly raising his head – now little more than a sickening ball of blood and shredded flesh – he managed to get himself up on his feet, but as he went to speak, his jaw fell slack and he clutched at his chest. He coughed once, spitting blood, then dropped to his knees and fell headlong onto the floor.

Billie-Jo thought for a second she was going to faint. She stumbled to the bench and picked up a piece of rag. Pressing it firmly against the entry wound, she counted to three and, stifling a scream, pulled hard. The chisel slid out. She took it over to her bag and dropped both it and the bloody rag inside.

Giving Bamford's prone body one last look – 'See how popular you are with the little boys with your face sanded off, you cunt!' – she limped to the door.

162

Peering out to make sure there was nobody around who might see her leave, she stepped outside and slipped quietly away into the woods.

CHAPTER 13

'Acid in a perfume bottle? That's barbaric!'

Landis nodded. His expression was grave.

DC Linda Duvall of the Hampshire Constabulary took a sip of coffee and set her mug down. 'What the hell was wrong with these people?'

'That was only part of it.' Landis picked up a digestive biscuit and slid the plate towards Duvall. She smiled politely and took one. 'Ever hear the name Carl Banks?'

Duvall shook her head and brushed a loose hair back over her ear. She was an astute woman and although Landis had only met her for the first time 15 minutes earlier, he had taken an immediate liking to her.

'No reason you should have, I suppose,' Landis said. 'It was all kept out of the press, but even if you'd heard about it internally, you probably wouldn't have taken much notice. I only learned about the incident myself a few months ago.'

'Incident?'

'Banks was... I don't know, a bit of a loose cannon I suppose you'd call him. Ex-military and, from what it seems, pretty much a mercenary for hire. Dirty work that nobody else would touch with a bargepole was his speciality. Anyway, his landlord found him dead in the

164

bathtub. Flesh burnt off his bones. It was a real horror show.' Landis suddenly didn't fancy his biscuit any more. He put it back on the plate. 'Somebody had emptied out a jar of fragrant bath crystals and replaced them with sodium hydroxide.

'*Somebody?*'

'Well, it certainly wasn't him. I mean, if you were going to commit suicide I'm sure you could come up with any number of less dramatic ways of doing it. The agony he must have gone through doesn't bear thinking about. No, it was premeditated murder.'

Duvall shuddered and washed down her biscuit with another mouthful of coffee. 'Did they collar anybody for it?'

Landis shook his head. 'Off the record, solving Carl Banks's murder wasn't exactly a number one priority on anyone's list. From what I understand, he was bad news, owed a lot of money to a lot of people. Any one of them could have wanted him dead, but it was impossible to pin the killing on any of them. The case is still open, obviously, but I don't think anyone's trying that hard. Anyway, here's the thing. Back in September I got pulled in on a case involving a number of murders on an island out in Greece.'

'Oh, Christ, really? That was all over the news. Mástiga and…'

'Terence Hallam. Which is why we're talking now.'

Duvall looked a little confused. 'Sorry, I don't see how this Banks guy fits in. I was only asked to come and speak with you about Hallam because of what was uncovered at Michael Bamford's house.'

Landis held up a hand. 'Hear me out.'

'What would someone like Hallam want with a shitheel like Banks?'

'Just what I asked myself. As I say, hear me out. Long story short, the Greek authorities were about as useful as a windscreen wiper on a submarine. As far as they were concerned, what Hallam got up to on that island wasn't their problem – he was a Brit, and that made it ours. They did the bare minimum necessary to observe protocol, then they washed their hands of it. I had a load of cleaning up to do over here, and that's when Banks's name came up. There was paperwork found at Hallam's apartment in Mayfair that connected them.'

'So, are you saying Hallam killed this Banks guy?'

Again, Landis held up a hand. 'Hold your horses. Hallam employed Banks to design the traps for his island and get them installed. The actual on-site work was carried out by someone else, but after completion they were conveniently killed in a boating...' – Landis made little air quotes – '...accident.' He shook his head. 'But that's another story. Hallam had a file full of ideas and designs for – well, to be blunt, imaginative ways of murdering people. People he deemed to be a blight on society. As I said, the Greeks weren't exactly forthcoming, but from the little information they did provide me with, what was uncovered on the island was only the tip of the iceberg. It seems a lot of these death-traps never got past the spitballing stage. They dreamed up some pretty sick stuff. That acid perfume, poisoned soft drinks, underground traps with spikes to skewer victims, something involving rotating blades on a waterslide...'

'You'll be telling me next Hallam wanted to put sharks in the bloody swimming pool.' Duvall saw the look on Landis's face. She stared at him in disbelief. 'You're kidding me, he did *not* put sharks in a pool. No way!'

'Piranha in the lake.'

'Jesus, that guy was certifiable!'

'To put it mildly. Anyway, the email trail that was unearthed on your man Bamford's computer was very interesting indeed. Thanks for sending all that stuff over yesterday, by the way. It made for some very enlightening reading. Did you read any of it?'

Duvall shook her head. 'No, I was just asked to forward everything to you. Kiddie porn is as sick as sick gets. Fortunately, when that kind of shit shows up it takes the investigation out of my hands. These people make me puke.'

167

'The kids stuff isn't what I meant by enlightening.'

'Oh, sorry, I just assumed… What then?'

Landis reached for the folder on the desk in front of him and opened it. 'In more than one of those emails to Hallam, Bamford actually referred to what he was doing as God's work. I'd say he went above and beyond the call.'

'Don't tell me we're talking about some sort of deviant paedophile old boys club and Hallam and Banks were part of it?'

Landis shook his head. 'No.' He extracted a sheet from the folder. 'I printed out one or two pertinent exchanges. There's no doubt whatsoever that Bamford was involved with what happened on Mástiga. But there was one small detail in particular that caught my attention.' He handed the sheet of paper to Duvall. 'From Hallam to Bamford. Third paragraph.'

Duvall's eyes widened as she read aloud: 'And if we decide to press ahead with the spa suggestion, we're definitely going with the idea of substituting bath crystals with sodium hydroxide. Tried and tested and wholeheartedly approved by our late friend, Mr Banks. LOL.'

She looked up at Landis. 'So Hallam *did* kill Banks!'

'Or had him killed. Either way, he was responsible.' Landis picked up his coffee. 'Which neatly clears up Banks's death. Another box ticked.'

Duvall smiled. 'Happy to have been of assistance.'

Through a mouthful of coffee Landis made a noise and waved his hand at her. He swallowed. 'That's not the end of it. There's also been a question bouncing around at the back of my head since I was assigned to deal with this whole sordid business. Where the hell did Hallam get all the money to finance the damned thing? I got what I *thought* was the answer to that conundrum a couple of weeks ago.'

'Well, from what I understand, he was pretty loaded. But maybe not…'

'Not so much that he could afford to buy his own island and convert it into a Disneyland for sociopaths, no. He needed an investor. As I said, Bamford was definitely involved, and there's irrefutable evidence in these emails…' – Landis tapped the folder – '…of substantial sums of money paid into one of three offshore bank accounts owned by Hallam. And before you ask, I'll be pushing for court orders to access the details of those accounts. But I've been down that road before and it's a nightmare. Data protection is tighter than a gnat's chuff where banks are concerned. I honestly reckon it'd be easier to get a free pass into Fort Knox.'

Duvall grimaced. 'Tell me about it!' She handed the printout back. 'So, Bamford was his investor then. Job done.'

Landis slipped the piece of paper into the folder and closed it. 'One of them.'

'*One* of them?'

Landis put the folder away in his desk drawer. 'You've heard of Crispin Partridge?'

'The financier guy who got shot dead last month? Sure.' Duvall emptied her mug.

'Then you'll know about the embezzlement.'

Duvall nodded. '*Alleged* embezzlement. He didn't live long enough to go before a jury.'

'Trust me, he was guilty as sin.'

Duvall raised her eyebrows. 'Okay. Oddly enough, you know, that's the second time Partridge's name has cropped up this week. I've got an old friend works for the Kent Police and I was talking to him a couple of days ago. I mean, Partridge only got mentioned in passing to be honest. But Tim – that's my friend – happened to mention he used to know his wife or something. Anyway, apparently they're working on the angle it was someone he defrauded who shot him, right?'

'That's the official version, yes.'

Duvall frowned. '*Official* version?'

'The truth is possibly more disturbing.' Landis leant forward, interlocked his fingers and rested his elbows on the desk. 'Since the charges of embezzlement were levelled at him, there's obviously been a lot of digging around into Partridge's financial affairs. Something came up after his death that gave Kent reason to get in touch with me. It seems that last year he poured five million quid into a certain offshore account.'

Duvall whistled through her teeth. 'Hallam?'

'Terence Montague Hallam.'

Duvall laughed. 'Montague? That's a new one on me.'

Landis rubbed his chin thoughtfully. 'Didn't use it, hated it apparently. Doesn't matter.' He sat back in his chair. 'I went down to Tunbridge Wells and spoke with the guys looking into Partridge's death. They were very helpful, gave me carte blanche to look through all the material they'd gathered. They even gave me access to his home computer and one that had been confiscated from his office. And guess what?'

Duvall shrugged. 'He was balls deep in Hallam's arsehole just like Bamford?' She saw Landis wince. 'Sorry.'

'Forget it. No, unlike your man Bamford's veritable orgy of email evidence, beyond that five mill payment I couldn't find another single thing to tie Partridge to Hallam. He was probably just more circumspect and covered his tracks, but there were no emails and no records of any communication between the two of them at all. Zilch. Nonetheless, it was worth the trip down there, because if nothing else it provided me with the answer to that niggling question about how the whole thing was financed. And after that I was happy to put the matter to bed.'

Duvall gritted her teeth. 'Until I sent you Bamford's emails.'

'Precisely.'

'But hang on, I still don't see the connection. Could Partridge and Bamford have possibly known each other?'

'Not that I've been able to ascertain. Yet. But don't you think it's more than a coincidence that two people who filled Hallam's pockets with money have died in the space of three weeks?'

Duvall shook her head. 'I see what you're driving at, but Michael Bamford's death was down to a nasty accident. Officers spoke with his live-in housekeeper and she said when he got up that morning, he'd told her he wasn't feeling too well. But he was Akela for the Stoney Cross cub scouts and there was a meet that day and he insisted on going. He'd been showing the kids how to carve wood apparently. His colleagues – two very nice ladies – said that at the end of the session one of the mothers was late picking up her kid and Bamford was more than happy to stay behind with him till she showed up. I'll be honest, given what we now know, the thought of him alone there with a little boy makes my stomach churn. Anyway, the mother was interviewed too and she claimed she only spoke with him briefly, but aside from maybe looking a little out of sorts when she first arrived, he seemed chirpy enough. When she and her kid went, he was left on his own in the village hall clearing up the woodwork tools, and sometime thereafter he had a heart attack and fell onto a motorised sander.'

Landis had been listening to Duvall patiently with an expression of mild disinterest on his face. He raised his eyebrows.

She frowned at him. 'What?'

'He *fell* onto an electric sander?'

'That's right. After suffering a heart attack. Coroner's report was conclusive.'

'And Crispin Partridge was shot dead in his own home by some disgruntled associate or other that he'd stiffed.'

'Exactly.'

'Or at least that's what the Kent Police think.'

'And you don't?'

Landis spun his chair towards the window and peered out at the overcast morning sky. 'There's a storm coming.'

Duvall pressed him. 'Come on, what are you saying? You *don't* think Partridge's death was related to the charges of embezzlement?'

Landis turned back to face her. 'If you'd asked me that question two days ago, I would have said yes, that was exactly what I thought. The fact that Partridge was helping Hallam bankroll his scheme was purely coincidental. Furthermore, I'd have told you that for that evil misdemeanour alone, maybe he got exactly what he deserved. But then you contacted me about Bamford.'

'I didn't know what it was all about. I certainly wasn't going to ask. I just did what I was told to do. But I suppose I kind of assumed it was about the kiddie stuff.'

'Naturally. But this has opened a whole new can of worms for me.' Landis sighed. 'I mean, think about it for a minute. Once is happenstance. And I'll concede that on face value twice could conceivably be coincidence. But I simply can't disregard the fact that two people who paid Hallam huge sums of money and were involved to some degree in discussions over how to kill innocent people are now dead themselves. And I just can't help but wonder...' He trailed off as he saw the look on Duvall's face; the penny had dropped.

'Jesus Christ! You think there might be more? Investors, I mean.'

174

Landis nodded. 'You have to admit it's a very real possibility. It would have cost more money than you or I could ever conceive to fund that set-up. Let's just say Partridge put in five million, and Bamford – from what I understand – something like three. Lumped together with whatever Hallam had, surely it still wouldn't have been enough. I mean, he bought a whole damn island!'

Duvall rubbed her eyes. 'This is absolutely insane.'

'It is. But what concerns me most right now is that if Partridge and Bamford's deaths *didn't* come about the way everyone seems to be thinking they did, whoever else gave Hallam money is probably in danger.'

'Don't tell me you're thinking some sort of vigilante shit?'

Landis didn't reply.

'Okay, assuming these other sick miscreants do actually exist, where would you even start to look for them?'

Landis sighed. 'Right now? I haven't a damned clue. But if there *were* more, there has to be something out there somewhere that will identify them.' He leant forward, wagging a finger. 'And I'll tell you this, Duvall. I'm not going to rest until I find it.'

'Call me Linda.'

Landis smiled at her. 'Call me Landis.'

CHAPTER 14

Five days had passed since Billie-Jo's visit to the New Forest and every part of her body was still aching.

The journey back to the station at Ashurst had been tough going, but – unlike her journey out, which had been punctuated by several breaks – she was running on adrenaline and actually covered the 18 miles without stopping. Having noticed that she had some of Bamford's blood on her coat, she had bundled it up in her bag and, although it had been cold to begin with, by the time she had arrived back at Pedal Power the sweat was pouring off her.

The old man had seemed pleased to see her and once again tried to strike up a conversation.

'Would you believe you've been my one and only customer today?'

That wasn't good. If Billie-Jo had been the only person he'd seen, he would definitely remember her. Grunting a brusque reply about needing to catch her train back to Basingstoke, she had all but thrust the bike at him and crossed the road to the station.

'Nice speaking with you too!' The note of sarcasm had been all too evident.

Her arrival home hadn't been as inconspicuous as she would have liked either. Tracy had been at the kitchen sink washing up, and as soon as Billie-Jo had walked through the door, she started on her.

'What you doin' home so early?' she snapped. 'I told you last night, Lionel's comin' over this evenin'.' She screwed up her face. 'What the fuck is that smell?'

Billie-Jo shrugged. 'I can't smell nothin'.'

Tracy took a step towards her, sniffed and recoiled. 'It's *you*!' She noticed that her granddaughter wasn't wearing her jacket. 'Where's your coat? It's fuckin' freezin' out there today!' She eyed her suspiciously. 'What have you been up to? You look like the wreck of the Hesperus!'

'The *what*?'

'The Hesperus.' Tracy saw the blank look on Billie-Jo's face. 'Fuck me.' She rolled her eyes. 'It's, er… it's… As it goes, I don't know *what* the fuck it means! My Nan used to say it. Point is, have a look at yourself in the mirror!'

Billie-Jo scowled. 'I've had a busy day!'

Tracy looked at her scornfully. 'You? *Busy*?'

Crossing the living room to the stairs, Billie-Jo paused at the bottom step. 'I'm gonna shower and change, then I'm goin' out again. I wouldn't want to ruin your evenin' with Lionel.' She puckered her lips and made little kissing noises.

'Oi!' Tracy pointed a finger of warning at her. 'I'll have none of your cheek.' She watched Billie-Jo

177

disappear off upstairs. 'And just you make sure you wash them clothes yourself,' she shouted after her.' She heard the bathroom door slam shut and, wafting a hand in front of her face, she went back out to the kitchen. 'I sure as fuck ain't doin' it.'

Billie-Jo removed her top and inspected the injury on her shoulder. It didn't look too serious, but it was throbbing badly.

Standing in the shower, she cleaned it up as best she could. Then, after drying herself off and taking care not to get blood on the bath towel, she took out a bottle of TCP antiseptic from the bathroom cabinet, removed the cap and sat down on the toilet seat. Taking a deep breath, she bit down hard on the end of the towel and applied a little of the clear yellow fluid to the wound. The searing pain almost made her cry out, but she managed to withhold it.

Happy that she had done as much as she could to prevent infection, she went to her room and taped a sanitary towel across her shoulder. It was crude but it would do the job.

She could still hardly believe she'd got away with committing three murders in cold blood – four if Tyler were to be included. When her heart-stopping confrontations with Partridge and Bamford played back in her head, which they did frequently, she still felt a little bit bad about Cressida. But circumstances had painted her into a corner and she was managing to keep any serious sense of guilt at bay by reasoning she'd been left with no choice. She had done the world a favour. She was invincible!

Just the same, in the days following her Stoney Cross trip, doubt had begun to creep in over the risks posed by continuing her vengeful spree. She had been lucky so far. But surely it would only be a matter of time before she slipped up badly. And what then?

Billie-Jo's fear of imprisonment was crushing; the very thought of it made her feel sick. Yet there was an indescribable rage blazing deep down inside her that wouldn't allow her to let it go. She *had* to continue, until every affiliate to Hallam's conspiracy had paid for taking her family away from her. Even if it meant there was a place waiting for her in hell, she would finish what she had started and be damned.

Two down, three to go.

Late on the following Thursday night, Tracy was watching the *BBC 10 O'clock News*. As usual, she had the sound down low. Billie-Jo was looking at a video on TikTok. She was just thinking about going up to bed when Tracy let out a little hoot of laughter and pointed at the TV.

'Here, isn't he that Detective Landon twat?!'

Billie-Jo looked up from her phone. There on the screen was Detective Inspector Landis.

'Put the sound up a bit, Nan.'

Landis was seated in the middle chair of three, with a uniformed officer on either side of him. He was addressing a small gathering of journalists.

'…And we now believe that the deaths of Crispin Partridge and Michael Bamford could be connected. Investigations have revealed that both men were associated with Terence Montague Hallam, the former government minister responsible for the death of eight British Citizens in Greece last summer. A photofit description of an unknown person who visited Mr Bamford's house asking after him just prior to his death has been provided to investigating officers by his housekeeper –'

Billie-Jo's heart skipped a beat.

'– and we're now appealing for witnesses who may have seen this individual either in the vicinity of Tunbridge Wells on Saturday 28th December, or in and around the Stoney Cross area of the New Forest, three weeks later on the Saturday 18th January. The person we wish to identify, possibly a male, was wearing…'

A photofit image that the witness had helped to create flashed up on the screen; it bore no resemblance to Billie-Jo whatsoever. The bottom part of the face was concealed behind a maroon-coloured scarf and the hair was blonde; Billie-Jo's was dark brown. Her beanie looked more like a beret in the photo and the glasses she had been wearing were, as they appeared in the photofit, a completely different shape.

Billie-Jo almost laughed out loud. She breathed a sigh of relief. Zero points to Anneka for observational skills.

'I still say whoever done that Partridge in deserves a fuckin' medal,' Tracy said through a mouthful of cheese puffs. 'And if this other cunt was part of what happened on that island, I'd give him two medals!'

Billie-Jo breathed an internal sigh of relief. It was bad news that the police had made the connection between Partridge and Bamford, which she assumed would have been evidence of the money they had given Hallam.

Worst case, the police might start looking for somebody who survived Mástiga – and that might put her in the frame. Best case? A man like Hallam would surely have had enemies in high places, and the sums of money that had been moving around can't have vanished into the ether. Billie-Jo consoled herself with the thought it was far more likely *that* would be the impetus behind the investigation.

She went up to bed that night thinking about the photofit picture. She was pretty sure nobody in Tunbridge Wells would remember her. The weather had been awful and she had hardly encountered a soul. It was possible the old guy at Pedal Power in Ashurst

181

would see the news, and if he did, he might be able to adjust some of Anneka's flaky recollections where description was concerned, and would certainly confirm that the bundled-up figure wasn't a *he*. But even then, she was confident no description anybody might provide would be likely to identify her.

Later that night, she laid in bed reading up on the woman she had selected to be her next target.

Apparently an author of some renown – although Billie-Jo had never heard of her – 52-year-old Samantha Ellis had made her millions with a prodigious succession of historical romance novels, all of them populated by not-so-demure damsels eager to lure unfeasibly handsome heroes into their beds. Ellis was a one-woman conveyor belt and her ability for churning out books at a rate of between four and five a year had earned her the label – not entirely meant without ridicule – "The 21st Century Barbara Cartland"; Billie-Jo hadn't heard of her either.

Ellis was a lesbian and, rather ironically given her literary persuasion, not one to submit to the trappings of romance. On the contrary, from the sound of it she had burned an extensive trail of discarded one-night stands and broken-hearted longer-term lovers, without so much as once pausing to look back with regret.

Billie-Jo scrolled down and clicked on the link headed Early Life.

The youngest child of three, born to parents Donald and Phoebe, Samantha Ellis had excelled in a private education that eventually landed her a prestigious place at the University of Warwick, where she studied history from 1972 to 1975...

Billie-Jo frowned. Something about that rang a bell. She opened a second browser window on the burner phone and typed Terence Hallam education into the search field. Sure enough, there it was: Hallam attended the University of Warwick between 1971 and 1974. *Hallam probably fucked her*, Billie-Jo thought. *That would have been enough to turn any woman lesbo*. She shuddered to shake off the image.

Closing the browser window, she returned to reading about Ellis. For all her fame and fortune, it appeared she wasn't a well-liked figure. She was a sought-after guest on the interview circuit but, when she actually deigned to turn up for bookings, she was more often than not inebriated, aloof and habitually rude. Such behaviour might normally have given rise to the question of why she hadn't simply been blackballed. The answer was simple: The public seemed to love her. She was erudite and witty, and her impoliteness was eclipsed by a remarkable knack to entertain. The article drew parallels with Oliver Reed – another name that meant nothing to Billie-Jo – and stated that the TV shows on which Ellis appeared would always figure high in the audience ratings.

She was also the nemesis of chefs up and down the country; renowned for complaining and refusing to pay for her food, once again her notoriety came with a certain prestige and it became an unspoken challenge between restaurateurs to be able to say they had served her a meal without receiving a tongue-lashing. Furthermore, she held extremist political views, which had on more than one occasion been likened to those of the 1930s Nazi Party.

In short, from what Billie-Jo had read, Samantha Ellis was a despicable, remorseless, gold standard bitch. She decided she would have no compunction whatsoever about wiping the woman off the face of the planet.

The next search result on the Google page stopped Billie-Jo in her tracks. It was a report on Ellis's death. Why hadn't she noticed that sooner? Cursing, she clicked the link and it took her to *The Guardian*'s website.

Just before Christmas, Ellis had been dining out with a group of friends in Manchester. She had been holding court as usual when she had suddenly suffered a severe allergic reaction to a dish of langoustines. She was rushed to hospital where, a few hours later, she passed away.

Billie-Jo clicked on several more reports across various sites, few of which rose above nominally sympathetic. She laughed out loud at the headline on the Daily Comet's piece:

WHAT A CRAY TO GO!

Old trout thwarted by dodgy prawn!

So that was that. Fate had intervened and beaten Billie-Jo to the prize. She had wasted her time reading up on Samantha Ellis, and she felt niggled that she'd been deprived of watching the harpy take her last breath. But was that really such a bad thing?

Looking at it practically, it was one less time she would need to venture out and put herself at risk. And that had to be a good thing, didn't it? At the end of the day, the woman was dead and that was all that mattered.

She smiled to herself: *Three* down, *two* to go.

Billie-Jo suddenly felt overwhelmingly tired. It was too late to even think about doing any more research tonight. Tomorrow would come soon enough.

Yawning, she glanced briefly at the first of the two profiles in Hallam's dossier, then leaned over and tucked it away underneath the bed. Shivering, she turned out the light and snuggled down under the

blankets. *Toyah Leaky*, she thought. *What a fuckin'
annoying name.*

*

'You skank! I'll bust your head and shit down your
froat!'

Billie-Jo grinned. 'Nice, Pengelly.'

Lynzi stared at her. 'Fink that's funny do ya?'

Lynzi Pengelly had been the bane of Billie-Jo's life
for the past two years. She was one of three girls in the
school that she had never seen eye-to-eye with. The
other two – Hannah Malone and Zoe Adams – had
more or less left her alone since Bobbi-Leigh had died
and she steered clear of them as best she could too.
Lynzi was another matter entirely though. Whether it
was on or off school premises she was always bruising
for a fight.

It was almost the end of lunch break and it had
started to drizzle. Billie-Jo had just stepped in out of
the rain and was loitering in the corridor waiting for the
class bell to ring when Lynzi had come storming over
and accused her of giving her the stink eye. Which of
course she hadn't.

'Well?!' Lynzi demanded, flicking the voluminous
mane of jet-black hair dyed with streaks of purple out
of her face. 'Do ya?'

'Yeah, I do. I mean, I wouldn't get caught dead looking at an ugly lezzie cunt like you.' Billie-Jo motioned to the two girls standing behind Lynzi – Emily Robinson and Maya Blake. 'Dumb and Dumber over there would get bent outta shape.'

Lynzi brought her face up close to Billie-Jo's. 'Call me that again. I dare ya!'

Billie-Jo continued to smile at her. 'Which? Ugly or lezzie?'

Lynzi's eyes were burning with hatred. 'Why you little...'

'Oh, sorry!' Billie-Jo laughed. 'You meant *cunt*.'

As Lynzi raised a fist, a large hand appeared from nowhere and grabbed hold of her arm.

'Enough!'

'Get off me!' Lynzi twisted her arm free, but her hand flew out and caught the owner of the hand a glancing blow that knocked off his glasses. Her attitude vanished as she saw who it was. 'Sorry, sir!'

Bending to retrieve his spectacles, the school's Biology teacher, Mr Gibson, looked up at her angrily. 'Right, Pengelly! I'll see you in my office at three-thirty for half an hour's detention.'

Lynzi looked at the teacher petulantly. 'But, sir, that's not fair!' Pouting, she pointed at Billie-Jo. '*She* started it.' She looked round for Emily and Maya's support, but they had scarpered.

187

'Don't lie to me, Pengelly. I saw exactly what happened. Hazelwood wasn't doing a thing.' He looked at Billie-Jo and added, 'For a change.'

Billie-Jo was about to say something when Lynzi cut her off.

'But half a fuckin' hour, sir?!'

Mr Gibson glared at her. 'Forty-five minutes!'

Lynzi was going to protest again when she saw the look on the teacher's face and thought better of it. She huffed. 'Yes, sir.'

Straightening his glasses, Mr Gibson turned and walked off towards his classroom.

Lynzi glowered at Billie-Jo. 'You just got me jail-time with the Gibbon!'

'Yeah, whatever,' Billie-Jo said, turning away.

Lynzi grabbed her sleeve and leant in close. 'Just you wait, skank. You're dead.'

She caught sight of Mr Gibson, who was watching her intently from the doorway at end of the corridor. Forcing a smile and nodding theatrically, she stepped away from Billie-Jo. '*Dead!*' she hissed through gritted teeth. Then she spun on her heels and took off up the corridor to where Maya and Emily were waiting for her.

Billie-Jo watched Lynzi giving her so-called friends a mouthful and couldn't help smiling to herself.

CHAPTER 15

For most children, Friday afternoons constitute the best few hours of the week. The seemingly endless drudge of five days at school is finally coming to an end and the moment of escape is at last in sight. And, of course, beyond that final three-thirty bell the weekend awaits. Niggling thoughts of assignments waiting to be written were easy to banish; homework could be dealt with just before bed on a Sunday night. Prior to that there were 56 hours of countless possibilities and, most importantly, glorious freedom.

For Billie-Jo, as much as she couldn't wait to get out, a note of gloom always tempered the jubilation of those last couple of hours; since the new term started in September, her final lesson of the week had been chemistry – a subject she loathed with a passion, tutored by an insufferably dull teacher.

Her step dad had often bemoaned the absurdity of the school curriculum: 'Who the fuck needs to know bollocks like what the coffee output of Columbo is? Or the chemicalness of possum nitrate? Why don't they teach useful shit that's gonna help ya later on in life?!'

Billie-Jo couldn't have agreed more. Yet today, sitting in class and listening to Mr Beecham drone on, she was actually paying attention. The teacher had opened the lesson with the announcement that they would be looking at the properties of hydrogen fluoride, and an idea that had been playing on Billie-Jo's mind for a few days had suddenly taken on very real possibilities.

She had woken before her phone alarm went off that morning and immediately immersed herself in Googling information on Toyah Leaky. She found a lengthy profile piece on an equestrian website called *Racing World*. It wasn't flattering. On the contrary, it didn't hold back on the more sordid details of the woman's life.

As she read it, Billie-Jo wasn't surprised to learn that Toyah Leaky had something in common with Crispin Partridge, Michael Bamford and Samantha Ellis. Yes, she had funded the death of Billie-Jo's family, so obviously she had money to burn; a sickening amount in fact. But the other aspect that had become something of a running theme among Hallam's cabal was that Leaky was also a thoroughly unpleasant human being.

Billie-Jo had looked at the portrait picture accompanying the article. If she hadn't already taken against the woman due to her annoying name, she certainly took a dislike to her at that moment; barely recognisable as the same person whose black and white snapshot was in Hallam's file, the picture showed a gaunt-faced woman with bright red dyed hair bundled up on top of her head in a style that could only be described as resembling a haystack. She was holding a glass of champagne and looking superciliously into the camera through the lightly tinted lenses of a pair of Dolce & Gabbana spectacles.

Toyah Leaky was born of mixed parentage. Her father, Crawford Leaky, was British, while her mother, Beatrix Volonté, had been born in Italy but emigrated when her diplomat father's work brought him to England. Crawford and Beatrix owned Tranquillity Meadows, a horse stables near the California Country Park where they trained racehorses...

California?! Billie-Jo's heart had leapt into her throat. Swiftly opening another browser window on the burner phone, she'd typed the name into the search field. Much to her relief, it had turned out that California Country Park was four miles south-west of Wokingham. Heaving a sigh, she had returned her attention to reading about Leaky.

She was the youngest of Crawford and Beatrix's four children, all of whom spent their formative years around horses. In her 2007 autobiography, *Raising a Gallop*, she had described her tough early teenage years. Short and skinny, she had been an easy target for bullies. Mercilessly persecuted by the other girls at the Queen Anne's boarding school near Reading, she had been given the nickname Stopcox.

In a passage in *Raising a Gallop*, talking about her final year in school, Leaky wrote:

Obviously derived from the fact I shared my Christian name with the famous singer and my surname suggested the need for a tap, Stopcox – the nickname everyone seemed to find side-splittingly funny and hurled at me at every opportunity – was harmless enough, I suppose. But at 13-years-old you don't see things that way, and my Mother telling me to ignore it did nothing to prevent the hurt. However, as time wore on, I did become somewhat inured to it. Greater humiliation was yet to come.

I had just started to take an interest in boys, and one day, much to the hilarity of everyone in the refectory, Iris Walker wiggled her index finger towards the floor and loudly announced, "Stopcox – one glimpse of her ugly mug is enough to make men go limp!" Suddenly what had been innocuous humour took on a new, far more spiteful connotation.

After that I was determined to have sex with the first man I could. As it turned out, it was a boy named Gareth. He was 18, just two years older than I, and he worked weekends at my parents' stables. He had bad breath, the foulest body odour, it lasted about 30 seconds and it was absolutely horrible.

But I was in heaven. I had proven Iris
Walker wrong, and that was all I cared about.

Billie-Jo had thought about her first time, with a boy
named Paul Weaver: if B.O., bad breath and premature
ejaculation was all that Leaky had to complain about,
she'd been lucky.

Young Toyah found solace with her beloved horses
in end-of-term breaks away from Queen Anne's. But
home life wasn't exactly a bed of roses either.
Crawford Leaky was a malicious man and never
hesitated to use his belt to administer punishment when
he deemed it required. Which in Toyah's case was
frequent. Unsurprisingly, she despised him. And
because Beatrix never once intervened, she hated her
even more.

When Crawford and Beatrix had died in a helicopter
crash whilst holidaying in the Bahamas, Toyah didn't
shed a single tear. Her three older brothers had already
moved on to careers away from the stables and had no
interest whatsoever in taking them on. Two of them
pushed for a fast sale, but Toyah had been adamant she
could run them herself, and her other brother backed
her up. He helped her to talk the other two round and a
deal was struck whereby Toyah would take over the
day to day operations and, in an advisory capacity, they
would all receive a percentage of the profits.

Much to everyone's surprise, not least of all her own, Toyah had made a real go of it, and within two years the stables were running at a profit far greater than anything it had seen in the hands of Crawford and Beatrix.

Unfortunately, perhaps as a response to her underdog childhood, Toyah's newfound power had quickly gone to her head. She would hire employees on a whim and then fire them for the tiniest misdemeanour. She had a fling with her stable manager, Marcus King, that saw them married three weeks later and divorced nine weeks after that amidst charges of domestic violence – specifically beatings with a riding crop; the abused had become the abuser. What would inevitably have been a bitter court case was avoided when Leaky's lawyers mediated a substantial out-of-court settlement for the bruised and battered King.

She soon became an objectionable figure at race meetings, where she would always drink too much and happily offend anyone within earshot.

As had also been the case with Samantha Ellis, none of this seemed to cause Leaky any harm where matters of business were concerned. The stables were producing the cream of the racecourse and, when money is at stake, people frequently seem to be prepared to turn a blind eye to anything. Latterly though, there had been accusations from ex-staff that her drinking had progressed to alcoholism and, worse still, reports of cruelty to the horses…

Billie-Jo had stopped there. She needed to get to school. At the outset of what she had been reading, she had actually started to feel a little bit sorry for Toyah Leaky. But the last few paragraphs had simply reinforced her resolve: the toffee-nosed bint had to die.

*

Hardly anybody in the classroom was listening to Mr Beecham and as usual he hadn't appeared to notice. Either that, or he had given up caring long ago.

He set down the small beaker that had been a part of his demonstration. 'So, as we have seen, hydrogen fluoride can exist either as a colourless gas or a liquid. It can also be dissolved in water. When that happens, we call it…?' He pointed to a boy at the back of the classroom who was looking out of the window. 'Chapman?'

The boy jumped. 'Eh?'

'What do we call it?'

The boy shrugged. 'Dunno.'

Beecham sighed. 'And you never *will* know if you don't pay attention, boy.' He rolled his eyes. 'We call it hydrofluoric acid.'

A disinterested look on his face, the boy picked up a pen and started doodling on the back of his textbook.

'Very well,' Beecham continued, 'for the benefit of everyone else except Chapman, it's important to remember that contact with hydrogen fluoride can be a very dangerous business.'

Unlike her classmates, Billie-Jo had been listening intently this afternoon. The idea of dousing one of the three remaining investors with acid – two now that Samantha Ellis was off the list – had occurred to her several days earlier. It seemed only fitting that one of them should suffer the same agonising death that they had inflicted upon her mother.

Beecham held up a small brown bottle. 'Hard to believe that something that looks so innocuous could be fatal, isn't it? But make no mistake. Breathing in hydrogen fluoride can cause what is called a pulmonary edema. This is when there is swelling and fluid accumulation in the lungs. Skin contact in concentrated form is capable of causing severe burns that in the best case will ulcerate, in the worst... Well, let's just say in short, you don't mess with hydrogen fluoride. And that is why, when we run our experiment next week, we will be taking all the necessary precautions. Any questions?'

196

Except for two girls over to his left, who sniggered about something unrelated to the lesson, the room remained silent.

Billie-Jo watched her teacher return the hydrogen fluoride to the cabinet behind his desk that was filled with similar bottles.

He turned back to face the class. 'Right then. Pens out. This is your homework for the weekend.'

As soon as the final bell rang, pushing against the throng, Billie-Jo made her way up a level to the toilets and locked herself in one of the cubicles.

Two girls came in chattering excitedly, went into the adjacent stalls and continued their conversation through the partition, giggling as they discussed what they wanted to do to the lead guitarist of a rock band that Billie-Jo detested. After what felt like an age, they washed up and left.

Billie-Jo remained in her cubicle, idly browsing Facebook on her phone and half-listening to the voices in the corridor outside. Gradually the noise abated until there was silence. She looked at the time: ten minutes to four. Beecham would have had more than enough time to clear up and he'd be heading for the staff room about now.

From detentions past, Billie-Jo knew the general routine observed by most of the members of staff.

Beecham would spend the best part of 40-minutes in the staff room, either marking homework or enjoying a coffee with his colleagues as they had their post-mortem chat on the week's events, or aired their grievances. He would then return to the science laboratory, collect his personal effects, lock up and leave. That gave Billie-Jo a clear window of at least half an hour to get into the lab and acquire the bottle of hydrogen fluoride.

She waited for another 15 minutes to minimise the chances of anyone still being around, then she made her move.

Leaving the cubicle, she crossed to the door, opened it an inch and looked out. She couldn't see or hear anything, so she opened it wider and stuck her head out, looking quickly up and down the corridor. There was nobody about. She was just going to step out when a door banged somewhere to her left and she ducked back inside.

Peering carefully out again, she watched as a cleaner carrying a bucket and mop crossed the corridor and disappeared into the classroom opposite.

As quickly as she could, Billie-Jo dashed up the corridor, through the double doors and down the flight of stairs to ground level. She paused and looked through the glass window in the doors at the bottom to ensure there was nobody coming; satisfied that there wasn't, she hurried out and along to the science lab. Taking a breath, she knocked the door. There was no reply. She cast another quick look to make sure no-one was around to see her enter, then she pushed open the door and went inside.

Much as she had hoped it would be, the key to the chemicals cabinet was still sitting in the lock. Pulling the sleeve of her jumper down over her hand, she took hold of the key, opened the cabinet door… and froze. There were voices coming from the corridor outside.

Her heart racing, she ducked down low behind Beecham's desk and listened. It was a man and a woman. Their voices got louder as they came to a stop outside the laboratory door.

Billie-Jo glanced up and saw the door of the cabinet hanging open. From where she was crouched it was out of reach; she would have to step out from behind the desk to close it. She started to sweat. If whoever it was outside the door came in, there wasn't going to be an easy way to explain what she was doing here. What on earth had possessed her to think that stealing chemicals from the school was a good idea?

The conversation was indistinct, but the man must have said something funny because the woman burst out laughing. Billie-Jo recognised the high-pitched whinny: it was the school's art teacher, Miss Bingham.

'Fuck off,' Billie-Jo whispered. '*Please* just fuck off!'

Almost as if they had heard her, the voices got quieter and then faded away to nothing.

Immediately, Billie-Jo was up on her feet. She ran a finger along the bottles until she found one labelled **Hydrogen Fluoride**. Taking it out it, she thrust it into her shoulder bag and scampered across the room putting an ear to the door and straining to listen. But there was nothing to hear.

She pulled out her phone and looked at the time: four-fourteen. There was a good chance she had a few minutes breathing space before Beecham returned, but she couldn't count on it for sure. She opened the door and looked cautiously out. There was nobody to be seen.

The main exit doors would be locked by now, but she had already considered that. There was a door to the indoor pool that would still be open; from five until six o'clock on a Friday afternoon it was used for extracurricular swimming classes by parents and their disabled children.

Billie-Jo scooted along the corridor, through a set of double doors, down a flight to basement level and out through another set of doors into the corridor that ran parallel with the pool changing rooms.

Sport had never been on Billie-Jo's list of favourite subjects at school – in fact she didn't actually *have* a list of favourite subjects; she hated them all. But for her there was something futile about every aspect of sport. She had never seen the point of exerting herself unnecessarily, and running around a netball court half-dressed in the middle of winter was about as pointless as it got. Whether it was her reluctance to undertake that unnecessary physical exertion, the chiding she always got from the teacher over her lack of competitive spirit on the field, or the brutal ignominy of compulsory shared showers in the changing room afterwards, sport had quickly become another thorn in her side.

As she reached the entrance through to the pool at the end of the corridor, she heard the double doors behind her clatter open and a voice shouted out.

'Hazelwood, you skank! What you still doin' here? Hangin' round waitin' to have your bony arse kicked are ya?'

Billie-Jo spun round and saw Lynzi Pengelly coming towards her.

'Oh, just fuck off Pengelly, or I'll rip yer tits off.' She started to turn away. 'Course, I'd have to find 'em first.'

'Don't turn your back on me! I owe you for stitchin' me up with the Gibbon! He spent the whole fuckin' detention pervin' at me!'

As Billie-Jo pushed open the swing door into the deserted pool area, Lynzi caught up with her. 'I said *don't* turn your back on me, ya cunt!' She pushed Billie-Jo hard and sent her sprawling forward onto the wet tiles. Bending down, she grabbed hold of Billie-Jo's bag and yanked it off of her shoulder. 'Got any dosh in here, have ya?'

'Give me that!' Billie-Jo shouted, scrambling to get up onto her knees.

Lynzi took a step away from her. 'Uh-uh! Why don't ya come and take it?' She held out the bag and waved it back and forth teasingly. 'If ya fink you're hard enough.' But, before Billie-Jo could get to her feet, the girl dropped the bag, launched herself forward and gave her a hard shove.

With a cry, Billie-Jo flew backwards, lost her footing and toppled into the pool. She went under for a few seconds, then sprang out of the water spluttering.

Lynzi burst out laughing. 'Told you I'd get you, ya cunty skank!' Picking up the bag, she knelt down at the edge of the pool and started to rummage around in it. Frowning, she pulled out the bottle of hydrogen fluoride. 'What the fuck's this shit?'

'Leave my stuff alone!' Billie-Jo shouted as she swam back to the side.

Reaching up, she grabbed hold of Lynzi's arm. The girl tried to pull away, but she lost her balance, the bottle flew out of her hand and rattled across the tiles, and she tumbled sideways and fell into the pool.

Both girls went under and tussled beneath the surface for a few moments, then burst out of the water in unison.

'Please!' Lynzi gasped. She desperately tried to cling to Billie-Jo in an attempt to keep her head above the water. 'I can't swim!' All trace of the loud-mouthed, stroppy teenager punching for a fight was gone; in her place, a terrified little girl.

'Too bad,' Billie-Jo said calmly. 'I can.'

Before Lynzi could reply, she grabbed hold of the girl's head and with all the strength she could muster forced her down and under. Lynzi's arms appeared as she thrashed violently around in a feeble attempt to find something to grab hold of. She squirmed around and one of her feet flew up out of the water, followed promptly by the other one. One of the Doc Martens caught Billie-Jo square on the jaw. She almost let go, but managed to wrap her arms tightly around Lynzi's legs and pushed her deeper under.

She was just beginning to wonder how long she could keep this up when Lynzi's body jolted slightly and Billie-Jo lost her grip.

Reeling away, she hoisted herself up onto the side of the pool. She turned, gasping for breath, expecting to see Lynzi right behind her, but she wasn't there. She stared at the spot where the girl had been, but all she could see was a pair of legs scissoring frantically beneath the surface.

Time seemed to stand still as Billie-Jo watched, trying to understand what was happening. As the feet seemed to lose their will to fight and slowly stopped kicking around, she slipped back into the water, took a deep breath and ducked down beneath the surface. The chlorine stung her eyes as she opened them, but after a few seconds her vision came into semi-focus.

Lynzi's body was suspended almost vertically, upside-down in the water. Her arms were moving gently at her sides and her skirt was billowing up around her waist. Then Billie-Jo saw what had happened.

The face, its mouth yawning wide, was twisted at an awkward angle on the bottom of the pool. The long mane of black and purple hair had become wrapped around Lynzi's neck and been sucked into one of the pool filters, effectively pinning her to the tiles.

As she climbed out of the pool, Billie-Jo remembered a day trip with Tracy to Stoke Park near Guildford when she was about five-years-old. She had stood on one of the filters in the paddling pool and it had felt like a magnet was pulling against her toes.

Pushing the strands of wet hair out of her face, she retrieved the bottle of hydrogen fluoride and dropped it into her bag. Then she walked quickly round the perimeter of the pool, through the open door and out into the car park.

CHAPTER 16

There were few people that Billie-Jo hated more than Lynzi Pengelly. But on reflection there was something about the girl's death which, in the cold light of the aftermath, was troubling her.

It wasn't the fact she was actually dead; even Maya and Emily, Lynzi's every-present cronies, had been intimidated by her. There was no doubt that the world would be a better place without Lynzi Pengelly in it. Aside from the slight concern that someone might have seen her on the school premises after hours, it didn't worry Billie-Jo that she was responsible for Lynzi's death either.

No, it was something far more disturbing than that.

The surge of euphoric empowerment she had experienced as she biked back to Ashurst after killing Michael Bamford was like nothing she had ever felt before. It had been more all-consuming and exhilarating than the day she received her first kiss from a boy and had floated round on cloud nine for the rest of that week.

An hour earlier, as she had watched Lynzi Pengelly's body floating in the school swimming pool, she had felt that same powerful burst of ecstasy. She liked it. More than that, she loved the way it made her entire body tingle, and she couldn't wait for an opportunity to feel that way again.

It was this thought that was running through Billie-Jo's head as she ran herself a hot bath that evening. And not in a positive way. It had occurred to her that if for no other reason than the electrifying thrill that killing gave her, she had somehow acquired a taste for it. And that thought actually scared her.

She undressed and stood in front of the bathroom mirror. Examining the puncture wound on her shoulder caused by Bamford's chisel, she was pleased to see it was healing well and barely even hurt to touch now. She had been lucky, it could have been far worse.

She turned off the bathtaps, stepped into the water and sank down beneath the blanket of white foam, stretching out and immersing herself until only her head and the tops of her knees were visible. It felt wonderful.

Before she had shot Tyler James, Billie-Jo would never have believed that killing someone could be so simple. Of course, there's the moral compass to overcome – the innate understanding in every decent human being that killing is inherently wrong. And that's no easy thing to conquer. If it were, people would be bumping each other off all over the place, and for the most trivial of reasons at that. But get past that stigma and the actual act of taking a life proves ridiculously easy.

As Billie-Jo luxuriated in the hot water, she realised that whatever sense of right and wrong she might have had was gone. What would her mum think of her? Vicky might not have been renowned for her morals, but murder? Maybe, Billie-Jo thought, it really was time to stop. Yet once again, as that sense of doubt began to engulf her, the rage inside swiftly eclipsed it.

There was something else she had read in the articles about Toyah Leaky that had been playing on her mind. As a wedding present, Marcus King had given his new wife two beautiful Hungarian Viszlas. After they divorced, she would beat the poor dogs repeatedly and without mercy. Maybe it was because of the way her stepfather had treated the family dogs, Bronson and Stella, but the very thought of the woman with the haystack hair beating two helpless dogs had incensed Billie-Jo beyond all reason.

*

The journey to California Country Park was much less straightforward than those to Tunbridge Wells and Stoney Cross. Billie-Jo would have to travel from London Paddington to Reading, then walk ten-minutes to catch a bus that would take her as near to the park as it was possible to go on public transport. Following that there would be a 2-mile walk; thirty-five-minutes or thereabouts. However, as Billie-Jo tried to commit to memory the details of the route she would be taking, she was at least pleased to see that there wasn't going to be any cycling required! And if nothing else, she thought, regardless of the motives for her excursions, she was becoming far more comfortable travelling independently and seeing parts of the country she might not otherwise have visited.

Her parents had seldom ventured out of London. To begin with, they had no vehicle of their own; Vicky Hazelwood couldn't drive and Jamie Trot's licence had been revoked for a succession of speeding offences before the two had met. Neither did they have the money to fritter on buses and trains – or, as Jamie not so eloquently once put it, "Spunk a load of dosh on a ride surrounded by old gits smelling of piss? No fuckin' way!".

Additionally, due to Jamie and Vicky's propensity for overindulging on alcohol, any fun there may have been on the infrequent occasions when they did head for the coast – usually to South End on Sea, occasionally Clacton – invariably started with bickering and, at some stage during the day, collapsed into a full-blown screaming match.

Billie-Jo had decided she would pay Toyah Leaky a visit on the morning following the incident at the school swimming pool. Unlike Partridge and Bamford, whose home addresses she had been able to locate without too much effort, Leaky had proven to be a more difficult nut to crack. However, from what Billie-Jo had read, the woman could be found at her stables, Tranquillity Fields, almost every Saturday and Sunday morning. So that would be where she would go.

It wasn't going to be ideal; almost certainly there would be other people around. But without the first clue of how to find out where Leaky actually lived, what choice did she have? She would just have to go for it and improvise if and when the moment arose.

As it turned out, she didn't go on the Saturday as planned after all. She had woken to find her Facebook timeline ablaze with messages of sympathy over the tragic drowning of Lynzi Pengelly.

As she read through them, Billie-Jo had scarcely been able to correlate the adoration expressed in the seemingly endless stream of commiseration with the Lynzi that she had known.

Beneath a photo of Lynzi, Maya Blake and Emily Robinson – locked in a group hug and pouting playfully for a selfie – Maya had written:

To my beautiful friend. Love you for always.
RIP. XXX

210

That had been fair enough, Billie-Jo supposed; Maya had been one of the dead girl's most devoted hangers-on.

There was also one from Emily:

Miss you hun. Love Emily xxxx

Not quite as over the top as Maya's then. There was something telling about that.

Billie-Jo scrolled on through. There were countless more messages of a similar ilk to Maya and Emily's, but she also noticed that a few of them were from people she knew for a fact had been targets of Lynzi's spite.

She felt her hackles rise when she saw that even her friend, Carly, had waded in with:

Taken too soon by the Angles X

Carly! Of *all* people! Her relationship with Lynzi had been just as fractious, if not more so than Billie-Jo's. Yet she had actually added a kiss! And to top it off, she hadn't even spelt Angels right!

As she made a mental note to tackle Carly on her message the next time she saw her, a thought flashed across Billie-Jo's mind and she could suddenly imagine how the police interrogation would go:

211

'So, Miss Hazelwood, we see you didn't leave a message of condolence on Miss Pengelly's Facebook page.'

'No.'

'We have it on very good authority that you *hated* Miss Pengelly. Is that true?'

'No.'

'Your friend, Carly hated her too though, didn't she? But *she* left a message and you didn't. I put it to you that you *did* hate Miss Pengelly. So much so in fact that you killed her. You did kill her, didn't you?'

'No. No. *No*!'

It was utterly ridiculous, of course, and Billie-Jo shook the scenario from her head. Yet whether it was a moment of paranoia or otherwise, the thought made her feel uneasy.

Her loathing for Lynzi had hardly been a secret. Carly's feelings about the girl were also well known, but she had risen above it to leave a message of sympathy. In the midst of such an outpouring of affection and grief, it might draw attention if Billie-Jo were to be the sole absentee. She hadn't successfully gotten away with the murders of Tyler, Partridge and Bamford just to go and get arrested, convicted and banged up for the accidental death of a worthless skank like Lynzi Pengelly. And it *had* been an accident. Well, sort of anyway.

Billie-Jo couldn't bring herself to write anything nice, so she settled for a simple **RIP** with the thinking that *her* RIP meant Rot In Piss.

The whole Facebook business left Billie-Jo feeling sick and she ended up spending most of Saturday in bed.

Tracy proved to be surprisingly compassionate; after initially giving her an ear-bashing, she realised her granddaughter actually did look a little peaky, so at lunchtime brought her up a bowl of chicken soup and a buttered roll. She even went as far as to cancel a date with Lionel that she had planned for that afternoon.

After a day of rest, Billie-Jo slept well that night and was up early the following morning and packing her bag for her visit to the California Country Park.

In the wake of Landis's appeal on the news and the revelation that the two dead men had been associated with Hallam and Mástiga, Billie-Jo had realised she would need to move quickly. If her last two targets had seen the news – and she had to work on the assumption they would have – it was unlikely they would be shaken enough to come out of the woodwork, holding their hands in the air and confessing their involvement with Hallam in exchange for police protection. But they would most definitely be on their guard.

Additionally, the police would not only have linked the murders of Bamford and Partridge by their association with Hallam; both men had been shot dead by someone using the same calibre pistol; ergo, most likely, it had been the same killer. Employing a different modus operandi this time round might at least delay Toyah Leaky's impending death from being connected to Bamford and Partridge's.

So, Billie-Jo decided she wouldn't take the gun. She didn't really need it this time anyway, at least not as an instrument of retribution. No, she had much more fitting plans for Leaky.

There had been little choice but to dispose of the coat she had been wearing when she killed Bamford. But on the previous Monday afternoon, Billie-Jo had gone shopping on the way home from school and managed to find another that was almost an exact match for the blood-spattered original. If nothing else, a like-for-like would prevent any questions from Tracy over her being able to afford a new one.

Adopting her usual disguise, she took the tube to London Paddington, then hopped on the nine thirty-two service to Bristol Temple Meads, which en-route would stop at Reading.

The train out of London was far busier than Billie-Jo had expected for a Sunday morning, but she managed to secure a single seat opposite the toilet, soon realising why it had been vacant in an otherwise heaving carriage: there was a horrible smell lingering in the air and Billie-Jo couldn't help but recall Jamie's thoughts on the odious delights of public transport.

During the journey, a sad-faced man wearing a scruffy coat with a grubby backpack slung across one shoulder came walking through. Without saying a word, he swiftly deposited a packet of tissues and a printed note alongside the occupant of each seat. As he stopped to place one on the armrest of Billie-Jo's, she caught the overpowering odour of stale sweat; it was even more pungent than the smell emanating from the chemical toilet.

She glanced at the note the man had left with her:

I AM WITHOUT A JOB. MY WIFE HAS DIED AND I HAVE ONE CHILD TO FEED. PLEASE BUY THESE TISSUES FOR MONEY.

She leant out of her seat and watched him as he returned to the far end of the carriage, then made his way back down towards her again, mostly retrieving the untouched packets of tissues and stuffing them back into his holdall. Billie-Jo heard a woman about half a dozen seats in front of her say, 'Sorry, no.' There wasn't even a hint in her disinterested tone that suggested she actually *was* sorry.

Not so long ago, just like the passenger in front of her, Billie-Jo would have also turned the man away. It was nothing more than begging and the number of people doing it on the tubes and the trains had been on the increase for some time. Moreover, there were stories of it being part of a web of organised crime, and on public transport it was against the law. Not that making it illegal had made the slightest bit of difference.

But there was something about reading that simple note that struck a chord with Billie-Jo.

How easy it was to go from relative comfort to a struggle-to-survive situation. She of all people knew that. Her home life had never been what anyone would have called a cheerful one. On the contrary, most of the time she had been miserable. All the same, compared to where life had positioned her now, she would have given anything to be back in the little flat in Churchill Hamlets with Jamie and Vicky and Bobbi-Leigh and the two dogs.

Only since losing her family had Billie-Jo realised what a happy life it had been before, she just hadn't known it at the time. It all felt like another world now, a lifetime away, and she desperately wanted it back.

The man begging was probably just a scam artist and the words about his dead wife and starving child a warped fabrication to pluck at the heartstrings of the gullible. But then again, perhaps not. Life, as they say, can change on the spin of a coin.

As the man stepped up alongside her and was about to pick up the tissues, Billie-Jo felt in her pocket and handed him a one-pound coin.

The man's sad expression changed into a grateful smile. He nodded his appreciation and without a word moved on through the connecting door to the next carriage.

When she reached Reading, Billie-Jo nipped into a hardware store in town to make a purchase, then caught the first available bus to Biggs Lane. The ride only took a little over an hour and a quarter, but to her it felt like an eternity. She was starting to feel a bit twitchy and couldn't wait for the familiar burst of adrenaline to kick in, which would quell her nerves and carry her through everything that lay ahead.

The weather had changed between her departure from Reading and her arrival in Biggs Lane. What had begun as an overcast, drizzly morning finally surrendered to bright blue skies and sunshine.

Alighting the bus, she maintained an impressive pace on foot and reached the California Country Park in just under 30-minutes. She had a good idea where Tranquillity Fields was located; she had repeatedly studied Google Maps until the geography of the place was pretty much imprinted in her head. But she was pleased to find that the stables were clearly signposted anyway, which removed any uncertainty from the equation.

Aside from the main entrance gates, Tranquillity Fields was completely ringed off behind eight-foot-high, poorly maintained Cherry Laurel hedging. Billie-Jo could hear the distant whinnying of horses from somewhere off on the other side. It wasn't going to be easy to breach – she had realised that when she looked at the gallery of online images of the place – but obviously she couldn't just go strolling in through the gates.

She circled the perimeter of the hedgerow until she came across a narrow break in the thick foliage. Slipping her bag off her shoulder, she removed her spectacles and dropped them inside. Then she laid down flat on her front and wormed her way in through the branches.

The inner side of the hedge was fenced with six-foot-high welded mesh wire. This Billie-Jo had also clocked on some of the online photos and she had come prepared.

Still positioned face down, it was a struggle to get into her bag, but she felt around inside and found the pair of heavy-duty clippers she'd stopped to buy in Reading. She had chosen well; they severed the wire strands with ease and in less than a minute she had created a hole big enough to get through.

She remained flat down in the hedgerow and waited for a couple of minutes, her eyes scanning the terrain for any sign of life. There was none. Maybe coming on a Sunday had been the best option after all, she thought. The less staff on site the better.

Giving it just one more minute to be sure, she moved forward to get through the hole in the fence. A protruding strand of wire that she hadn't bent back far enough scratched her cheek. She put a hand to her face. It felt wet. Looking at her fingers she saw blood. Cursing silently to herself, she wriggled carefully forward until she was completely through, then stood up and looked about her.

Over to her left were the wooden-fenced paddocks she had seen in the photos. Aside from one, in which there was a beautiful chestnut brown stallion sauntering aimlessly around, they were empty. Detecting movement, the horse spotted Billie-Jo and stood watching her inquisitively for a moment. Then it lost interest and trotted away to the far side.

Behind the paddocks, stretching away into the distance, there was a mile-long grass gallop, running almost parallel to which there were shorter length sand and all-weather shavings gallops.

Away to the right, Billie-Jo could see a cluster of fenced-off areas containing hurdles and various other training equipment, beyond which was an expanse of open grassland. Then, on the far reaches of that, there were wash-down bays and the two large stable buildings themselves.

Thanks to the photos she had pored over, everything was as familiar to Billie-Jo as if she had been there before and she couldn't have picked a better spot to access the place if she had planned it.

Her nerves now gone and adrenaline firing on all thrusters, she made a mental note of her point of entry, then took off at speed, running swiftly along the length of the fence. The early rain had left the unmown stretch of grass squelchy under foot.

As she drew level with the stables, she could hear music playing from inside. Glancing about again to ensure that there was nobody around, she was just about to cross the wide stretch of dirt track towards the door of the nearest stable block when an elderly bearded man wearing Wellington boots and dungarees and carrying a bucket in each hand stepped out.

Billie-Jo froze for an instant, then dropped down onto her haunches. It wasn't as if the manoeuvre would save her; if the man turned his head just a fraction to the left, he would almost certainly spot her. Fortunately, he didn't. With his back to her, he paused in the open doorway and shouted cryptically back over his shoulder: 'These may be your stables, ma'am, but let it be known I don't agree with what you're doing. Just you be aware, if it happens again…'

Without finishing whatever it was he was about to say, the man turned away to the right and walked off towards the wash-down bays, then disappeared around the far corner of the building.

Without any further hesitation, Billie-Jo quickly stood up, scurried across the track and peered in through the open doorway. The music was louder now. With a final look around, she stepped inside.

The interior was much darker than she had expected. As her eyes adjusted to the half-light, she saw that it comprised some twenty or more divided stalls arranged in two long, opposing rows, between which ran a central walkway. Only half a dozen of the stalls appeared to be occupied.

She couldn't see anyone, but behind the music there was the sound of someone talking. It was definitely a female voice and it sounded angry, but whatever it was she was saying was drowned out by the song; it was a slushy romantic ballad that Billie-Jo didn't recognise.

Hoping that the volume of the music would drown out her approach, Billie-Jo moved forward.

From her left there came a sudden snorting noise and a horse stuck its head out over the top of the stall gate, startling her. She took a sideways step to walk around it and her foot clipped a hayfork that had been left propped up against the gate on the opposite stall. Before she could grab hold of it, the fork toppled and clattered down onto the stone floor.

The music abruptly shut off.

CHAPTER 17

Billie-Jo stopped stock still. There was a moment of silence that felt like an eternity, then a voice called out from somewhere down at the far end of the stables.

'Hello? Is that you, Mills?'

With her heart pounding, as Billie-Jo stood deciding whether or not she should answer, a short, wiry figure stepped out of the gate of the left-hand stall at the end.

Billie-Jo immediately recognised Toyah Leaky's bright red haystack hair-do.

'Oh!' the woman exclaimed. 'You gave me a bit of a start.' She was well-spoken but the voice was slurred. She hiccupped and swayed slightly. Reaching out, she put a hand on the gate to steady herself.

Billie-Jo's mind was racing. Every fibre in her body was screaming at her to turn and run, but she knew if she did she would never come back.

Leaky peered at her through the gloom. 'What are you doing sneaking around in the dark? Come down here so I can get a better look at you.' She hiccupped again.

Billie-Jo came to a decision. Why was she hesitating? It had to be now or never. And never wasn't an option.

Leaky was wearing mud-spattered riding boots over stone-washed denims and a padded navy-blue gilet, beneath which was a bulky, pale blue long-sleeve double-knit sweater.

As Billie-Jo got closer to her, she could see that the woman had a large, half-filled glass of white wine clutched in her hand. Behind her, perched up on the dividing wall between two stalls, there were two empty bottles of Chablis Premier Cru.

Leaky looked wearily at Billie-Jo. Her eyes were sleepy. 'We're not open on Sundays.' She waved an idle hand in the air. 'And if it's stable space for a horse you're after, you should know that we don't do that here. Besides…' – another hiccup and the head lolled slightly – '…it's protocol to telephone first. If you had, you would have saved yourself the trouble of a wasted trip.'

'It's not a wasted trip,' Billie-Jo said quietly.

'What *do* you want then?' There was impatience in the tone now. 'This is private property.' Another hiccup.

'I know that. I'm not here about stabling a horse. It's you I wanted to see. I have to talk to you about something important.'

Leaky tutted. 'Well, you still should have called ahead.' She pursed her lips, apparently considering the matter. She made up her mind. 'I'm not happy about

224

this, but you're here now, I suppose.' She reached out and took hold of Billie-Jo's arm. Her grip was surprisingly firm. 'Come and meet Silver Moon Star.'

Billie-Jo allowed Leaky to wrangle her into the stall.

The horse that she had been admonishing when Billie-Jo arrived was a Bay Roan Appaloosa. There was tangible sadness in the dark pools of its eyes and she could almost hear the poor creature willing her to liberate it from its cruel mistress.

'Moony, this is…' Leaky looked at Billie-Jo inquiringly. 'What did you say your name was?'

'I didn't.'

Leaky's brow furrowed. 'Well, don't bugger about, what is it?' There was that impatience again.

'Lynzi.'

'Moony, this is Lynzi,' Leaky said, turning to address the horse. She patted it on the side of its muzzle. 'Been a naughty girl, has our Moony. Let us all down rather badly at the Ascot two-thirty yesterday, she did.'

The horse looked at her blankly.

'You did, *didn't* you?' Leaky repeated, this time with unrestrained annoyance. She brought the flat of her hand down hard on the front of the horse's nose. It flinched and its nostrils flared. 'And. She. Was. Warned. Last. Time.' Each word was punctuated by another short, sharp slap.

225

Stamping its hooves, the horse tried to back away from her, but there was nowhere to go.

'Don't do that!' Billie-Jo cried.

Leaky spun round to face her. There was a sadistic smirk on her face. 'Don't do *what*?' She hiccupped. '*This*?' She slapped the animal's nose again, this time with even more force.

The horse snorted and shied away.

The woman glared at Billie-Jo. 'Who the hell do you think you are exactly, coming onto *my* property and telling me what I can and can't do with *my* horses?'

'You shouldn't treat her like that. It's cruel.'

'Cruel?' Leaky almost laughed. 'It's called *discipline*, girl. And if this useless nag doesn't start improving her form, she'll be pulling Steptoe and Son's cart around the streets.' Her hand flew out and she slapped the horse again. It whinnied and stamped its hooves. 'Shangalang will be replacing you if you don't start minding your Ps and Qs.' She raised her hand to strike again.

Billie-Jo grabbed hold of the sleeve of Leaky's sweater. 'Stop!'

The woman yanked her arm away and stared at her fiercely for a moment. Then, as quickly as it had come, the anger subsided. 'You said you wanted to speak to me about something important.' It was as if striking Silver Moon Star had never happened. She took a mouthful of wine and swallowed. 'So get on with it and make it snappy.' She smiled but there was no humour there. 'Or I'll have you thrown out.'

'By who?'

Leaky flapped a limp hand in the direction of the entrance. 'By my man, Mills. And it's "by *whom*", not "by who".' She took another swig of wine. 'Come on. Take that silly hat off and tell me what you want.'

Billie-Jo shook her head. 'It's funny how you lot got off perving on us and watching us suffer, yet you don't recognise me when I'm standing right in front of you.'

'What on earth are you on about you silly girl?' Leaky drained her glass. 'You're not one of my riding school students are you?'

Billie-Jo removed the beanie and pulled the scarf down from the bottom of her face.

Leaky's quizzical expression slowly changed to one of recognition. 'Oh!'

Billie-Jo nodded. 'Yeah. Oh.'

Suddenly Leaky thrust a bony finger at her accusingly. 'It's you! You killed those two men they were talking about on the TV. Partridge and...' – she hiccupped – '...you know, the other one.'

'Bamford.'

Leaky touched a finger to the end of her nose. 'That's him.' Then the realisation of what Billie-Jo had just said dawned on her. 'It *was* you. You *did* kill them!'

Billie-Jo nodded. 'And you couldn't even remember their names. Your buddies.'

'Buddies? *Remember* them?' Leaky scoffed. 'Don't be so ridiculous. I'd never even heard of them until that item came on the news this week. It was only when the report mentioned that they were connected to Terence that I realised they were fellow investors in the Mástiga Project.' Leaky frowned. 'Wait.' She waggled the bony finger at Billie-Jo again. 'You thought we knew each other?' She huffed. 'What a rank amateur you are. Of course we didn't know each other. There could have been five or fifty-five.' She shrugged. 'Don't know, don't care. All I knew was that there *were* others.'

'Not any more.'

Leaky's eyes widened defiantly. 'Well, you're not going to kill me!'

Dropping the wine glass, which smashed on the stone floor, she moved forwards, but Billie-Jo was too quick for her. Grabbing her by the shoulders, she pushed the woman backwards. Leaky slipped in a dollop of horse dung, lost her footing and landed flat on her backside. She wiggled quickly backwards across the floor into the corner of the stall, letting out a little squeal as she caught her hand on the broken wine glass. She pointed up at Billie-Jo, attempting to preserve an air of defiance but failing miserably. 'You… You just stay away from me, do you hear?'

'I hear.' Billie-Jo stood over her. 'Horrible, isn't it? Being in fear for your life.'

At that, the fight seemed to leave her and Leaky physically sagged back into the corner. She suddenly seemed to have sobered up.

'When I saw that news report linking those two men to Terence, I knew whoever killed them would probably be looking for me too. One of the newspapers said something about a mad serial killer on the loose.' She curled her index finger and tapped it against the side of her head. 'But I knew. I knew it had to be someone connected to that damned island. I have to say though, I never considered for one moment it would be a child.' She looked up at Billie-Jo sorrowfully. 'A *child*!'

'What you did to us on that island was fuckin' evil. You deserve to pay for that.'

Leaky pursed her lips and shook her head slowly. 'Let me tell you something, little girl. There's a crawling sickness infecting this country…'

'It's you that's sick. You and your buddies.'

Leaky laughed. 'Don't be obtuse. We were going to be the *cure*.'

'Oh, bore off! You sound just like the others. That's *really* what you think?'

'Absolutely.' Leaky squinted up at her. 'Tell me. Did you do this irksome little dance with *them*?' She made a little circling motion with her hand. It was bleeding quite badly from where the glass had gashed her, but she didn't appear to be too concerned.

Billie-Jo screwed up her face. '*What*?'

Leaky made the little circular motion again. 'You know. The chitchat. It's like a dance. You say one thing, I say another. You threaten me, I plead for my life. Back and forth, back and forth.'

'What the *fuck* are you chattin' about?'

Leaky sighed. 'You really are obtuse, aren't you, girl?' She looked at her hand and seemed to notice the blood for the first time. 'Whatever. Look, if you're going to kill me just get on and do it, but for God's sake please just stop trying to talk me to death.'

Billie-Jo nodded. 'You know what? You're right. This is the third time I've tried to get you people to say somethin', absolutely *anythin'* that makes sense to me about what went down on that island. Somethin' that at least tries to justify what you did.'

She reached into her bag and felt around for the pair of old gardening gloves she'd found in one of the storage boxes in her bedroom.

'But I'm just wastin' my breath, aren't I? There isn't any justifyin' it. There's nothin' any of you can say that will *ever* defend what you did to me and my family. You're all fuckin' psychos.' She pulled on the gloves. 'My Mum might not have been the greatest mum in the world, but she was *mine*. And she sure as fuck didn't deserve what you done to her.'

'Your Mum… I don't…'

Billie-Jo let the fury take her. 'You remember! You melted her fuckin' face off!'

'Ah, yes, of course. The woman with the melted face.' Leaky smirked. 'I'll have you know I admired her for the fortitude she exhibited in protecting you and your sister from that vile paedophile. But that acid atomiser. It was inspired. And that face of hers…' She all but sniggered. ' Well, let's be honest, it was a vast improvement afterwards.'

Billie-Jo's reached back into her bag and withdrew a slender steel canister. It was about eight-inches long and resembled a small thermos flask, only with a nozzle and flip-up steel siphon fitted to the top.

Leaky's eyes were now registering fear. 'What's that?'

'The last thing you're ever going to see.'

'Wait! I'm sorry. I didn't mean what I said. Please don't kill me! We *can* talk.'

Billie-Jo shook her head and held the canister out at arm's length in front of her. 'Let's see how *you* fuckin' look with your face melted off. Let's be honest, it'll be a vast improvement afterwards.'

She pressed the nozzle and jet of liquid spewed out through the steel siphon, dousing the right-hand side of Leaky's face.

Before leaving home that morning, Billie-Jo had gone into the bathroom, locked the door and spent several minutes carefully decanting the contents of the stolen bottle of hydrogen fluoride into the canister. Although she had Googled some harrowing images and had a pretty good idea what the effects of the acid making contact with flesh would be, nothing – not even having seen her own mother fall victim to acid burns – could have prepared her for the horror that unfolded in front of her now.

The noise that came out of Leaky's mouth was barely even human. Billie-Jo desperately wanted to turn away, but her body was disobeying the cry from her brain; they seemed to have become separate entities. Memories of watching Vicky in the throes of torment came rushing into her head, and as if in a trance she stared in terror as Leaky's nose seemed to lose its form; the thin layer of flesh forming her right nostril melted away from the cartilage and hung limply in a sinewy streak across her cheek.

The cheek itself had turned scarlet and become swollen and as Leaky, now blubbering incoherently, touched her face, several of the blisters burst, smearing her fingers with viscous yellow pus.

The iris in her right eye had gone from bright blue-grey to a dark, opaque smear. Then the surface of the eyeball itself started to bubble and contract into a glutinous blob. The eyelashes had shrivelled as if singed by open flame, and soft skin surrounding her eye blistered and puckered as what was left of the eyelid curled upwards and the decimated eyeball began to seep out of its socket.

Leaky was trying to scream, but there was no sound, only a strangled hiss. As her mouth with its two rows of impossibly perfect teeth yawned wide, Billie-Jo raised the canister for the second time and pumped down hard on the nozzle. A second burst of acid squirted out and straight into the woman's open mouth. She started to choke and spat out the residue, but the damage was already taking effect. The tongue seemed to distend before Billie-Jo's eyes, and as Leaky made a throaty guttural noise, it lolled out of the side of her mouth amidst foaming bloodied sputum, which dribbled in rivulets down her chin and dripped steadily onto her sweater.

As if she were moving in slow motion, Leaky slumped onto her side, twisted and started to drag herself across the floor towards the stall gate.

Billie-Jo felt her gorge beginning to rise; it was time to get out. Leaky was as good as dead; her work was done. As Leaky continued to advance on her, she

233

stepped back out onto the walkway, set down the canister and removed her gloves, dropping them into her bag.

Suddenly, Leaky's arm snaked out and tried to grab her leg. Billie-Jo stepped deftly to one side, and with a last death rattle, Leaky sagged, her head dropped onto the floor and she lay still.

Billie-Jo turned to leave and her heart skipped a beat.

The elderly man she had seen when she arrived – presumably the person Leaky had referred to as Mills – was standing at the far end of the stable, watching horrified from the open doorway.

CHAPTER 18

Two minutes earlier, Harry Mills had been busy mopping down one of the wash-bays when he thought he heard someone scream

He stopped what he was doing and cocked an ear. Resting his elbow on the end of the shaft for a moment, he listened intently. He had been almost certain, but now there was nothing but the distant whinny of Bad Moon Rising in his paddock.

He was about to resume his toils when the sound came again. This time there was no doubt about it; it was a scream and it had come from the south stables. Dropping the mop, he ran across the yard as fast as his old legs would carry him.

Later on he would admit he was expecting to find that one of the horses his boss was always so quick to lash out at had finally turned on her. But what he saw as he reached the stable entrance made his blood run cold.

Partially silhouetted against the light streaming in through the second set of doors at the far end of the block, someone was standing over a body laying on the walkway. Mills's eyesight had been deteriorating for some time, but even from this distance he could see the shock of red hair. As he stood rooted to the spot trying to rationalise what he was seeing – surely there had to be *some* explanation for this! – the figure standing over the body turned and locked eyes with him for an instant. Mills couldn't be sure, but it looked like a girl.

For both of them there was a fleeting moment of indecision, during which time seemed to stand still. Then Mills started forward. He saw the girl kick something, which flew into Misty Moon Star's stall with a hollow clang, then she turned and hopped over the safety barrier spanning the doorway.

She caught her foot, stumbled, bounced off a stack of hay bales and with a squeal of pain catapulted away to the right out of sight.

Mills hurried down the walkway and stopped beside Leaky's prone body. He bent and rolled her over and his mouth fell open. 'Holy Mother of God!'

Glancing into the stall, he saw the discarded canister laying at Misty Moon Star's feet. The horse was idly munching on some hay and seemed to be totally unfazed by the events that had unfolded in front of it. Mills patted her on her muzzle and, climbing carefully over the barrier, he hurried to the corner of the building and looked back along its length. The girl had reached the far end, but she was hobbling.

He shouted to her. 'Wait!'

Billie-Jo limped to the edge of the dirt track. *Wait? For what?*, she thought. To get arrested, tried for triple murder and spend the rest of her life – the next sixty years, or even longer – locked up behind bars? *Not happening!*

She had twisted her ankle when she struck the hay bales and the pain searing up through her calf was agonising. But she managed to make it to the fence. Looking back, she was alarmed to see that Mills was in pursuit.

'Damned well stop, would you?!' The accent was broad Cornish and he sounded breathless.

Moving as fast as she could along the line of the fence, Billie-Jo picked the wrong moment to look back over her shoulder; her foot snared in a rut and she was sent sprawling down onto the damp grass. In an instant she was up again, but the second she put weight on her foot, a searing pain shot up through the already injured ankle and into her calf. She let out a cry. The pain was intense and her leg almost gave out beneath her. She had to hook her fingers through the mesh wire for support.

She had so very nearly made it to her exit spot, but Mills was advancing on her fast now.

Holding onto the fence, she managed to hobble the last few metres to the hole that she'd cut in the wire. She dropped to her knees and thrust her bag through into the gap ahead of her. Then, laying down flat on her front, she started to squirm through into the Cherry

Laurel hedgerow. But her coat sleeve got caught on the wire. She tried to pull herself free, but the severed tendrils just embedded themselves even further.

'Fuck!'

Managing to twist onto her side, her fingers scrabbled to find the zip on her coat to try to undo it. She tugged at it, but it snagged and jammed.

That's when she felt the hand grab hold of her leg.

'Got you!'

Before Billie-Jo knew what was happening, she was being dragged backwards across the ground, her coat sleeve ripped free and she was out in the open again. She squirmed free and rolled over onto her back as the old man stood over her.

Was this it then? After all she had been through? Game over? She lashed out her foot, but Mills stepped nimbly to one side.

'Woah there!' he exclaimed breathlessly. 'Calm yourself down. I'm not going to hurt you.' Puffing hard, he bent and rested his hands on his knees. Then, moving his hands round to the small of his back, he winced as she straightened himself up again. He looked down at the frightened girl splayed out on the ground in front of him. He could see her face clearly now and it disconcerted him; she could barely be much older than his granddaughter. 'What on earth brought a young girl like you here to do such a terrible thing?'

Billie-Jo pushed herself up on her elbows. She didn't know where to begin. 'I... I...'

Mills held up a hand. 'It doesn't matter. I'll tell you now, Ms Leaky was an evil woman. She was cruel to animals and humans alike. As far as I'm concerned, you've done the world a favour. Our beautiful horses too.' He reached out to her. 'Come on, get yourself up off that wet grass. You'll catch a chill.'

Billie-Jo allowed the old man to help her up onto her feet and she leaned back against the wire fence. The fight had all but abandoned her.

Mills pointed at her. 'Here, look. You've ruined your coat. Your mum ain't going to be too pleased with you.'

Billie-Jo glanced at the jagged tear in her sleeve. She shrugged.

'You've cut your face too.' He tapped his cheek.

Billie-Jo nodded. She stared down at her feet. 'What are you going to do?'

Mills ran a hand through his beard thoughtfully. 'Can't say as I rightly know. But I suggest you make yourself scarce.'

Billie-Jo raised her head and looked into the old man's eyes. She couldn't quite grasp what he was saying. Surely he wasn't letting her go, was he?

'I don't understand.'

'Just go.' Mills bent and held the wire mesh aside for her. 'Get out of here before I change my mind!'

He watched Billie-Jo as she got down on her knees and crawled through the fence into the dense hedgerow. As her feet disappeared, he let go of the mesh and it sprang back into place. Sighing, he turned away and slowly made his way back across the grass towards the stables. He paused at the door, fumbled in the pocket of his dungarees and pulled out a mobile phone.

*

Detective Inspector Landis pulled a generous pinch of Old Holborn from his initialled tobacco pouch and fed it carefully into the bowl of his favourite rosewood pipe. Using the tip of his thumb to tamp it down, he put the well-chewed end of the stem between his lips, struck a match and touched it to the surface of the tobacco. He moved the flame slowly around the bowl, puffing rhythmically until it was lit and burning evenly. Satisfied, he exhaled a wisp of smoke, closed his eyes and rested back in his chair.

Being a police officer had given Landis first hand experience of some terrible things over the past 18 years; all manner of death and depravity, which the ordinary man on the street couldn't imagine or begin to conceive of. He had always prided himself on being able to separate his work from his private life. But since the loss of his wife, Erin, a year ago things had changed. He'd had more time on his hands, and work – over which he had become obsessive – had started to infiltrate his weekends.

For no reason beyond that – at least none that he was able to pinpoint – he had allowed personal feelings to creep into the ongoing Hallam investigation. The lack of progress was getting him down and he didn't mind admitting it. In fact, he had been distinctly vocal about it when he'd spoken with Superintendent Nash on Friday afternoon. Just as he had anticipated, she had reeled off the requisite spiel about the benefits of tenacity and assured him that she had every faith in his ability to catch whoever was killing off Hallam's investors. But that didn't obviate the dispiriting feeling that he was getting nowhere.

He had reached the point where, not only didn't he share Nash's confidence in him, he wished he had never heard of Terence Hallam.

There had been zero response to his televised appeal earlier in the week, although that hadn't really surprised him. It had been worth a try, of course. But no matter what the stakes might be, people are naturally averse to coming forward for fear of reprisal. Besides which, nobody would be willing to confess to their involvement with the Mástiga murders.

His trip out to see Nick Mason on the Friday morning hadn't helped his burgeoning malaise either. Mason had made it clear on the phone that he didn't really want to speak to him again; he'd said all he had to say during the initial investigations the previous September. But when Landis had told him the ripples of what occurred on the island hadn't yet abated, the man's interest had been sufficiently piqued that he'd acquiesced.

When Landis arrived at Mason's home in Slough, however, the reception had been distinctly frosty.

Landis had asked him about his final conversation with Hallam, and specifically whether he might have said anything at all relating to his mysterious cabal of private investors.

Nick Mason had listened patiently enough to what Landis had to say, but he'd refused to let the detective speak with Kirsty or Charlie. He had been able to provide ironclad alibis for his whereabouts during the murders of Partridge and Bamford, and when he'd shown Landis to the door, he had made his feelings abundantly clear: 'If somebody really is out there tying up the loose threads, they have my blessing. But we've moved on, Detective Inspector. We just want to be left alone.'

Landis had left Slough thoroughly satisfied that the Masons had no involvement in what was happening, but even more dejected than when he'd arrived.

Staring out of his living room window at the rain lashing against the glass, Landis puffed thoughtfully on his pipe. The crossword resting on his lap had hardly been started; he had only managed to answer two questions in the half hour he'd been working on it; his mind was inescapably elsewhere this afternoon. 'Obvious disagreement for one in court,' he mused aloud. 'Nine letters.'

From the coffee table, his mobile phone suddenly buzzed into life. Setting aside his pipe, he picked it up and looked at the screen: **DUVALL**. He tapped the accept option.

'Linda?'

'Hi, Landis.'

'To what do I owe this pleasure so late on a Sunday afternoon?'

'I think I may have something of interest for you.'

Landis felt his heartbeat quicken. 'Go on.'

'As we agreed the other day, I put the word out among a few old colleagues to keep me informed of any homicides in their districts – strictly off the record, of course. I wasn't expecting much to be honest, but there was nothing to lose.'

'And?'

'It looks like it might have paid off.'

Landis sat bolt upright. 'I'm listening.'

'I've just got off the line to Neil Marsh at Thames Valley Constabulary. They had an emergency call out to a racing stable over Wokingham way a couple of hours ago. A Toyah Leaky. She was victim of a brutal acid attack. I know it may be nothing, but I couldn't help thinking of that woman on the island.'

Landis stood up and walked to the window. 'I don't suppose for one second there were any witnesses?'

'As a matter of fact, there was. One. Old guy who works at the stables on weekends. He told Nash that he was cleaning out the wash-bays when he heard Leaky's screams and saw two lads wearing black hoodies scarpering hell for leather out of the stables – and I quote – "like their feet were on fire". As I say, it may be nothing, but…'

'Where did they take the victim?' Landis wedged the phone between his ear and his shoulder and reached for his shoes.

'The Copse.'

'Never heard of it. Why not the Royal Berkshire?'

'There's a specialist burns unit at The Copse. She's in a seriously bad way. The old man had the wherewithal to call the paramedics first. They were there when Nash arrived. They got her stabilised and helicoptered her to The Copse.'

'Where is this place?'

'A couple of miles west of Wokingham.'

Landis finished tying his shoes. 'Thanks. I'll GPS it. I'm going to head over there now. Any chance you could give your man Nash a buzz back? Pave the way for me? Let him know I'm coming?'

'I already did.'

Landis smiled. 'You're a sharp cookie, Linda.'

He went out into the hall and took down his jacket from the coat stand beside the front door.

'I want you in on this if you're up for it. What are you doing this evening?'

'Nothing that can't wait.' Duvall suddenly sounded a little breathless.

'Wokingham is just over an hour from here. Sorry, you probably mentioned it the other day, but I've got a brain like a sieve at the moment. Where are you?'

'My flat in Winchester.'

'Similar distance then. What do you say we meet there at...' – Landis glanced at his watch – '...six-thirty?'

'I'm on my way.'

CHAPTER 19

The return trip from California Country Park had been misery incarnate. It took Billie-Jo almost three times as long to get back to the bus stop as it had on the way down. Her ankle had started to swell and she was forced to take several rest stops, sitting on the verge and waiting until the pain had subsided enough for her to continue. While she walked, the skies had clouded over, and just as she got there – only to see the one-an-hour bus disappearing off up the road – the heavens had opened and it had tipped down. Having waited another hour in the pouring rain for the next bus to come, she then sat out the thirty-minute ride back to Reading completely soaked to the skin.

At the station, a young woman had come walking along the platform shaking a collection tin. Spotting Billie-Jo, she had sidled up to her and thrust a leaflet into her hand, informing her that there was an alternative to living rough and it could be found in the arms of God. All she had to do was open her heart to Him.

'Or Her,' Billie-Jo had said.

The woman had given her a funny look and continued preaching at her, relaying her own past as a vagrant until the day she'd seen the light.

246

Billie-Jo had only managed to escape by going into the ladies' toilets, where she caught sight of herself in the mirror. She could certainly see why she had been targeted by Doris Do-gooder; her hair was hanging down in tangled clumps from beneath her sodden beanie, the cut on her cheek was worse than she'd realised, and there was a black smudge of dirt on her chin. As for her coat, it was scuffed and spattered with mud where she'd climbed through the hedge and the six-inch long rip in her sleeve was flapping wide.

What Mills had said to her about her mum being angry might have been wide of the mark by virtue of the fact she no longer had one, but getting past her nan in this state was going to be no easy feat.

On the train journey back to Paddington, her mobile phone had rung. It was Tracy.

'What you up to?'

'I'm out with Carly.'

At that moment the conductor decided to fire up the tannoy to loudly announce that the next stop would be Iver.

'Where exactly *are* you?' The question was wreathed in suspicion.

'We took the train into town to see a film.'

'Ah, okay. What film?'

What's showing at the moment? Billie-Jo's mind went completely blank. 'No, we er… we changed our

minds in the end. We went to Burger King instead.'
She needed to nip this conversation in the bud pronto.
'What did you call for?'

'Oh, yeah. I was just wonderin' what your plans are
for tonight.'

'Loverboy Lionel comin' over tonight, is he?'
Billie-Jo made little kissing noises.

'You can cut that shit out! As a matter of fact, since
you mention it, Lionel won't be comin' round here no
more.'

'Oh! I'm sorry.' Billie-Jo meant it.

'Don't be. Turns out he's a fuckin' arsehole just like
every other man I've ever known.'

'So what *did* you call for?'

'I was thinkin', if you pick up a pizza on the way
home maybe you'd like some quality Nan time and we
could watch a DVD together or somethin'? I ain't
watched that one you gave me for Christmas yet.'

Billie-Jo squinted at her reflection in the window
and silently mouthed 'What the actual fuck?' Why was
her nan suddenly being so nice? But even as the
thought flashed through her head, the answer came to
her. For all her outward bluster, Tracy was probably
quite lonely. Since Billie-Jo had been living with her,
aside from Lambeth's aged lothario, Lionel Palmer, she
had never even heard Tracy mention having friends, let
alone seen evidence of any.

'Sure, Nan. That'd be nice.'

The bonhomie didn't last long.

When she got home, Billie-Jo let herself in as quietly as she could. There was no sign of Tracy. Hoping to get to her room before she was seen, she made her way stealthily up the staircase. But as she got to the top, the toilet flushed and Tracy stepped out onto the landing.

'Fuck a duck, you made me jump! Why are you sneaking around like creeping Jesus?'

She flipped on the light, took one look at her bedraggled granddaughter and her jaw dropped open. 'You look like you've been dragged through an 'edge backwards!'

That's exactly *what happened*!, Billie-Jo thought. 'You might not have noticed, but it's pissing down out there,' she said sullenly.

'I *know* it is! I'm not talkin' about that. Look at the state of you! What the hell have you been up to?'

'Nothin'.'

'Don't you nothin' me, you little scrote. Here, you'd better not have been brawlin'!'

'I haven't!'

'Well, what…' Tracy trailed off and she put a hand to her mouth. 'Oh fuck me! You've been raped, haven't ya!'

Billie-Jo screwed up her face. 'No! For fuck's sake, Nan!'

Tracy's expression visibly changed to one of relief. 'Well, what *have* you been doin' then?'

'We was play fightin' with Carly's dog, that's all.'

'Shit on a stick! *Play* fightin?!' It's torn you to bits!' She frowned as something occurred to her. 'Hang on a sec. Didn't you tell me Carly's dog's a toy poodle?'

'Yeah. Brutus. Vicious little cunt!'

'*Brutus*? Who calls a fuckin' poodle Brutus?' She looked at Billie-Jo's torn sleeve. 'Look at your coat too. Fucked! I gave that to you for Christmas an' all.'

Billie-Jo changed the subject. 'Hey, look, I got the pizza.' She fished the box out of her shoulder bag and handed it over. 'A Five-Cheese Feast. I hope that's okay.'

Tracy licked her lips. 'That looks lush. I'll go heat the oven. You'd better get yourself in the shower first too. You smell like…'

'I know. A tramp's arsehole.'

Tracy cackled and shook her head. 'Like you've been rollin' in horseshit actually.'

Billie-Jo didn't know whether to laugh or cry. 'I'll be ten minutes.'

Tracy watched her limp along the landing to her bedroom. 'That Brutus have a chew on your foot too, did he?' she said sarcastically.

The truth was, she didn't believe a word she'd been told. But if there was one thing she'd learned since her granddaughter moved in, it was that the harder she pushed, the tighter Billie-Jo clammed up.

It's been said about some of the most notorious serial killers that they reached a breaking point in their trail of death where they actually longed to get caught – and were relieved when they actually were. Or so a myriad of psychoanalysts have observed. Something about the realisation that capture would be the only thing that could stop their murderous spree.

Billie-Jo had always thought that was a facile conclusion to draw. Why the hell would anyone responsible for multiple murders actually *want* to get caught and have to face the damning consequences of what they'd done? It made no sense to her whatsoever. But as she stood under the fine needles of hot spray, cleansing herself of the day's events, she at last had an insight into why: killing people is *so* exhausting!

Briskly towelling herself down and finally feeling human again, she opened the bathroom door to be greeted by the heavenly scent of pizza wafting up from the kitchen.

After the awful day she'd had, it was beginning to feel as if the net might be closing in around her. Mills would have reported her to the police and it was only a matter of time before they came knocking on her door. And whether what the shrinks had said was right or not, unlike the Bundys and Dahmers and Nilsens of the world, Billie-Jo had no desire to get caught. At least not until her odyssey was complete.

There must be no further delay now. She couldn't wait until next weekend, that was for sure. She had intended to do some digging for information on the final investor named in Hallam's file this evening – she would be bunking off school and paying him a visit tomorrow. But it would have to wait until bedtime now. Putting on the favourite onesie that Bobbi-Leigh had given her for her birthday, she went back downstairs to spend some "quality Nan time" with Tracy.

CHAPTER 20

Having got snarled up in traffic due to a bad accident on the M4 between Windsor and Wokingham, it was a little after eight o'clock when Landis finally reached The Copse. He'd initiated a hands-free call to Duvall to explain what was happening. She had promised to wait and, sure enough, as he pulled into the hospital's small car park, she was there.

She climbed out of her car and waved a hand.

Landis parked up in the space opposite hers and got out. 'Linda. I'm so sorry about the wait. Bloody nightmare.'

She shook her head. 'Don't worry about it. I'm afraid I've got bad news though.'

Landis screwed up his face. 'Oh, Christ, don't tell me she's...'

'No, no. She's very much alive. She got out of surgery half an hour ago. But it's not going to be possible to speak to her until tomorrow morning at the earliest.'

Landis shook his head. 'Not good enough. It's imperative we see her tonight. She's the first of Hallam's investor bods to survive. There's a chance she might actually be able to identify our pair of vigilantes.'

Duvall looked doubtful. 'They wouldn't let Nash speak to her. He left just before you arrived. He knows you were coming though and you have his blessing to give it a try. Just be aware there's a whole heap of doctors' orders to get past.'

'Yes, well, we'll see about that.'

'On the plus side, the old man who saw the two lads running away is still here.'

'Really?'

'Yeah. He insisted on accompanying Leaky in the helicopter. He's inside waiting for a taxi.'

Landis sighed. 'Okay, well that's a starting point at least. Let's go and have a word with him.'

They found Harry Mills sitting in the waiting room, shoulders hunched and staring at his feet. As the door opened and they came in, he looked up hopefully. Then his face fell.

'Oh. I've been waiting for a taxi to come and take me home.' He sounded tired. 'Fully booked – and on a Sunday night too. Just my flippin' luck. They told me it would be at least an hour, but it's already been two.'

Landis extended a hand. 'I'm DCI Landis, this is DC Duvall.'

Mills didn't stand up, but he reached out and shook his hand. 'I already spoke to the other officer when I first got here.'

'Nash?'

Mills nodded.

'I realise that. And we're very grateful for the information you've been able to give us. But I was just wondering if you would be kind enough to quickly take me through what you saw again?'

Mills sighed. 'Very well.'

Landis and Duvall sat down.

'As I explained to your Mr Nash, I was cleaning out the bays where we wash down the horses.' He chuckled. 'It never ceases to amaze me how filthy they get. No sooner have you got them clean than...' He trailed off as he saw the look on Landis's face. 'Anyway, I was busy doing that when I heard screams coming from the south stables. I hurried over and I saw two men wearing black hoodies running like hell out and across the field. There was no way I could chase after 'em. I've got arthritis in my left knee, you see, and even if I hadn't, they was moving way too fast for me. Like jackrabbits they was. Anyway, when I went into the stables, I found Ms Leaky on the floor with...' – he swallowed hard – '...with her face all burned.'

Landis looked at him sympathetically. 'I can't begin to imagine what a shock that must have been for you.'

'Too right. I ain't never seen nothin' like that in all my born days.'

'Two men, you say.'

'Excuse me?'

'You said you saw two men running away.'

Mills nodded. 'Yes, sir.'

'How can you be sure they were men if they were wearing hoodies?'

'Well, I… I just assumed, I guess.'

'Then you couldn't say with any certainty that they were definitely men?'

Mills hesitated. 'My eyesight isn't what it used to be, sir. I suppose I could have been wrong.'

Landis exchanged glances with Duvall. He smiled at Mills. 'That's fine.' He changed tack. 'Any cameras on site?'

Mills shook his head. 'Not on the stable blocks themselves. There's cameras on the main gate.'

Landis looked at Duvall. 'Make a note we need to check that footage.' Her turned back to Mills. 'Miss Leaky must mean a lot to you. You coming here to the hospital with her, I mean.'

'*Ms* Leaky and myself, we didn't always see eye to eye on everything. I'll make no secret of the fact I didn't like the way she treated the horses. But she doesn't have anyone else, you see. So I *had* to come. I guess you'd call it a sense of duty.'

Duvall smiled at him pleasantly. 'You're a very decent man.'

Mills looked awkward. 'I don't rightly know about that. It's no more than anyone else would have done in my shoes.'

The door opened and a young nurse in her early twenties popped her head round the corner. 'Your taxi has arrived, Mr Mills,' she said, and promptly ducked out again.

'At bloomin' last!' Mills stood up. 'If you don't need me for anything else, Detective Inspector… sorry, I forgot your name.'

'Landis. No, it's fine, we're done for now. You've been very helpful, Mr Mills. Thank you. You get yourself on home now.'

Mills bid them both a goodnight and left.

Duvall opened her mouth to speak but Landis cut her off. 'You don't need to say it. Our key witness isn't as reliable as we might have hoped.'

They stepped out of the waiting room. The nurse who'd spoken to Mills had resumed her station at the desk beside a set of double doors at the top end of the corridor.

Landis moved in close to Duvall and spoke quietly. 'How do you feel about helping me with a small deception?'

She looked at him quizzically. 'What have you got in mind?'

'I've got to speak to Toyah Leaky. I just need to get past that nurse and find her room.'

Duvall looked at him apprehensively. 'And how exactly do you propose we do that?'

'Not we. *I*. It's about as clichéd as ruses get, but I want you to create a distraction. I don't know, faint or something.'

'*Really*?' Duvall grinned. 'I can do better than that. Just wait by the water dispenser. You'll know when to move.'

As she approached the desk, the nurse looked up from the chart she was filling out.

'I know it's a bit of a pain,' Duvall began, 'but...'

The telephone on the desk rang. 'One moment.' The nurse held up a finger to Duvall and took the call. 'Yes... yes, doctor... I'll come right down.' She ended the conversation and stood up. 'I'm sorry, one of the doctors needs me urgently. I'll be back in a minute.'

'Of course.'

The nurse punched the release button on the double doors, there was a buzzing sound and she went through. Quick as a flash, Duvall stepped over and stuck out her foot to stop the door swinging shut. She urgently beckoned to Landis, who had been stood by the water dispenser watching. He hurried up the corridor.

'What were you going to say to her?'

'Doesn't matter. Just be quick!'

'Wait here. I shan't be long.'

Landis slipped past her and she stepped away to let the door swing shut behind him.

A long corridor running at 45 degrees to the main one stretched out in front of him. He moved swiftly along past rows of closed doors on either side, checking the name holders mounted on them. He passed one on the left that was slightly ajar and he heard a giggle come from inside. Flitting past, he caught sight of the reception nurse locked in a passionate clinch with a young doctor.

Landis smiled to himself and moved quickly on.

Three doors further down he found what he was looking for. The handwritten card in the name holder read: LEAKY. T. Opening the door as softly as he could, he stepped inside.

The room was in darkness, but as his eyes adjusted, he could see the woman laying in a bed beside the window. Her head was entirely wrapped in gauze and bandages. There was a drip in her arm and she was hooked up to an electronic vital signs monitor, which was beeping rhythmically.

Landis moved quietly over to the bed.

'Miss Leaky…'

The body stirred and, painfully slowly, the head turned an inch towards him. One of the eyes was hidden behind the bandages, but the other stared out at him fearfully.

She made a little gurgling sound.

'Please, don't be afraid. I'm a police officer.' Landis bent in closer. 'I need to ask you a couple of vitally important questions. Can you understand me?'

Leaky gurgled again.

'Are you able to nod?'

There was no movement. The one frightened eye continued to stare at him.

'Okay.' Landis gently took hold of her hand. 'Do you know who it was that did this to you? If you can manage it, one squeeze for yes, two for no.'

Although the movement was barely discernible, he felt the fingers tighten around his own.

'Was it two men?'

Two soft squeezes.

'A man and a woman?'

Two more squeezes.

This was ridiculous. Landis tried again. 'Two women then?'

Once again, two squeezes.

Landis frowned. He started to wonder if she could actually understand what he was asking.

'Not two men, not two women, not a man and a woman... I don't understand.'

Leaky released his hand and very slowly raised her index finger.

'One? *One* person? A man or a woman? Sorry.' He took hold of her hand again. 'Was it a man?'

Two squeezes.

'A woman?'

Another two squeezes.

Landis sighed. This was getting him nowhere. Leaky clearly wasn't compos mentis.

'I'm sorry, I really don't...' He trailed off as a thought flashed through his mind. 'Was it a girl?'

One squeeze.

Landis could have punched the air. '*Definitely* a girl?'

Again, a single squeeze.

So. One assailant – a girl – with what must have presumably been an accomplice outside keeping watch then.

Landis released Leaky's hand. 'Thank you,' he whispered.

As he stepped out of the room, the young nurse was coming down the corridor towards him. She didn't look happy.

'Detective! What exactly do you think you're doing?!'

'It was important I spoke to Miss Leaky tonight. This investigation stretches far wider than one acid attack.'

'Doctor Saunderson will be furious when he finds out. I'm going to have to ask you to leave!'

Landis looked past her to where Duvall was standing in the open doorway at the end of the corridor. She shrugged at him apologetically.

'Certainly. Thank you so much for your co-operation.'

He pushed past the nurse and she glared at him as he walked away up the corridor.

When they got out, Landis walked Duvall to her car and told her what he'd learned from Leaky.

'A girl?!'

'Yes. There are two teenage girls who survived Mástiga. Billie-Jo Hazelwood and Hollie Page. And both of them lost their entire family there. And it was Hazelwood's mother who was doused with the acid perfume. That would be a pretty good motive to want these shysters dead, wouldn't you say? An eye for an eye?'

Duvall nodded. 'You think they're working together?'

'It's a very real possibility.' Landis looked at his watch. 'It's too late to do anything more in an official capacity tonight. But I'm going to be paying the pair of them a visit first thing in the morning.'

CHAPTER 21

It was no surprise to Billie-Jo to learn that Cole Smythe was every bit as reprehensible as his fellow conspirators in Hallam's scheme. He was what her nan would have called "a privileged tosser".

The recurrent theme in half a dozen online interviews that Billie-Jo read was of his deprived teenage years as an only child, with a father and mother whose exacting standards had been impossible to meet.

Smythe's perceived hardship was something about which he seemed eager to bleat at every given opportunity. Yet, however loveless a relationship it may have been, in terms of material wealth he had it all; far more than any child could want for. And with holidays abroad, he saw more of the world in a few years than a lot of people get to see in their entire lifetime. But you can't put a price on love and it was that emotional connection between them that was conspicuous in its absence.

Smythe was a zealous movie buff and when he announced that he wanted to attend film school his parents had once again opened their chequebook.

So that was being deprived was it?, Billie-Jo thought. *How awful for him!*

Throughout the late 1990s, young Smythe spent every May stalking the Promenade de la Croisette in Cannes, becoming such a familiar figure at the world-famous film festival that he was eventually able to worm his way into marketplace screenings. It was there that he developed a taste for extreme European horror.

It was also in Cannes that he met a couple named Derek and Penny Savage, with whom he struck up a firm friendship. They had been in attendance to hawk the international rights to a low budget sci-fi horror they had made – essentially a rip-off of *Alien*. They took young Smythe under their wing and helped him get a foot though the door into the film industry. Being a fast learner, he was soon running their production company, DPS Pictures.

The relationship had come to a calamitous end when Derek caught Cole and Penny in bed together. A month later, Derek was dead – he threw himself under a train – and two months after that Cole and Penny were married. They launched their own production company, Pencol Unlimited, and enjoyed moderate success with a line in British-shot horror films that rivalled the prodigious output of American independents like Full Moon Features and Troma Entertainment.

Billie-Jo laughed as she read some of the titles on their catalogue: *Carnage on Campus*, *Attack of the Killer Woodlice*, *Rabid Space Werewolves*, *Cannibal*

Babes in Chains, *Django Undead*, *Virgin Fangs* and *The Incredible Melting Whores*. One titled *The Lycan Lads* actually sounded quite good though; it had apparently scooped plaudits at Cannes in 2011 and had gone on to become the darling of the same year's festival circuit.

But for Smythe the grass was always greener. And a little further digging on Billie-Jo's part revealed a much darker side to this respectable British success story.

Under the banner Colpen Triple-X, the Smythes masterminded a slew of adult films, shot, produced and distributed in Europe. Colpen's most infamous line was their *Studentesse Troie* series.

Billie-Jo looked up the meaning on Google Translate: *Schoolgirl Sluts*.

The series' infamy was born of the fact the couple liked to use the youngest performers they could legally get away with. There had been allegations that underage girls appeared in their films, but they had always managed to wriggle out of litigation on some technicality or other.

Cole Smythe claimed to have slept with all his actresses too. This hadn't been a problem for Penny; no-strings affairs were just fine with her, indeed she was as sexually adventurous as her husband. She actually appeared in two of their adult films, and that was where she met and fell head over heels for a

266

Cypriot girl named Tonya, who performed under the screen name Misty Sinn.

The Smythes' marriage didn't last long after that, and a messy and hostile divorce ensued, which was finalised in 2015.

Two years later, Smythe married Ashley Winters, better known as Suzie Kravesit, an actress he had used often and whose lack of inhibition and willingness to do anything on camera had turned her into something of an internet sensation. A little over a year later they were parents to triplets.

Smythe continued to produce adult films at a phenomenal rate under Colpen Triple-X's re-monickered company, One Hand Fun Creations. In 2019 alone, 23 new titles had been added to their catalogue. Diversifying from schoolgirl fantasies, the line dipped into humiliation and faux snuff scenarios.

Again Billie-Jo had to turn to Google to find out what "faux snuff" meant. She was alarmed to learn that it had something to do with faking death. So there it was right there: the reason that Smythe had bought his ticket into Hallam's enterprise. He enjoyed watching humiliation and death. She refrained from clicking the links to further details.

From what she had read, Smythe was an outspoken advocate of the legalisation of recreational drugs, despite having fought to kick a ruinously expensive cocaine habit at the age of 21. She found a video clip of him being interviewed on the set of one of his horror films in which he bragged about there not being a single opiate in existence he hadn't experimented with. When the young woman interviewing him asked if he was still a user, he merely grinned and winked at her: 'Not that I'd admit on camera. Come back to my room and we'll talk about it.'

All in all then, Smythe was an arrogant and thoroughly contemptible specimen. And despite the fact that Penny had taken him for a fortune in divorce proceedings, still an extremely wealthy one too: at the age of 43, his estimated personal fortune apparently ran to some £130 million, most of which had been derived from his dubious pornography empire.

As Billie-Jo had been reading, an idea had been forming in her head. It actually made her feel sick, yet it seemed so perfect. She had been unable to discern where the man lived, but there was other information that she could use. By the time she switched out the light and rested her head on the pillow, she had decided precisely how she was going to get to Cole Smythe.

*

'Oh, dear Lord, no.' Landis sighed heavily. 'How? *When*?'

Having endured a night of sporadic sleep, he had arrived at his office at seven-thirty in the morning. His trip out to The Copse the previous evening had given him a lead he had cursed himself for not having given serious consideration before. If only he'd had photos of Hollie Page and Billie-Jo Hazelwood that he could have shown to Toyah Leaky. She might have been able to identify one of them.

Promptly at eight he'd telephoned the social services in Peterborough where it had transpired Hollie had been temporarily placed in care in October. Primarily he'd wanted to confirm she was still living there, but it was also a courtesy to call ahead and let the social services administrator know he was coming and wanted to speak with one of their wards. The last thing he'd expected to hear was that she had taken her own life.

He listened as the woman tearfully explained how Hollie had been found dead on New Year's Eve: 'She was found in a bathtub fully clothed. She'd slashed her wrists. The razor blade she had used was floating in the water beside her.

'It was a terrible shock to us all. She was a lovely girl, but after what happened to her on that holiday, and the mental scarring from years of parental abuse... well, she had problems.'

Landis offered his sincere condolences and hung up.

Terence Montague Hallam's diabolical initiative continued to cast a dark shadow, bringing death and destruction to everything it touched.

New Year's Eve then: that didn't entirely preclude Hollie from some level of involvement in the murders of Crispin and Cressida Partridge between Christmas and New Year. Maybe she *had* done it, or at least aided and abetted. And then, unable to live with the guilt, committed suicide. Yes, that was possible. But the more Landis thought about it, the more he was convinced that wasn't the case.

Whether Hollie Page and Billie-Jo Hazelwood had been in cahoots at the outset was irrelevant now. The old man, Mills, claimed to have seen two people fleeing the stables at Tranquillity Meadows. If one of them had indeed been Billie-Jo, who the hell was the other? Who was she in cahoots with now? Of one thing Landis was certain: he was damned well going to find out today.

Draining his tea, he tossed the Styrofoam cup into the wastebasket and set off for Islington.

*

Billie-Jo felt sick. She had woken just before six and a virulent case of nerves had kicked in the moment she opened her eyes.

She couldn't believe she had come as far as she had without getting caught. But she was under no illusions; it was luck rather than judgement that had brought her here and the end was finally now in sight. Just one more trip out of London – one more risk, one more person to be disposed of – and it would all be over.

Spooning Shreddies into her mouth from a breakfast bowl and struggling to keep them down, she was pacing back and forth in the kitchen.

Tracy, still wearing her pyjamas, was seated at the table and watching her with mild amusement.

'What the fuck's the matter with you this mornin'?' She scratched at the rats' nest of hair that was begging to be brushed. 'You got servitus dance or somethin'?'

'You what?'

'Don't tell me you ain't never heard of servitus dance!'

Billie-Jo stared at her blankly. 'Nope. What is it?'

'It's when… well, it means… How the fuck am I supposed to know? It's somethin' my Nan used to say when I wouldn't sit still.'

Billie-Jo raised an eyebrow. 'There's a lot of things your Nan used to say.'

'Yeah.' A far away look appeared in Tracy's eyes. 'She was full of 'em, bless her.' She frowned. 'Anyway, what *is* the matter with you?'

Putting down her bowl of cereal, Billie-Jo took a seat. 'We've got a shitty maths test today.' She started tapping her foot nervously against the table leg.

Tracy looked at her sceptically. 'Since when did maths tests bother you? You're good at maths.'

'It's trigonometry. I don't understand it and it's totally pointless, plus I'm crap at it and I fuckin' hate it!'

'I remember that trigomitty bullshit when I was at school and I ain't never needed to use it in all my life. Not once.' Tracy reached over and patted her granddaughter's hand. She glanced down. 'And will you *please* stop tappin' your soddin' plates!'

Billie-Jo stood up. 'Yeah, well, I'd better get goin'.'

Tracy looked at the barely-touched bowl of Shreddies. 'You not eatin' them?'

'Nah. I ain't feelin' too good this mornin'.'

'Well they ain't goin' to waste.' Tracy grabbed up the bowl and started to tuck in.

Billie-Jo picked up her bag and walked to the front door. She stopped in the open doorway and looked back. 'Love you, Nan.'

The spoon paused at Tracy's mouth and some milk dribbled down her chin. She looked at Billie-Jo suspiciously. 'What you after?'

'Nothin'! I just love you, that's all.'

Tracy smiled. 'Yeah, well, I love you too, babe.' The smile vanished. 'Now fuck off to school and smash that bastard maths test!'

Two minutes later, Billie-Jo was on her way up the street with all thoughts of school gone. Destination: Sutton Coldfield.

At the same moment she reached Essex Road station, Landis was pulling up outside Tracy's house. Temporary lights for gas works on Archway Road had held him up and the trip had taken twenty minutes longer than it should have. He hurried up to the door, knocked and waited.

When Tracy saw him, she defensively wrapped her arms tightly around herself.

'You again?' She stared at him angrily. 'Don't tell me this is still about that fuckin' island! When are you gonna leave us alone?'

'Good morning, Mrs Hazelwood.'

'It was until you showed up. What do you want?'

'I was wondering if I might have a word with your Granddaughter please.'

'She ain't here.'

'May I ask where she is?'

Tracy guffawed. 'Seriously? It's fuckin' Monday mornin', where do you *think* she is?'

Landis had to bite his tongue. 'I realise it's Monday morning. I was just hoping I might have caught her before she left for school. It's very important.'

'Well, you should have got here sooner if it's that important. She left early. She's got a test today.' Tracy's stomach tightened as she remembered the state Billie-Jo had been in when she arrived home the previous afternoon. 'What exactly is this about?'

'I'm afraid I can't say.'

'Hypothermically, it wouldn't be about an assault or somethin', would it?'

'Hypo*thetically*, that would be between me and Billie-Jo. She's a student at Stoke Street Secondary, isn't she?'

'How'd you know that?' Tracy's eyes narrowed. 'You been checkin' up on us?'

Landis ignored the question. 'I'm guessing I'd need a warrant to come in and look through her things.'

'You guessed right! Look through her stuff? Fuckin' nerve of ya! Did you see a sign on the door that says "Drop-in Centre for Nosy Cunts"? *Did* you? No, you fuckin' well didn't! Now, if you'll excuse me, I've gotta take a shit.'

Without giving Landis a chance to respond, she slammed the door in his face.

He returned to his car. It wasn't ideal, but he was going to have to go to the school and speak with the girl there.

Picking up her phone, Tracy called Billie-Jo. It went straight to answerphone, but that didn't stop her launching into a rant.

'The filth have just been here askin' for you. I don't know what you've been up to, young lady, but we're havin' a talk when you get home. And I swear, if I see that fucker's face round here again, I'm makin' an official complaint!'

She angrily hit end call and, muttering under her breath about police harassment, went upstairs to the bathroom.

While she was dressing, a thought occurred to her. Out of the goodness of her heart – and certainly against her better judgement – she had allowed Billie-Jo to have the privacy of the box room all these weeks. But what if the kid was abusing the privilege? What if she was up to no good? Detective Dipshit had *probably* just come to open old wounds about what happened on the island, but he hadn't actually said so one way or the other. If not that though, what *had* he wanted? And why did he ask to look through her stuff? Maybe there *was* something else going on.

The more Tracy thought about it, the more it didn't feel right. And she certainly wasn't happy with the tale Billie-Jo had spun her about Carly's dog; something more serious had happened there. She wasn't going to allow herself to be taken for a mug. This was *her* house and she had a right to know if something was going on.

When she walked into the spare room, she was met by a heap of unwashed clothes lying on the floor beside the unmade bed.

'Lazy little cow.'

There was a small selection of celebrity gossip magazines on the bedside table. She picked one up and leafed through the pages. 'Garbage,' she muttered, looking at the flash on the front cover: **Brad's beach budgie-smugglers – exclusive pix inside!**

She sat down on the bed to take a closer look.

A minute or two later, she put the magazine back on the table and got down on her knees, feeling them crack as she did so. She peered under the bed and moved aside a couple of boxes of old DVDs.

'Christ, I've really got to get rid of some of this shit!'

Then her eyes fell upon a small cardboard box that appeared to be decorated with snowmen and robins. She pulled it out. It was a box of Christmas cards. Opening it, her eyes nearly fell out of her head. It was packed to busting point with money; hundreds and hundreds of pounds in loose notes and elastic-banded rolls. It was more cash than Tracy had seen in one place in her entire life.

'Where the *fuck* did this come from?!'

Replacing the lid, she reached back under the bed and felt around. Her fingers found something lumpy and she pulled it out. It was a black drawstring bag and Tracy immediately recognised it as the one Billie-Jo had returned with from Mástiga.

Getting up off her knees, she perched on the edge of the bed and emptied the contents of the bag onto the blanket beside her.

It was mostly an assortment of the sort of fripperies one might find in any girl's bag: a lipstick, a packet of mints, a purse with three pound coins in it, a foil packet of painkillers – four had been punched out – and two sets of headphones with their wires all tangled up. But there were two other items that caught Tracy's interest: one was a box of sanitary towels, which looked perfectly normal but felt inordinately heavy, the other was a sheaf of folded paperwork with multiple paperclips sticking out of it. Both items stood out incongruously among the others.

Tracy turned her attention to the box. Whatever it was she might have been expecting to see when she opened it, a handgun certainly wasn't on the list. She gasped and dropped the box on the floor, scattering bullets across the carpet. She quickly bent down and, with her fingers trembling, gathered them up and returned them to the box. She examined the gun.

'Fuck!'

Was it real? It was heavy enough and certainly looked the part.

Carefully putting it back in the box, she picked up the wodge of paperwork. She started to look through it, unsure of exactly what it was all about. Then her eye caught a name at the top of one of the pages: **CRISPIN PARTRIDGE**. Where the hell had she heard that name before? Was that a singer? An actor? She knew the name, but it wouldn't come.

Then suddenly it dawned on her. He was the scumbag who had been on the news for fraud, wasn't he? Then he and his wife had been found shot dead and there was something about him having been involved with the island.

Feeling her stomach do a somersault, Tracy glanced at the box of sanitary towels. Surely Billie-Jo hadn't…

She shook her head. No, that was a ridiculous idea.

But then she saw the photograph paperclipped to the next page. It was a head and shoulders portrait shot of a man, except the face had been scratched out. On the back someone had scribbled the initials CP.

Tracy flicked quickly through the rest of the paperwork. There was another name that rang a bell: **MICHAEL BAMFORD**. She couldn't be sure, but wasn't that the name of the other man that had been mentioned on that news report? He too had been connected to the island and was now dead.

She looked at the other names on what were now clearly profiles of various people. **SAMANTHA ELLIS**, **COLE SMYTHE**, **TOYAH LEAKY**… they meant nothing to her, but all except one of the accompanying portrait photos – Smythe's – had the faces scratched from them.

CHAPTER 22

On the way to Stoke Street Secondary School, Landis's phone rang. He wasn't going to take the call, but when he saw the name on the screen he changed his mind and tapped his Bluetooth earpiece.

'Linda.'

'Morning, Landis. How goes the battle?'

'Truthfully? It's not started well. I found out that Hollie Page is dead. Took her own life on New Year's Eve. Then I got stuck in traffic and...'

'*Again?* You seem to be making a habit of that.'

'Flippin' road works. And, as always, not a soul in sight actually *doing* anything!'

'Are you driving now?'

'Yes. I'm headed to the Hazelwood girl's school. Thanks to the road works, I missed her at home. Had a delightful conversation with her grandmother though.'

Duvall laughed. 'Do I detect a note of sarcasm there?'

'Possibly. Anyway, I assume this isn't a social call?'

'It isn't. I've got some good news and some bad news. Which do you want first?'

'Let's buck tradition. I'll take the good news first. I could certainly use some.'

'Hang onto your hat then. I called in a couple of favours on Friday and it paid off. I had an email just now from the Cayman National Bank and I have the names of Hallam's investors for you.'

Landis braked hard and swerved to the side of the kerb. The car behind him blew its horn and, as it passed by, the driver angrily mouthed something and stuck up his middle finger.

Landis shut off the engine. 'Say that again?'

'I have the names you needed.'

'You're kidding me! Why didn't you tell me you were working on that?'

'Because the way I got the information wasn't exactly ethical. Or even legal for that matter. Plus I didn't want to offer hope that I couldn't deliver on.'

'You're a genius, Linda.' Landis laughed. 'I owe you a drink.'

'I haven't given you the bad news yet.'

'Go on.'

'There were just five people who deposited sums running to millions into the Cayman account two years ago: Michael Bamford, Toyah Leaky, Samantha Ellis, Crispin Partridge and Cole Smythe.'

'And three of them are already dead.'

'Four.'

'Four?' Landis frowned. 'Which of the other two?'

'Samantha Ellis.'

'Why do I know that name?'

'I'd not heard of her, but she was a prolific author by all accounts. Romantic fiction.'

'That's it! My wife used to read her books. And Ellis has just been murdered? How the hell did that one slip under the radar?'

'Because she *wasn't* murdered and it didn't just happen. She died of natural causes a few months ago. Well, sort of. An anaphylactic reaction to a plate of bad fish.'

'Okay. So that leaves just one then. Smythe did you say?'

'Cole Smythe.'

'We need to find out everything we can about him ASAP.' Landis started the car and pulled back out into the traffic.

'Already have,' Duvall continued. 'He likes to think he's a film producer. Actually, that's a bit unfair. He *is* a film producer, but it's all junk. He makes crummy horror pictures, but it seems he's also the money behind a whole load of dodgy films from a company called – get this – One Hand Fun Creations. How tacky is that?'

'One hand...?' Landis winced as he realised what she meant. 'Okay, we need to find out where he lives. With luck it'll be on the other side of the world. That would put a spanner in our killer's works.'

'Sutton Coldfield.'

Landis smiled and shook his head. 'Are you trying to do me out of a job?' He punched his horn as a motorcyclist cut him up.

Duvall chuckled. 'Just trying to help. There's a production office for his legitimate films in Birmingham. Pencol Unlimited.'

'Pencol?'

'It's a conflation of Penny and Cole. Penny's his ex-wife. Acrimonious divorce. Seems the only reason he didn't change the company name is because it was well-recognised in the industry.'

Landis shook his head. 'Money dictates all. Well, thank you, Linda, you've been a huge help. Let's scrap that drink and make it dinner.'

'It's a date. There's one more thing though. You're going to have to tread *very* carefully on this. The information from the Cayman National Bank was obtained as underhandedly as underhanded gets. If you go in all guns blazing with Smythe and he kicks off, it won't just be you and me hauled over the coals. My contact will be swinging from the yardarm too. And that cannot happen.'

'Understood. Listen, can I ask you one more favour?'

'Sure.'

'Can you call that Birmingham office and...' He trailed off as he saw the standstill traffic up ahead. 'I don't believe this! *More* temporary lights!' He brought the car to a stop behind a white van. 'And I can't see round the flippin' van in front of me to see what's going on. Sorry, what was I saying?'

'Call Birmingham.'

'Yes. Check on Smythe's movements for the day. If you can get me a home address too, regardless of the outcome of my chat with Miss Hazelwood, I'm going to be driving up there straight afterwards.'

'Will do. But Landis. I'd really like to come along for the ride.'

Landis nodded. 'I owe you that much. Where are you now?'

'In the office. But that's not a problem. I have a couple of things to clear up first, so if you let me know where we can meet up, I could be there… I don't know, two o'clock maybe?'

'How about you come to me and we'll go up in my car?'

'That works for me.'

'Excellent. I'll buzz you back when I leave the school.'

'Cool.'

Landis smiled as the traffic started moving. 'Thanks again, Linda, You're a diamond.'

Only twenty-five minutes later, Landis was back on the phone.

'Landis?' Duvall sounded surprised. 'That was quick.'

'I'm still at the school. Hazelwood didn't show. The woman I spoke with in the office said it was possible she might just be late – seems it's not an unusual occurrence – but we know she left the house early. So where the hell is she? I thought I'd kick around here for a few minutes on the off chance she might show up, but it's looking less and less likely. I don't think I'll waste any more time here now.'

'So what's the next move?'

'I'm afraid treading carefully on this one just went out the window.'

'I don't have a problem putting myself on the line, but my contact mustn't…'

'Don't worry, we'll be the living embodiment of tact. This isn't about Cole Smythe being one of Hallam's investors, it's about preventing a murder. We need to locate him now.'

'And the girl!'

Landis shook his head. 'Smythe is our priority. Wherever he is, if she really is our vigilante, it's a safe bet she'll turn up there too. Did you make that call for me?'

'I did. They weren't very helpful. Apparently he's taken a couple of days off and he likes to be left alone when he's not working. So effectively he's incommunicado. I called his house – he's got a place at Four Oaks, about seven miles north of Birmingham city centre – but there was no answer. Same with three different mobile numbers.'

'*Three*? How the other half live. I struggle to afford the bill on one.'

'Two business ones for Pencol and One Hand Fun, and a private. I left messages and asked him to call me as soon as he gets them, but if he's as insistent on being left alone as his office claim, it's unlikely we'll hear from him any time soon.'

Landis sighed. 'So basically he's gone AWOL. He could be anywhere.'

'Yeah. But perversely, that works in our favour. If *we* have no idea where the hell he is, neither will your girl.'

'Technically I agree. But I wouldn't count on it. I repeat, *if* Hazelwood really is our vigilante – and I'm pretty certain now that she's at least involved – she's managed to pull off three murders in just about as many weeks.'

'The woman at Pencol did mention a couple of places he likes to frequent in the Sutton Coldfield area. A gym, a couple of clubs he hangs out at where he sources young girls for his films, that sort of thing. There's apparently one club in particular he spends a lot of time at: Pussy Galore.'

Landis scowled. 'This Smythe guy sounds like a real sleazy predator.'

'From what I read about him while I was waiting for you to call me back, I think that's putting it mildly.'

'Okay, this Pussy Galore is a good starting point then. But if *we* found out about it, Hazelwood could easily have done so too. Like I say, she's a smart kid. And it sounds like exactly the place a young girl with murder in mind might put herself up as bait for a shark. We can GPS it. You said you can be here by two?'

'One-thirty if I get a wiggle on.'

Landis smiled. 'Get that wiggle on. I'll see you soon.'

*

As Billie-Jo stood outside the sports centre in Sutton Coldfield she couldn't help smiling to herself as she thought about how easy it had been to locate her final victim. In a day and age when the protection of personal data is prioritised above all else – sometimes to the point of absurdity – all five members of Hallam's hideous cabal had been remarkably easy to track down; all the information she had needed to locate them was out there and it had taken little more than a few taps on her phone screen to find it.

The world wide web has a lot to answer for.

Cole Smythe was a dedicated and well-respected squash player and within a few minutes of digging around on the internet, Billie-Jo had found that he not only helped to build a state-of-the-art squash court in the grounds of Slade Park, he also played there regularly.

A phone call to his film production office in Birmingham had paid dividends. Introducing herself as Miss Carter, Billie-Jo had enquired as to the possibility of an appointment that evening with Smythe in order to discuss an idea for a film. His PA had told her that he religiously played squash on a Monday evening and would therefore be unable to meet with her. However, she had offered a number of other dates in a few weeks' time when he would be available. Billie-Jo had said she would check her diary and get back to her.

So now here she was, primed and ready to finish her mission. Smythe was obviously a fit man and she had taken into consideration that maybe he might prove difficult to handle. But from her research she had ascertained that as well as hitting a stupid little rubber ball against the wall, he of course had one other passion: attractive young women – with the emphasis on young.

Billie-Jo shuddered as the cold north wind whipped around her bare legs.

Before catching the train from Euston, she had popped into the Ann Summers shop in town and acquired an outfit that even she deemed tarty. But she was certain it would appeal to "Kinky Cole", as he had been dubbed in one tabloid newspaper piece she had read online. She had changed into the short red skirt – which only just covered her bottom – and black lacy top on the train, stuffing her own clothes into a carrier bag which she dumped in a waste bin when she arrived at Sutton Coldfield station. Fortunately she'd had the foresight to hang on to her hoodie, but with her legs exposed to the elements she was really starting to feel the cold.

She reached into the small PVC handbag that she had also purchased in Ann Summers and pulled out a packet of chewing gum. As she did so, a small Ziploc bag fell out onto the pavement.

'Bollocks!'

As she bent over to retrieve the plastic packet, a man's voice sounded from behind her.

'You alright there?'

Billie-Jo turned around and her eyes widened. Holding a squash racket, the man was bundled up in a Ralph Lauren tracksuit and had a black woollen beanie pulled down over his ears, but there was still no mistaking him. It was Cole Smythe.

'Oh, yes. I'm okay, thank you,' Billie-Jo stammered. 'I just dropped my gum.' She waggled the packet of Mint Extra at him.

As she straightened up, Smythe noticed her cleavage protruding from the insubstantial top beneath her gaping hoodie. He smiled at her. 'Are you a member?'

'Huh?'

Smythe pointed towards the entrance of the leisure centre. 'Of the gym.'

'Er, no.' Billie-Jo replied. 'Actually, I'm a bit lost.'

Smythe was still smiling at her. 'I didn't want to presume, but I must say you don't exactly look like you're heading for a workout.' His eyes once again dropped to Billie-Jo's chest.

'No. I'm a dancer. I was actually looking for the Lizard Lounge. I have an audition for a job there. Or *had*.'

'As a dancer?'

'Yeah. The pay isn't great, but I'm kinda desperate. You know, rent to pay and all that.'

'So where is this Lizard Lounge?'

Billie-Jo feigned a look of sadness. 'It's in town somewhere. But my audition was at five o'clock, so I've missed it now anyway.'

Cole looked at his watch. 'It would appear you have! It's gone six-thirty now.'

'Damn!' Billie-Jo exclaimed, again adopting a sullen expression. She looked at Smythe and emitted a little sob.

He was peering at her with an odd expression on his face. For a moment she wasn't sure he was buying her act, but then he reached out his hand and rubbed her shoulder. 'Now, now. Don't get upset.'

'You don't understand. My landlord is going to kick me out if I can't pay my rent!' She sobbed again.

Smythe thought for a moment and then he took Billie-Jo's hand. 'Listen. It might not be exactly what you're looking for, but I have a suggestion.'

'What?'

'Let's get out of the cold first. Why don't we go over there?' He pointed towards a cafeteria on the other side of the street. 'I'll buy you a nice hot drink and tell you what I have in mind.'

Billie-Jo eyed him uncertainly. 'I don't know…'

'Oh, come along. It's freezing out here. You look like you could use warming up.'

Billie-Jo smiled at him coquettishly. 'What should I say to an invite from a complete stranger?'

'You should say yes, of course!' Smythe grinned. 'I don't bite.'

Billie-Jo thought for a moment and then nodded. 'Yes. Okay.'

The fly had behaved exactly as anticipated and now the spider had him hooked in her web.

CHAPTER 23

They chose a corner booth in the café and sat down with two steaming mugs of hot chocolate.

Smythe reached out and tucked a loose lock of Billie-Jo's hair back behind her ear. 'You're an incredibly attractive girl, you know.'

Billie-Jo pulled a face. 'Not really.'

'No, you are. Trust me.'

'So what was this suggestion of yours?'

Smythe nodded approvingly. 'Straight to the point. A girl who knows what she wants. I like that.' He saw that Billie-Jo was waiting for an answer. 'I'm a film producer and I think you'd be great in one of my movies.'

'Yeah, right,' Billie-Jo scoffed with just the right level of conviction.

'I am!' Smythe drew a little cross over his heart with his finger. 'God's honest truth.'

'What's your name?'

'Cole Smythe,'

'I never heard of you.'

Smythe smiled. 'I don't suppose you've seen *Zombies vs Teenage Bitches from Hell*?

Billie-Jo shook her head.

'*Cannibal Babes in Chains*?' he asked hopefully.

'You're making this shit up!' She took a sip of her hot chocolate.

Smythe chuckled and pulled out his phone. He found his Movie Database profile and held out the screen for her to see. 'There you go. That's me. Cole Smythe.'

Billie-Jo tried to look impressed. 'Okay, so you *are* a producer. But why would you want to put me in some cheesy horror film?'

'Well, let me see.' Smythe reached out and ran his middle finger down the V between the soft mounds of her breasts. It came to rest on the centre gore of her bra.

Billie-Jo desperately wanted to bat his hand away and punch him in the face. Instead she matter-of-factly continued the conversation as if it was no big deal he was touching her. 'Go on.'

'I don't *only* make horror films – which *aren't* cheesy by the way.' He winked at her. 'No, I have a rather lucrative sideline in another genre. Films for... well, let's say for discerning gentlemen.'

Billie-Jo shook her head. 'You mean pornos?'

'That would be the derogatory term for them I suppose. I prefer specialist adult entertainment. There's good money to be made by a pretty young thing like yourself.'

Billie-Jo took another sip of her drink. 'You only met me five minutes ago. Why would you be telling me all this?'

Smythe smiled. 'Because I've been in this business a long time. I have a sixth sense for lost souls.'

Billie-Jo had to rein in the urge to laugh. If this was the best line the guy had...

He reached over and dabbed a smear of chocolate away from the corner of her mouth with his thumb. 'I know talent when I see it. And trust me, young lady, you have it in spades.'

Billie-Jo smiled at him. 'You're a handsy bastard, ain't you?'

Smythe grinned. 'Guilty as charged. So sue me.'

She pretended to be considering what he'd said. 'So you want to put me in one of your porn... I mean adult movies, do you?'

Smythe nodded. 'I do. Very much.'

'I'm only 16 you know.'

'That's not a problem for me.' He raised his eyebrows. 'Is it for you?'

Billie-Jo frowned. 'I don't know.'

He suddenly sat back away from her. 'If you're not interested, of course, there's a thousand more girls waiting behind you who will be. Girls smart enough to seize a golden opportunity when it jumps up and bops them on the nose.'

'I didn't say I wasn't interested, did I?'

Smythe sat forward again and caressed Billie-Jo's hand. 'Look. I know a place not too far from here. If you want, you could come and audition for me.'

You fuckin' filthy piece of shit, she thought. But she managed to force an innocent smile. 'Audition, eh?'

'I guarantee, if you're good you'll earn way more than you ever would dancing.'

Billie-Jo nodded. 'Okay.'

'Excellent!' Smythe stood up. 'Let's go.'

Taking her by the hand, he led her outside and back over the street to the leisure centre car park. As they approached a flashy red sports car, he touched his keyfob. There was a pipping sound, followed by a clunk as the doors unlocked.

'Nice ride,' Billie-Jo remarked.

'Beautiful, isn't she?' Smythe said proudly. 'Drives like a dream.'

'My stepdad would have absolutely loved this.'

'*Would* have?'

'Yeah. He's not around any more. I bet it cost you a bit.'

'My dear girl, this is a BMW i8 Roadster. The 2020 model. Limited edition in the metallic red. If one has to *ask* how much it costs, one certainly can't afford it.' He grinned. 'But since you *did* ask, I didn't get much change out of a hundred and thirty-five grand.'

He pipped the fob again and both the driver's and passenger doors opened, hinging smoothly upwards.

Taking Billie-Jo's hand, he helped her into the low slung seat, and she swung her long, slender legs inside. He felt a tingle of excitement as he caught a glimpse of underwear beneath her short skirt.

'Where I'm from, someone would jack this in seconds.'

Smythe reached across her and helped her put on the seatbelt. 'And where is it you're from?'

'Doesn't matter.'

'Beautiful *and* mysterious, eh? You intrigue me.'

He pressed a button on the fob and the passenger door hinged shut. Walking around to the other side of the car, he climbed in. 'You sure you're up for this?'

Billie-Jo smiled at him sweetly. 'Yes. Definitely.'

Less than a mile from the leisure centre, Smythe took a left into a side street. He parked up outside a dingy building and switched off the ignition. Putting a hand on Billie-Jo's knee, he gave it a little squeeze. 'Wait here a sec.'

As he hopped up the steps and disappeared inside, Billie-Jo peered out of the car window and up at the tired-looking guest house. Pulling down the visor, she checked her reflection in the small mirror, then opened her handbag and moved the contents aside. Lying flat at the bottom was the small paring knife she had purloined from the utensils drawer that morning before Tracy got up. She smiled and zipped the bag back up just as Smythe reappeared.

He opened the passenger door and helped Billie-Jo out. 'Follow me.'

'Hang on.' Billie-Jo didn't want him to suspect she had been too easy a pick-up. 'What would your wife think about this?'

'My wife?' Smythe was suddenly looking at her distrustfully. 'What makes you think I'm married?'

Bollocks, Billie-Jo thought. *Why didn't I just keep my fuckin' stupid mouth shut*? She inwardly sighed with relief as she caught sight of his hand. 'Well you are, aren't you?'

He followed her gaze and saw the ornate gold band on his ring finger. 'What sharp little eyes you have.' He smiled at her. 'Pretty ones too. Don't you worry yourself about that. Come on.'

They walked into what appeared to be an insalubrious guest house from another age. The air was thick with the nauseating smell of damp, and the wallpaper – its hideous pattern suggesting it had been there since the 1970s – was peeling away along its seams. Every inch of the place was crying out to be gutted and renovated – including the man sitting at the desk at the bottom of the stairs. He looked to be in his mid-60s. The grey hair on one side of his head had been grown long and combed across the top of his scalp in that laughable attempt men make to disguise their balding scalps. There was at least three days' worth of white stubble on his face.

He didn't even acknowledge Smythe and Billie-Jo. Hunched over the desk, he was engrossed in a video that he was watching on his mobile phone.

Taking the lead, Smythe led her swiftly up the narrow staircase. It was poorly lit and at the top there were several hallways branching off, all of them lined with doors. Billie-Jo couldn't help but notice how instinctively Smythe negotiated the corridors to get to the room he was looking for; he'd obviously been here before, she thought.

He unlocked the door to reveal a space barely bigger than her nan's sitting room. Just inside on the right there was another door into an ensuite bathroom. On the left was a wardrobe. A double bed dominated the centre of the room and a small table with tea-making facilities on it sat to one side of a small window. There was a television set on a wooden unit beside the far wall. The maroon carpet, patterned with black swirls, was stained and felt disconcertingly spongy underfoot, and there were occasional patches where it was completely threadbare.

Billie-Jo heard the key turn in the lock.

Smythe smiled at her. 'We don't want to be disturbed, do we?' He gestured to the bed. 'Take a seat. I just need to use the little boys' room.'

Billie-Jo sat down on the edge of the mattress as, giving her an encouraging smile, he stepped into the bathroom and closed the door.

She took her bag off her shoulder, got up and tried the window. They were only one floor up and it might be a convenient escape route. But it was jammed and she couldn't free the latch. If the dank, sweaty smell of the room was anything to go by, it probably hadn't been opened for years. There wasn't going to be any other way out except past the old fart downstairs.

She sat back down and surveyed her surroundings, wondering what degradation the walls might have witnessed.

The bathroom door opened and Smythe emerged with a white towel wrapped tightly around his waist. He placed his neatly-folded clothes on the table next to the kettle. 'Would you like a cup of tea?'

Billie-Jo shook her head. 'No thanks'.

He sat down on the bed beside her and placed a hand on her knee. His fingers felt hot and as they danced up to caress her thigh, she couldn't help but notice the man's large biceps; there had to be considerable strength in those arms. As she had imagined, he was indeed a fit man.

'Why don't you take that sweatshirt off? I'd love to see what you're wearing underneath.'

'Sure.' Billie-Jo nodded and stood up.

Smythe sat back, his eyes watching her hungrily, as she pulled the hooded sweatshirt up over her head. The lacy top she had on underneath clung to the fleecy lining and lifted with it.

Smythe took advantage of the moment and reached forward, placing his hand on her midriff. 'What lovely soft skin you have,' he said salaciously.

Billie-Jo pulled away. 'I'll just hang this up,' she said. Her mind was racing. How the hell was she going to be able to overpower this man?

As she stepped over to the open wardrobe, she noticed an iron on the shelf above the rail. She took down a clothes hanger and hooked it inside her hoodie, then turned back to look at Smythe.

He had got up and was standing looking out of the window into the darkness. His back was to her. 'You're going to be delicious in *Forgive Me Father, For I Am Sin*,' he muttered, seemingly talking to himself. 'A star in the making.'

Billie-Jo quietly took the iron down from the shelf. But as she did so, the plug whipped round and clattered on the side of the wardrobe.
Smythe spun round just as Billie-Jo thrust the iron out of sight behind her back.

Returning to the bed, he sat down and patted the mattress. 'Come on, don't be shy, young lady.' His brow furrowed. 'How remiss of me! I never asked you your name.'

Billie-Jo walked forward. 'My name?'

'Yes. If we're going to be working together, I need to know what to call you.'

She stopped next to him, her arms out of sight behind her back. 'Does it really matter?'

Smythe shuffled round on the bed to face her. 'I suppose not. We'll have to come up with a stage name for you anyway.' He grabbed her waist with both hands and pulled her towards him. 'Come here!'

His towel fell open and Billie-Jo saw that his penis was erect. Pressing his face against the soft warmth of her stomach, he inhaled deeply. 'Hmmm. You smell really good.' He moved a hand up across her rib cage and tried to push the lacy top up. 'Let's see what you're hiding under here.'

With one swift movement, Billie-Jo swung her right arm round and cracked him hard across the side of his head with the iron.

With a startled yelp he toppled sideways, fell off the edge of the bed and hit the carpet with a dull thud.

She looked down to see a pulse of thick red blood seeping from just above his left ear.

CHAPTER 24

Much to Landis's exasperation, a succession of further traffic delays had meant that he and Duvall didn't reach Sutton Coldfield until well after six o'clock.

On the way up, Duvall had filled Landis in with a little more information about Cole Smythe, which only added cement to his opinion that the man was indeed thoroughly detestable.

When she mentioned the fact that he drove a metallic red BMW i8 Roadster, his jaw had dropped.

'Seriously?! Jammy devil! That's my dream car. You've got to have serious money to burn to buy one of those beauties. Even second-hand, they cost well over a hundred grand. I tell you, Linda, if I didn't hate this guy before, I sure do now!'

Their first port of call on arrival had been Smythe's home at Four Oaks. It was a large, modern, detached property located on an avenue lined with mature oak trees. They suspected as they approached that they had wasted their time; the place appeared to be in total darkness and there was no sign of the BMW on the drive that Landis had been looking forward to seeing.

While he waited in the car, Duvall had tried the doorbell several times anyway, but to no avail. They had reasoned Ashley Smythe might be at home,

303

especially as she had young children. But if she was inside, she was either sound asleep – which didn't seem likely at six in the evening – or sitting in the dark and ignoring the door, which made even less sense.

They had moved on to the leisure centre at Slade Park. What they learned there only served to compound the frustration of their visit to Smythe's home at Four Oaks.

The young woman on reception had been very helpful, informing them that Mr Smythe had indeed been in that afternoon and had played squash with a fellow club member, Mr Patrick Hartman. Smythe had won the match and was exultantly vocal about it when he'd signed out at six-twenty. However, he hadn't left immediately. He'd remained flirting with her for about five minutes – as he always did when he'd triumphed on the court – and was in a jubilant mood. He'd invited her to go for a drink with him at The Circus, a club in town, but she had politely declined; could he not see she was working? He'd told her not to worry about trivialities like that and repeated what he'd said to her many times before: she would earn a lot more money working with him. After a little more banter, he had finally accepted she wasn't going to surrender and left at six twenty-five.

It seemed Landis and Duvall had missed the man by just over three quarters of an hour.

They visited The Circus and Pussy Galore, which it transpired were only a couple of streets apart, and drew blanks. The barmen in both establishments claimed to know Smythe well and they reported not having seen him that evening.

When they stepped out of Pussy Galore, a light sleet had begun to tumble from the sky.

'Where next?' Duvall asked as they got back into the car. She shivered. 'God, it's cold.'

Landis sighed. 'He's likely to be in town somewhere. He didn't go home and from what the girl at the leisure centre told us he was in a celebratory mood.'

'There are those two other clubs to check out.'

'Indeed.' Landis started the car. 'We'll find him. We have to.'

The sleet was coming down hard now. Landis turned on the windscreen wipers and they set off.

*

Billie-Jo stood for a moment staring down at Smythe's body. Then, nonchalantly dropping the iron onto the bed, she walked round to the side where he had fallen and looked out of the window.

It was dark and there was a steady fall of sleet twinkling against the hazy glow from a streetlight across the road. She pulled the curtains closed and lashed out her foot at Smythe's shoulder. 'Cunt!'

He groaned.

Billie-Jo's eyes flashed as she looked down at his seemingly lifeless body. She kicked him again – harder this time. He made another low moaning sound and his eyelids started to flicker.

'Shit!' she hissed through gritted teeth. In a panic, she picked up the iron. She could wallop him again; that should finish him off. Then she remembered the paring knife.

Scooting around the bed, she grabbed up the patent red handbag and withdrew the sharp blade. But as she turned her attention back to Smythe, she saw he'd reached out and was gripping the black metal rail of the bed's footboard.

'Oh no you don't!' Billie-Jo shrieked and kicked his arm away.

He fell limp again.

Holding up the iron, she gripped the flex and ran it through her fingers to the plug at the end; it was a good three feet long. Using the knife, she deftly cut through it and threw the appliance onto the bed. Taking hold of the plug, she severed that too and held out the length of white flex. Yes, that would do the job. Carefully tucking the knife into the waistband at the back of her skirt, she squatted down beside Smythe.

Looking up at her through glassy eyes, he held out his palm. 'Wait,' he gargled weakly. 'Stop!'

Billie-Jo fiercely batted his hand away and grabbed hold of him by the arm. He was even heavier than she had imagined and it took all her strength to hoist him up. Nevertheless, by hooking her arms underneath his armpits, she managed to drag him around the bed and propped him up in a sitting position against the footboard.

Smythe's head lolled to one side and he mumbled something unintelligible.

'Shut up!' Billie-Jo snarled.

She pulled his left hand out roughly from behind his back and slapped it up against the footboard, winding the flex around his wrist to strap it to the bars. Glancing at his muscular arms, she decided not to leave anything to chance; if he were to come round properly, he could easily free himself. She hastily unplugged the power lead from the television, yanked it from the back of the set and knelt back down beside him. Then, taking hold of his right hand, she bound it firmly to the bed.

Rocking back on her haunches, Billie-Jo assessed the helpless man. His chin was resting on his chest and his head was swaying gently. She could see a thick glob of blood had collected around his earlobe.

Pulling the knife out of her waistband, she lightly tapped it on her knee while she pondered her next move.

Suddenly Smythe coughed loudly, giving her a start. He slowly lifted his head and their eyes met.

'My head... Christ, it's banging,' he groaned hoarsely. He peered at his restraints through bleary eyes, blinking as he tried to comprehend what was happening.

'A headache is the least of your problems right now.'

Smythe squinted up at her. 'Why?' he whispered. 'Who are you?' His eyes followed her as she stood up.

'You know, this is starting to get really fucking annoying!' She reached over and pulled on the flex. Satisfied that he was firmly restrained, she leant over and looked into his eyes. 'It's incredible how quickly you wankers forget all the shit you've done and the people you done it to. I wish I could forget so easily.'

Smythe frowned. He seemed to be a little more lucid now. '*What* things have I done?'

Billie-Jo put her face right up close to his and he shuddered as he felt the cold blade pressing against his left breast. His eyes dropped towards his chest.

'Look at me!' Billie-Jo barked.

His eyes shot back up.

'Look *real* hard. Don't you recognise me at all?'

Smythe's eyes narrowed. 'Were you in one of my films?'

'No!'

'Look, I never force anyone to do anything they aren't willing to do. If you have a grievance…'

'For fuck's sake, I wasn't in one of your sick films!'

Smythe stared at her. There was a vacant look in his eyes as he searched for an answer, but it was evident he didn't have a clue. 'If I've done something to you, I'm really, really sorry. Honestly I am. But I just don't know…'

'*Sorry?!*' Billie-Jo stood up quickly. As she did so, the end of the knife nicked Smythe's nipple and he winced. He looked down and his eyes filled with fear as he watched a trickle of blood run down and pool in his navel.

'I've stood in front of four of you cunts now and not one of you knew who I was. Have you *any* idea how much that pisses me off?'

'Who are you? *Please* just tell me,' Smythe implored her.

'I'm Billie-Jo Hazelwood. And you and your sadistic, privileged mates murdered my whole family last September on that bastard Greek island!'

Smythe looked at her in disbelief, then jerked forward in an attempt to free himself.

Billie-Jo watched in amusement as he fruitlessly thrashed his bound hands about.

Realising he had no chance of escape, he stopped struggling and breathlessly spoke. 'Look. Billie-Jo. Can I call you that?' He waited for a response but nothing came. His expression was similar to that of a rodent cornered by a cat moments before its untimely demise. 'You don't need to do this. I have money – more then you could ever dream of. If you let me go I'll make sure you're set for life.'

Billie-Jo glared at him. 'Money. With you people that's the answer to everything, isn't it?'

She squatted down in front of him and pressed the knife onto the centre of his chest.

Smythe flinched. 'Wait! Come on. Don't tell me your life wouldn't be better with a bit of money in the bank?'

Billie-Jo twisted the knife, exerting just enough pressure to hurt him but not pierce the skin. 'Do you know what would make my life better?'

Through gritted teeth, Smythe replied. 'Tell me.'

'Going back to my flat in Southwark and having a ruck with my kid sister for stealing my make-up whilst my Mum and Dad yell at us to shut up and stop bickering.' She gulped hard. 'But that ain't gonna happen…' – she raised her voice – '…because you and your fucking mates killed them!'

'So now you're going to kill me. And that will make everything okay will it?' Smythe's demeanour had changed. He'd become a little more defensive. 'You're no better than me, you know. In fact you're worse.'

'*Worse?*' Billie-Jo smirked. 'How do you figure that?'

'Can you untie me? These cables are biting into my wrists. We can talk about this, but it's *really* uncomfortable down here.'

Billie-Jo laughed 'Dream on!' She leant forward and rested the blade sideways across Cole's neck. 'Tell me. How am I worse?'

'The Mástiga initiative was devised to provide a solution to the backward degradation of our country. You have no idea how important Terrence Hallam's work was, do you?'

'Backwards degradation?'

'Yes. Where did you say you lived?'

'Southwark'

'On a council estate?'

'Yeah.' Billie-Jo removed the knife from Smythe's throat. 'So what?'

'Those estates are a breeding ground for crime and filth. People languishing in low rent hovels, sponging off the state whilst men like me work every hour God sends to pay for it.'

311

Billie-Jo was breathing heavily through her nose whilst Smythe continued his rant.

'The UK economy is in ruins and do you know why?'

'I'm sure you're going to tell me,' Billie-Jo replied sarcastically.

'Benefits! Unemployment benefits for people that would rather sit around on their arse all day than do an honest day's work. Housing benefits to put people in homes they don't deserve. Child benefit for women who can't keep their legs together. And sickness benefits for people who are just plain lazy or should never have even been born! Terence was a genius and had things not gone to the wall... well, let's just say we would have been revered for our cleansing of these vermin.

'I won't deny, there's a certain level of voyeuristic pleasure in what we were doing, but the reason I got involved, the reason I ploughed a great deal of money into Terence's company was simple: I'm sick to death of watching the country go down the pan and our useless government pulling the flush!'

'Have you finished?'

Smythe looked at Billie-Jo quizzically. 'Yes.'

'Nice speech. Those vermin you're referring to were my family – my Mum, my little sister and my Stepdad. We might not have fitted into your toffee-nosed world, but we still deserve to live. Who the fuck made you judge and jury anyway?'

'We *made* ourselves judge and jury. Someone had to step up. You wouldn't understand. It's not your fault really, just your unfortunate upbringing. But sooner or later this country will drown under a tidal wave of feckless, dirty criminals and...'

'*Criminals?*! And what you're doing is totally legit is it?'

'You said it yourself, little girl; if my car was parked on your street, it would be stolen straight away.'

'Fuck you. I've had enough of this bollocks.' Billie-Jo reached for her handbag and withdrew the small Ziploc bag full of the pills that she'd stolen from Tyler's flat.

'What's that?'

Billie-Jo ignored him. She looked around the room. Through the open bathroom door she could see two small glasses beside the sink. She stood up and crossed the room. Filling both glasses she returned to Smythe.

'I hear you're a bit of an adrenaline junkie.'

CHAPTER 25

'This is ridiculous,' Landis grumbled as he and Duvall stepped out of Hot Surrender, the fourth and last of the clubs that Cole Smythe patronized with any regularity. 'We're wasting time and getting nowhere fast. I think I'm going to have to contact Birmingham City Police to put out an APB. I really didn't want to have to. I didn't inform them we were coming. I was probably being naïve, but I was hoping we could deal with this as quickly and unobtrusively as possible.'

They dawdled beneath the fabric awning over the steps and looked out at the thick sleet, which was building up along the length of the kerb.

Landis stared at the slushy mounds dejectedly. 'That's going to freeze. And it's not easing off either. The roads are going to be like skating rinks before long.' He frowned. 'You know what? I wouldn't want to be out on a filthy night like this if I didn't have to be. Maybe we're out here chasing our tails and Smythe is back at home warming his feet by the fire.'

'It's possible.' Duvall cupped her hands together and blew into them a couple of times, flexing her fingers to work the stiffness out of them. 'We could have just missed him earlier, I guess.'

'That's what I'm starting to wonder.'

'Back to Four Oaks then? One last shot before we contact BCP?'

Landis sighed. 'We've nothing to lose. We've kind of run out of options.'

There was a bus coming along the street quite fast. They waited under the awning for a few moments for it to pass. As it flashed by in a blur, they caught a glimpse of a sea of faces, devoid of expression, staring out into the night.

They hurried quickly over to the other side of the street where they'd left the car.

'My feet are like blocks of ice,' Duvall muttered as she climbed in.

Landis started the engine and turned on the heater. 'It's on high. You'll soon be toasty.'

'Thanks, Landis.' Duvall smiled at him gratefully. 'I'm glad I came along.'

'I'm glad too.'

Five hundred yards up the street the bus had pulled up at a request stop. There was no way round – the gap between it and the vehicles parked on the opposite side was far too narrow – so Landis was forced to stop and wait.

A minute passed and the bus hadn't moved off. Then one more minute.

'What the heck is this joker playing at?' Landis muttered, impatiently tapping his fingers on the

315

steering wheel. He tooted the horn with the bottom of his palm.

Still the bus didn't move.

'This is daft!'

Landis hit the horn again and was about to get out to see what was happening when a man in uniform appeared from the pavement side of the bus. He came over to the passenger door of the car and tapped the glass.

Duvall wound down the window. 'What's going on?'

The man leant down and peered across her at Landis. 'Sorry, pal.' He spoke wearily. 'She's kaput.'

Landis frowned. '*What*?'

'The bus. Buggered. Broken down.'

'I know what kaput means,' Landis replied irritably.

'Calm down, pal. It's not my fault. It's probably the cold ballsed up the transmission fluid. Or maybe the antifreeze. I don't know, I'm not a mechanic, I just drive the bastard.' He shook his head. 'I told the boss there was something not right before I left the depot. Didn't *sound* right, you know?' He tapped his ear. 'But would he listen? No, he wouldn't. Now we're going nowhere.'

'We're in a hurry! I need to get past!'

'Nothing I can do, pal. I've called the depot, they're sending an engineer out, but even if he can fix it fast,

I'd say we're probably going to be stuck here for at least an hour. Anyway, I've got a bus full of pissed-off passengers to deal with.'

With that the man turned and sauntered away.

Duvall wound up the window. 'There was a turning on the right about a hundred yards back.'

Landis grimaced. 'We'll have to reverse. There isn't enough room to turn.'

Fortunately nobody was on the road behind them and they quickly backed up to the turning and pulled into the side street.

Landis looked at his GPS. 'If we follow this down, it bends away to the right, but there's a T-junction at the end. If we take a left there, we can get back on track about half a mile further up the road.'

There were cars parked on both sides of the narrow street and manoeuvring room was tight. Landis proceeded slowly. As they took the bend, he was forced to brake.

There was an old man in the middle of the road not more than ten yards ahead. At his feet was a small black poodle that had stopped to relieve itself.

The man looked up at the car, squinting against the headlights, and waved a hand of apology. But rather than getting the dog to move, he stayed put, waiting patiently for it to finish its business.

'This is turning into a farce!' Landis exploded.

He started to wind down the window to give the man a mouthful when something caught his eye. 'Linda! Look!'

'What?' She turned her head to look at him.

He was staring out at the street ahead. 'Do you see what I'm seeing?' He pointed.

Duvall followed his gaze and her eyes widened. Surely it couldn't be...

Beneath a streetlight on the left, just beyond where the man and his dog were loitering, parked neatly between a Vauxhall Astra and a Kia Creed, was what looked every bit the part of a shiny red metallic BMW i8 Roadster.

'There can't be too many of those around,' Duvall said breathlessly. Her heart was pounding. 'What do you think?'

'I think we owe that flippin' bus driver a drink!'

*

Billie-Jo set down the two glasses of water on the carpet and opened the Ziploc bag. At a rough guess there were maybe a hundred small, circular, white pills in it. More than enough to kill someone.

'What *is* that?' Smythe asked her again. Any trace of defiance or bravado was gone now.

'What are you worried about? Aren't you the man who claimed to have taken every drug going?'

'Every drug going?' His eyes flickered at a memory. 'Oh! That stupid interview! That was years ago and I made it up.'

Billie-Jo laughed. 'Why would anyone make up shit like that?'

'Because journalists love it. It sells papers. Causes a bit of controversy. Keeps your name relevant. It's smoke and mirrors, that's all. Haven't you heard there's no such thing as bad publicity?'

'Well let's see if you're familiar with these.'

'Aren't you listening to me?'

Scooping a small handful of pills out of the bag, Billie-Jo knelt down beside him.

'What are they?'

'Speed or something.' She sniggered.

Smythe stared at her. 'You're crazy!'

Billie-Jo reached over and picked up a breakfast menu that was laying on the table. She opened it to create a V-shape and poured the pills from the bag into the crevice. 'Open wide.'

'You can't make me.' Smythe turned his head away.

Billie-Jo picked up the knife and pressed the tip to his throat. 'Make your choice.'

Smythe turned his head back to face her. 'Please. You really don't have to do this. I have kids.' There were tears in his eyes now. 'Name your price. Anything!'

Billie-Jo applied pressure to the blade and a bead of blood formed around the tip. Smythe winced. 'I *said* open wide.'

Making a small sobbing noise, he opened his mouth.

'Wider.'

He complied.

'Head back.'

'Please... Don't.'

'Head *back*!'

Billie-Jo pressed the flat of the knife against his brow. Tears running down his cheeks, he did as he was instructed. She rammed the end of the menu into his mouth and tipped it up and the pills cascaded down the folded spine. As he started to gag, she dropped the knife and threw aside the menu. Quickly grabbing up the glass of water and forcing it between his lips, she emptied it into his mouth. He tried to spit it out, so she grabbed hold of the top of his head and the underside of his jaw, forcing it shut. Some of the liquid squirted out of the corner of his mouth and splashed onto her lacy top.

'Swallow!' Billie-Jo commanded. She watched his Adam's apple rise and fall as, with a horrible gurgling noise, the amphetamines went down. 'Good boy.' She released his head and, as he gasped for air, a streak of sticky foam appeared around his lips.

In all the weeks her vendetta had been progressing, Billie-Jo had never felt as calm and in control as she did now.

'You said you like to keep your name in the press. This should get you on the front page. "Scumbag porno producer ODs in sleazy hotel room"!'

'You won't get away with this,' Smythe spluttered.

Billie-Jo shrugged. 'Maybe I will. Maybe I won't.'

'You're fucking insane! Killing me isn't going to take away the pain, you know!'

'Enough chat.' Billie-Jo picked up the Ziploc bag and looked inside; there were a couple of stray pills and some powder in the bottom. 'Waste not, want not. Open up.' Billie-Jo picked up the knife.

'What you're doing… everything you've *done*, it's going to haunt you for the rest of your life. And it's not going to bring your family back.'

'I said open your *fucking* mouth!' She pressed the end of the blade against his left eyelid.

Squeezing both his eyes tightly shut, Smythe opened his mouth and she emptied the remains of the bag's contents down his throat. As he started to choke, she tossed the bag and knife aside and forced his mouth shut again.

He arched his back and strained against the bonds, kicking his legs for all he was worth, but she held on tight and didn't let go until she was certain he had swallowed.

As she got up off her knees there was a knock on the door. Her head shot round and a muffled woman's voice sounded: 'Room service.'

There had been little doubt that the BMW belonged to Smythe. Any that there had been was quashed when Duvall looked at the licence plate: CS 1.

She and Landis had tried several doors on both sides of the street before they struck gold. When the man with the comical comb-over opened the door and they'd asked about Smythe he had been hesitant. Duvall had shown him a photo of Smythe on her phone and he had shaken his head. Immediately suspicious he wasn't telling the truth it was only when she flashed her police badge, he'd started to sing like a canary.

'Oh, how silly of me!' His tone had become sickeningly obsequious. 'Its not a very good picture, I must say I hardly recognised him. Yes, of course. Mr Smythe. One of my regulars. I run a very discreet establishment here, that's why I have to be careful. It's…' He trailed off as he saw the expression of disgust on Duvall's face. 'He's upstairs in the company of a young lady. Room 211.'

Landis's face fell. 'How young?'

'Not that it's any business of mine and I certainly don't judge my guests for their peccadilloes. I wasn't really paying attention and...'

Landis grabbed the man roughly by his shirt collar.

'*How* damned young?'

The man tried to pull away, but Landis had a firm hold of him. '*Very*. She's very young, a teenager maybe.'

Landis shot Duvall a glance. 'Hazelwood!'

They pushed through past the man.

'You'd better call this in!' Landis cried to the Duvall. 'Fast.'

The landlord yelled something at them about not being allowed to come barging into his hotel without a warrant, but his protestations faded behind them as they dashed full pelt up the narrow staircase and into the maze of dingy, interconnecting corridors peppered with numbered doors. The place was far bigger than its outward appearance suggested.

Duvall finished her call. 'They're on their way.'

As they approached room number 211, they slowed down to a trot and stopped.

Landis put an ear to the door. All he could hear was the blood pounding in his ears. Shaking his head, he ushered Duvall over. 'See if you can hear anything,' he whispered.

She stepped forward and listened for a moment. Then she nodded. 'There's someone talking,' she whispered back. 'But I can't hear what they're saying.'

Landis thought for a second. 'You knock,' he said quietly. 'Say it's room service.'

Her face panic-stricken, Billie-Jo spun back round and looked at Smythe. 'What the fuck is this?' she hissed.

His head was starting to swim. But he saw an opportunity and seized it. 'I…' he started. He felt the edge of the blade at his throat. 'It's room service. I ordered champagne,' he mumbled. He was almost incoherent now.

The knock came again. 'Room service,' the voice repeated.

Billie-Jo looked at Smythe warily. She pressed the knife up underneath his jaw. 'I'm going to answer it,' she said quietly. 'If you scream it'll be the last fucking sound you ever make.'

Standing up, she crossed to the door and rested her hand on the end of the key. 'Who is it?'

'Room service,' the voice said again.

Billie-Jo looked back at Smythe. There was foam around his mouth and his head was lolling again. His eyeballs rolled up into his head.

She steadied her breathing. 'Leave it outside please.'

There was a pregnant pause. Billie-Jo was about to put her ear to the door when the voice replied: 'Of course.'

Billie-Jo waited for almost a minute. She glanced back at Smythe again. His head was rested against the footboard.

Holding the knife behind her back, with fumbling fingers she turned the key in the lock.

What happened next unfolded so fast that she barely registered what was happening.

CHAPTER 26

Billie-Jo had opened the door no more than an inch when it flew open, sending her sprawling backwards across the carpet. She looked up and recognised the face of Detective Inspector Landis as he burst into the room. Behind him in the open doorway there was a woman.

In an instant, Billie-Jo was on her feet again as Landis advanced on her. 'Miss Hazelwood... Billie-Jo...'

'Back the fuck off!' she shrieked. She lashed out with the knife, narrowly missing Landis's outstretched hand.

'Okay. Calm down.'

'Don't fucking tell me to calm down!'

Landis looked over Billie-Jo's shoulder. He could see Smythe sitting slumped with his head to the side. His face was crimson and there was a sticky white froth around his mouth, dripping slowly onto his bare chest. The glassy eyes still showed signs of life as he stared first at Landis, then at Duvall, a pleading look on his face.

Duvall remained in the doorway, watching intently.

Landis's eyes flicked back to Billie-Jo. 'My name is William. You can call me Will if you like.' He smiled at her. She looked absolutely terrified and the knife was still pointing directly at him. He had learned from experience that cornered animals don't always act rationally.

Holding up a hand of surrender, he took a single pace back. 'I've spent a lot of time looking into your case and I fully understand what brought you here today and why you believe your actions are justified. But this has to stop. Now.'

Billie-Jo stared at him in silence. She was still pointing the knife at him but her arm was visibly shaking.

'It would be very much in your favour if we can get Mr Smythe out of here and into hospital,' Landis continued soothingly. 'That way we won't have to add his murder to your list of misdemeanours, will we?'

'He ain't going nowhere!' Billie-Jo snapped back.

'Well then, we have ourselves a bit of a problem.'

'You might do. I'm just fine!'

Landis smiled inwardly. The young woman's insolence reminded him of his 15-year-old granddaughter, Sienna; in fact, he thought, this girl, however much she looked an adult in the attire she was wearing, was only a couple of years older than Sienna.

'Okay, he said. 'I hear you. But this puts me in a very difficult position.'

'How's that?'

'Well, I'd like to be able to take you in quietly and prevent you from doing something that will further impact your life. But if I have to call the local Bobbies, it'll be completely out of my control what happens. I want to help you, Billie-Jo.'

With her arm now trembling uncomfortably, Billie-Jo lowered the knife. 'I ain't going down the nick with you.'

'The landlord of this establishment has already called the local police. It's only a matter of time and they'll be here, then this is all over and I'm out of the equation anyway.' He looked into her frightened eyes. 'It's up to you.'

Billie-Jo thought for a moment. There was no easy way out of this now. No way at all, in fact. It was over.

'Okay, take the gammon cunt. I was bored listening to his whining anyway!'

Landis smiled. 'Thank you, Billie-Jo. My colleague will untie him and if we can get him out into the hallway, you and I can talk.'

Billie-Jo moved round to the far side of the bed and Duvall stepped past Landis and squatted down beside Smythe.

Billie-Jo stood quietly whilst she undid the binds.

Smythe groaned weakly as Duvall and Landis hooked their arms through his, lifted him onto his feet and gently walked him out.

Billie-Jo gasped as Duvall opened the door. Clustered outside in the hallway were five or six police officers wearing flak jackets and riot helmets. Two of them were holding guns.

Landis came back in and closed the door behind him.

Billie-Jo raised the knife again and waved it at him. 'You said…'

'I'm sorry. Like I said, they'd already been called.'

'Bit fuckin' heavy-handed ain't it? Why didn't you send for the army as well?!'

Landis took a step towards her.

'Back off!' Billie-Jo snarled. 'I ain't kidding!'

'Come on. You know this needs to stop now. Put the knife down and we'll talk.' Landis smiled at her warmly and Billie-Jo felt a lump in her throat. 'Come on, kiddo. Time to give it up now.'

A memory flashed though her mind; her grandpa used to call her kiddo. With a sigh, she dropped the knife onto the bed.

'Good girl,' Landis said softly. Making no attempt to take the knife, he rested his backside on the small table and gestured for Billie-Jo to sit down. She did as he asked. 'What a mess eh?'

'Yeah,' Billie-Jo replied with her head low. A tear ran down her cheek. 'I'm going to jail, ain't I?'

Landis searched for the right words. Even though it was patently obvious this frightened young woman would probably spend the rest of her days in prison, he saw no benefit in discussing it now. 'Look, how about we get out of this thoroughly unpleasant room and we can sort it all out down at the station?' He held out his hand to her. 'Come on, kiddo.'

Billie-Jo slowly raised her head to look at him. Her face was streaked with tears and she suddenly looked like a helpless child.

'They killed my little sister,' she sobbed. 'She was only 14. Yeah, sometimes she could be a bit of a bitch, but I loved her so much and now I'll never be able to tell her that ever again.' The sobs became more intense and Billie-Jo wiped the mucus from her nose. 'I have no-one now. Bob's gone, my Mum and Dad are gone. I'd rather be dead with them.'

She reached for the knife, but quick as lightning, Landis grabbed it away.

'Don't say that. You wouldn't rather be dead.'

'I *would*. Please. I have nothing left to live for. *Please!*' Her eyes were imploring him.

Landis felt his heart breaking. In all his time as a police officer, he'd had no sympathy for the felons, especially murderers. But this girl had been through hell and, Lord forgive him for thinking it, but the people she had killed were sadistic and evil and – some

330

might say – deserved it. But regardless of how he felt, justice had to be served. And if he could help this young lady through the system as painlessly as possible, he would.

He stood up, put the knife down on the table and reached for Billie-Jo's hand to help her up. 'You're shivering.' Of course she was, it was the middle of winter and the girl had barely any clothing on. He pulled the threadbare blanket from the bed and wrapped it around her. Gently helping her to her feet, he led her around the bed towards the door.

'I'm really sorry!' Billie-Jo said through her tears.

Five minutes later Landis and Duvall paused outside on the steps.

The sleet had finally stopped and the walls of the surrounding buildings were bathed in flashing blue lights.

The landlord appeared behind them with a worried look on his face. 'I hope this incident isn't going to harm my reputation! What was going on up there?'

Landis gave the man a disparaging look. Deeming the question unworthy of a reply, he turned away and walked down the steps to the pavement. Duvall joined him.

Two paramedics were stretchering Smythe into the back of an ambulance. Billie-Jo was standing between two police officers beside the open door of one of the three patrol cars parked in the middle of the street.

Landis raised a hand to her and smiled. She didn't return his smile, but she raised her hands up in response; they were handcuffed. Then one of the officers rested a hand on the crown of her head, carefully assisting her into the back of the car, and closed the door.

The last Landis saw of her was the ashen face staring out of the window at him as the car moved away.

Duvall put on her seatbelt and sighed. 'Doesn't this all seem a bit strange to you?'

Landis looked at her. 'What do you mean?'

'Well, that Cornish chap at the stables was absolutely certain he saw two people fleeing the scene when Leaky was attacked.'

Landis pinched his chin. 'I'm not sure that our friend Mr Mills was telling us the whole story there. We'll have to speak to him again.'

'You think it's over then?'

Landis shook his head sorrowfully. 'Not for Billie-Jo Hazelwood it isn't. For her it's only just the beginning.'

'What do you think will happen to her?'

'There's no way she isn't going inside for what she's done.' He put on his own seatbelt. 'There are some mints in the glove box. Grab one for me, would you?'

Duvall opened the compartment and pulled out half a tube of Trebor Extra Strong. She handed them to him and he held out the packet to her.

She shook her head. 'Too hot for me.'

Landis popped one in his mouth and gave her the packet back. She returned it to the glove box.

He looked at his watch. It was approaching nine. 'How about we go have that dinner I promised you. Are you hungry?'

'Starving! Thanks, William.' Duvall grinned. 'Is it okay if I call you William? Or Will perhaps?'

'Just call me Landis.'

Acknowledgements:
The authors would like to thank Sandra Watson and Sara Greaves.
A special thank you to our loyal readers, especially those
who championed the writing of this sequel.

Cover photography and design by Rebecca Xibalba

Also from Rebecca Xibalba and Tim Greaves:
Misdial (2020)
The Break (2021)
The Well (2021)
Reset (2022)
3.2.1 (2022)
Available from Amazon, for kindle and in paperback

From Rebecca Xibalba:
Shootin' Starz: 20 Years Behind the Lens
Available in hardback from Amazon

The following titles are available in Audiobook format
from Audible and itunes:
Misdial (read by Paul Kendrick)
The Break (read by Sally Swift)
The Well (read by Sally Swift)
Reset (read by Keith Cruden)

Printed in Great Britain
by Amazon

21739101R00192